Cruel Crossroads

In the sun-drenched courtyard of the vast California
ranch of Simon Reyes, Kathleen felt suddenly alone
amidst the fiesta revelers.

Standing before her was the man she had thought never
to see again—Edmund Woodsworth, his cultivated
face a smiling mask of evil, and in his hands the
papers that put Kathleen in his power.

Next to Kathleen stood Simon Reyes, whose arrogant
features still filled her with hatred even after his
long, lean, hard body had conquered her will
to resist.

Only two choices lay before her.

She could return with Edmund to Boston. Or she
could surrender her name and the last remnants of
her freedom to Simon.

But what did it matter?

Either way led straight to hell. . . .

SAVAGE ENCHANTMENT

A NOVEL BY

Parris Afton Bonds

POPULAR LIBRARY • NEW YORK

SAVAGE ENCHANTMENT

Published by Popular Library, a unit of CBS Publications, the Consumer Publishing Division of CBS Inc.

ISBN: 0-445-04332-6

Printed in the United States of America

10 9 8 7 6 5 4 3 2 1

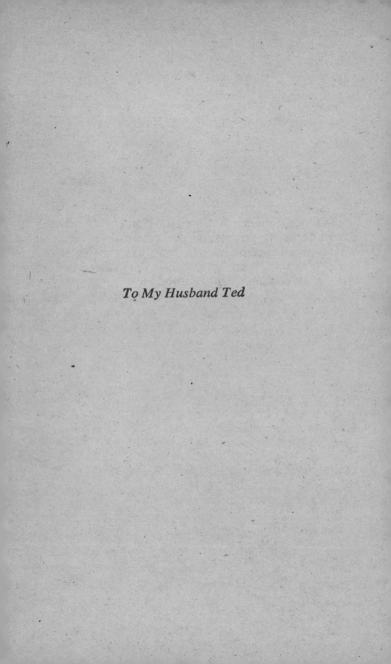

To My Husband Ted

Although some of the characters are drawn directly from California's romantic past, the majority are created purely from imagination. In some cases the dates of certain historical events have been slightly altered in order to retain the continuity of the story.

Savage Enchantment

1

1836

With a howl that more resembled that of an animal than of a human being, the middle-aged woman flung herself against the heavy wooden door, her skeletal fingers wrapping themselves about the iron bars of the door's window. Shrieks of bestial rage poured out of the spittle-flecked lips, directed toward the man on the other side.

The stately gentleman with the shock of silver hair stepped back from the door with a grimace of distaste. Drawing a linen handkerchief from the pocket of his dark blue waistcoat, he dabbed fastidiously at his upper lip as he propelled his twelve-year-old daughter back down the cold corridor of Boston's Northhampton Asylum.

"You can understand now, Kathleen, why I've been unwilling to let you see your mother more often these last few years. Only the fact that the doctors assure me her end is near—and not your persistent clamoring—has induced me to let you see her one more time."

The well-manicured hands formed clenched fists within the folds of the mauve-colored velveteen skirts that almost, but not quite, matched the deep purple of almond-shaped eyes. Eyes which at that moment blazed in impotent fury.

Kathleen Whatley stood before her father, who sat imperiously in the black and gold Sheraton chair, a crocheted blanket draped across his lap. His stringent features yielded nothing, in spite of the cough that racked his body.

"Kathleen, dear," he said in a chilling tone between spasms of hacking, "you've always been a spoilt and pampered child. A child determined to have her own way. You're twenty now. High time you grew up—accepted the responsibility of your station."

"And if I refuse, Papa? If I refuse to marry Mr. Woodsworth?"

"You surely don't wish to distress your father

further, do you, Kathleen?" Edmund Woodsworth asked, his silky voice tinged with a subtle threat.

Kathleen's heavily fringed eyes glared at the slim, fashionably dressed Englishman who stood languidly before the fireplace. Only barely did she repress a shudder while Edmund's glassy eyes slid over her with contemptuous indifference.

But his contempt was equaled by her own as she watched him raise a beringed hand to smother the yawn escaping from the lipless mouth—a defect he disguised with a thick blond mustache and Vandyke beard. Except for this imperfection, the pale, finely sculptured face was almost beautiful.

However, Kathleen was not deceived by the man's foppish mannerisms. For, in spite of the fact that Edmund was her father's lover—the homosexual relationship having begun when the two met in Madrid years before, as ambassadors for Great Britain and the United States respectively—there was a latent air of cruel strength about the Englishman. Indeed, the fortyish Edmund was renowned for his deadly expertise in swordsmanship.

"A man of steely purpose," the Boston *Times Herald* had punned about a recent duel between him and the now-deceased gentleman who had dared voice his opinion about Edmund's peculiarities.

Now Kathleen saw Edmund's lower lip droop petulantly when she refused to answer him, and braced herself for whatever cutting tirade might follow. But he merely turned to her father with a sigh of impatience, as if wearied by a recalcitrant child.

"My dear James, I'm afraid your daughter sadly needs disciplining. A job I shall certainly undertake once she is my wife."

Her father emitted a half-grunt of exasperation. "You're like your mother, Kathleen. Emotional and unstable. You understand, it was with a great deal of mental anguish that I forced myself to have her committed."

A shiver of irrepressible fear crept up Kathleen's spine. She understood. Her father did not have to say more. His power and influence were still great enough that unless she complied, she could well find herself languishing in some such place as her mother had for nearly ten years.

Kathleen had been too young to understand everything when the whole affair began. But she later picked up bits and pieces from servants' gossip.

"A sordid affair, indeed!" Amanda, their cook, had whispered to the housemaid, Becky. "There Mr. Whatley was in Spain as our President's minister to the court, and Mrs. Whatley—never did like the madam—too proud—she ups and takes herself a lover."

"What happened then?" Becky asked, leaning closer over the kitchen table to catch every word.

Amanda halted in the midst of peeling the onion. "The madam was the scandal of all Madrid. That's what! Didn't bother to hide her peccadilloes, that

one. There's them that say the Mistress Kathleen is
the love child of the madam's Spanish lover, and
not poor Mr. Whatley."

Amanda ignored the housemaid's smothered
gasp and went on with her story, delighted to have
a listener. "A heathen country, Spain was. Didn't
like it one bit, meself. Anyway, when Mr. Whatley
came down ill with consumption and had to give up
his post, the madam refused to return with him. Declared she'd stay in that pagan land with her daughter, she did!"

Becky's lashless eyes rounded with avid curiosity.
"What did the master do?"

The bony cook resumed peeling the onion. "Mr.
Whatley had a doctor there give the madam seda-
tives. She fought like a tigress. But after she was
unconscious, he whisked her aboard a ship bound
for Boston. Had to tend to her meself the whole
crossing. Heavily drugged, the madam was."

Kathleen had inadvertently made a noise at the
kitchen doorway then, and the conversation
abruptly ceased. But she could imagine the rest. It
was only a matter of a few signed papers, and the
estranged wife had been incarcerated in the hellhole
that served as an asylum.

She was sharply recalled to the present by her father's "Well, what's it to be, Kathleen?"

"I don't have any other choice, do I, Papa?"

Edmund's lipless mouth stretched in a hideous
curl of triumph, and he glided to the side of her fa-

ther's chair. "That is more like it, Kathleen. You and I shall deal quite famously with one another—as long as you are obedient."

Kathleen lowered long lashes over mutinous eyes. She too was quite sure Edmund would deal famously with her . . . and her inheritance. Within a year of their marriage he would no doubt be in complete control of the Whatley fortune if, as the reputable Boston doctors speculated, her father's declining health lasted even that long.

The Whatley fortune was nothing to her, except as a means to remain free from male domination. The thought of marriage, even if it were based on mutual consideration and respect, was repugnant to her. To some wives, it was an unpleasant experience one had to endure. But to her it was a thing of horror and disgust. To have to submit to the demands and pleasure of a man who had all rights over her—Kathleen was physically sick at the very thought. To be a helpless pawn as her mother had been—no!

And for Edmund—of all men—to have control over her person; to be a tool of his whim and used however his sexual perversions dictated—that was unthinkable!

But rebellion? If she refused to marry her father's lover, could she really face the living death of the Northhampton Asylum? Yet if she capitulated and married Edmund, what guarantee was there that Edmund would not do the same—incarcerate her, claiming inherited insanity?

After long moments of indecision, of mentally searching for any escape, Kathleen knew her only chance lay in stalling. The eyes, a startling lavender in the honey-gold face, raised meekly to the two men. "Give me a month to prepare for the wedding, will you, Papa?"

James Whatley and Edmund Woodsworth flashed conspiratorial glances of victory at one another. But such is the nature of tyrants that they fail to notice the small things that make and break empires—as the two men failed to notice the determined set of the full lips and the stubborn lift of the clefted chin that, along with the small childhood scar running under one cheekbone, detracted from the strong beauty of the woman facing them.

That night, as Kathleen lay in bed, staring vacantly at the lace-edged tester above, she conceived a plan. A plan that was rooted in the clipping the Whatleys' young butler Robert had hesitantly showed her, from the Boston *Times Herald*, six months earlier. She had not known then that the advice she had given him would be the shaping of her own destiny.

Over the aromatic breakfast of hot English blended tea and one of Amanda's freshly baked cinnamon rolls, Kathleen had scanned the clipping advertising for a tutor. As ever, she was oblivious of Robert's adoring gaze resting on the graceful column of her neck where wisps of sunlit curls escaped the carefully tended coiffure.

"I'd go ahead and apply, Robert," she answered, returning the clipping to him with a smile. "The trip in itself would be an adventure. And as for working in that wild wasteland—on the rim of the world, as you've put it—I certainly wouldn't let rumors of daily revolutions and Indian uprisings stop me."

Her smile faded, and one hand gestured at the wintry view of the crowded city that presented itself from windows framed by tasseled blue-velvet draperies. "Anything's better than this, Robert—Boston's stifling boredom. Here, you're pigeonholed to your station in life from birth . . . destined to a dull existence by Boston's proper conventions!"

Her grimace faded as she looked up into the face of the young man who hovered anxiously at her side. Robert Patton was the same age as herself—twenty. But why did she feel aeons older?

"Yes, go ahead, Robert," she had said with a conviction that surprised herself. "Apply for this tutor's job. Anything's better!"

Yes, anything was better than—and preferable to—marriage to Edmund Woodsworth. She knew her father to be a mercenary man, but, sweet Jesus, was there nothing he wouldn't stoop to? To actually barter her as if she were one of his stocks or properties. In return for the obscene caresses of another man! Who could believe it? This was 1844, not the seventeenth century, when marriages were understandably arranged.

The day following her confrontation with her father and Edmund, Kathleen launched her plan by bribing Robert to let her take his place, her diamond earrings setting the butler up in the bookshop he had often spoken of.

By the time her father discovered her disappearance, it would be too late. She would be on her way to the Mexican province of California. She would have her independence . . . but at a costly price.

2

Captain Nathan Plummer of the two-masted brig *Tempest*, his azure eyes surrounded by tiny weather lines that etched his ruddy face, watched the proud young woman at the railing. She turned, taking the thick, hideous spectacles from her nose, and lifted her face to catch the salty sea breeze as it swept the honey-streaked mass of golden curls from the severely arranged bun at her neck.

His breath sucked in at the startling revelation of beauty. Christ, what a wench! And willful, too! Captured in that moment's pose, she could have been the embodiment of the *Tempest*'s figurehead. Drawing men to her with those incredible wine-

colored eyes and then vanquishing them with the
unpredictable winds of her volatile nature—which
he had more than once experienced during the voy-
age. Nay, she was more than a tempest. With that
apricot complexion and sun-kissed hair she was
more a tawny lioness . . . of which one should be-
ware, he thought grimly, inhaling on the briar pipe.

But, by all that was holy, how he would love to
kiss away the polite coolness. It was like a Sierra
Nevada glacier, freezing a man foolish enough to
approach her. Damn her Yankee coldness! If she
was a Yankee, as he had at first supposed.

Or was it true, as one of the passengers whispered—the spinster Merriwitten—that the girl was
the cast-off mistress of a Panamanian politician? He
would never have thought so, hidden as she was by
the ugly spectacles and dour clothing. But to look
at her now . . . Nathan drew thoughtfully on the
pipe stem held between his teeth.

No, probably gossip. In spite of the fact that she
had been waiting, unchaperoned, on Panama's Bal-
boa docks with only the one valise, it was probably
just as she had told him, her low voice crisp and
aloof, when she had given him the passage fare to
the Mexican province of California. She was to be
a tutor at one of those ranchos.

But the tutors the Californios hired had always
been men. Whoever the wealthy *don* was who had
advertised for a tutor—what would he think when
he found his new employee was a woman?

Kathleen wondered, too, as she looked out over the Santa Barbara Channel toward the mist-shrouded coast, what her new employer, Señor Reyes, would say. But then, did it really matter? It was either face the anger of Señor Reyes or submit to her father's and Edmund's perverted plans for her.

Kathleen laughed softly, thinking how outraged her father must have been when he read her note informing him she had run off with the butler. For a Whatley to condescend to such a thing would be unthinkable to him.

However, it was no laughing matter, she thought, reflecting on what had happened since. The hardship of the journey had been much greater than she, accustomed to the comforts of wealth, could have imagined. A hearty February gale off the Atlantic Coast had confined her to her berth for the entire trip to Panama. And crossing the Isthmus, the jungles had been even worse.

She caught her lower lip between small white teeth, remembering the tropic's sweaty stickiness and the steaming swamps, and—the worst—the voracious mosquitoes! And the times when she half expected the coach to sink in quicksand. The Pacific portion of the two-month trip had been somewhat better, thanks to Nathan Plummer's solicitude.

She glanced at the massive captain through the thick layers of black lashes. Yes, with those locks as yellow as freshly churned butter and the warm blue eyes, he might certainly be called attractive. But that was as far as her appraisal went. It was best to keep him—and all other men—at a distance.

She would wander through hell the rest of her life before she would give up her independence, to be helplessly dominated by a male again. The cold, isolated life under the domineering rule of her father—if he was her father—had been quite enough to convince her of the folly of being bound to one man.

No, better to bide her time hidden in the vast emptiness of California until news of her father's death reached her—as surely it must, for the death of such a prominent man would travel even to California, part of New Spain. She would yet outwit the cunning man she called her father, and the libidinous Edmund. If nothing else, she had time on her side.

After her father's death, after her twenty-first birthday, she should then be free to return to Boston and resume her life, God willing.

Kathleen realized her hands were clenched on the brig's railing, and she forced herself to relax, to enjoy the view from the deck. The morning mist was already lifting so that the porpoises could be seen arcing in graceful dives among the swelling waves.

And in that sparkling sunlight Kathleen first

glimpsed the pueblo of Santa Barbara, built on a low, flat, and treeless plain and surrounded on three sides by an amphitheater of mountains.

There were maybe a hundred mud-brick houses with red tile roofs, and in the midst of them rose the wooden palisades of the presidio, with the Mexican flag—the cactus and the eagle—rising above the old Spanish fort.

A little way off were the Indian huts, and above their thatched roofs towered the splendid, newly plastered spires of the mission's church. The Santa Barbara Mission was queen of the twenty-one missions that lined El Camino Real, the Royal Highway, which ran almost the entire length of the province's coastline.

Since Santa Barbara had no harbor, Kathleen was forced to wait for the brig to lower its oarboat to take the few passengers ashore. But her patience had worn thin, and she walked the vessel's deck anxiously. She had no wish to postpone any longer than necessary her meeting with Señor Reyes—to know after four months of nervous waiting if her plans had succeeded.

There was already the unfortunate fact to nag at her that the *Tempest*'s home port was Boston. Yet she doubted that anyone aboard had recognized her, so discouraging was she at attempted conversations. Even the old maid Merriwitten and her equally aged companion Mamie Harding had given up their prying, and sat uneasily in the stern of the boat as the oarsmen waited for a large swell of the ocean to roll in, breaking up the heavy surf.

Once the oarboat beached, the sailors, clad in duck trousers and striped red cotton shirts, carried the passengers ashore. But it was Nathan himself who lifted Kathleen out of the boat and waded ashore with her cradled in his arms like a child. He set her down on the sandy beach, and, as her eyes scanned the people gathered there, looking for her prospective employer, she was barely conscious of Nathan's farewell offer—that he could be reached at La Palacia Posada that week, should she need anything.

Among the crowd Kathleen saw Indians, dressed only in rawhide breechcloths, soldiers, and the lower-class Mexicans and half-breeds that Nathan said were called *cholos*. But nowhere did she glimpse a ranchero—or Californio, as he had told her these men were called—native sons of upper-class Spanish colonists who had come to ranch nearly seventy years earlier.

The passengers who had come ashore had gone on to their destinations, and the crowd that gathered for the ship's arrival was already dispersing but for the few curious ones who eyed Kathleen's extraordinary golden coloring, rare there among the dark skins and black-eyed, black-haired natives.

But Kathleen lingered there, waiting, savoring the climate that was so different from that of Bos-

ton. The air was softer, the ocean bluer. And there
was a lazy, radiant warmth that permeated everything. However, as the lemon-colored sun began to
fall rapidly into the sea, she grew anxious. She was
half tempted to return to the *Tempest* and seek help
from Nathan, who was already aboard, busying
himself with the ship's cargo papers, when the
crunching of hooves on the smooth sand brought
her head around.

"*Espérame!*" the officer ordered sharply to the
three soldiers who rode behind him. He swung
down from the cream-colored palomino and approached Kathleen, his sword gleaming in the sun
and his scarlet taffeta sash swishing with the wind.

Removing the low-crowned hat piped with the
yellow braid of the cavalry, he said, "Señorita, are
you awaiting someone?"

The Spanish of childhood came facilely to her
lips. "*Sí,*" she told the stocky officer, who was only
a little taller than she, maybe five and a half feet at
the most.

"That is, I—can you tell me where I might find
accommodations for the night?" she asked, decid-
ing it was wise to say as little as possible. "Is there
a hotel near?"

Kathleen was unaware that the sea wind vividly
outlined her high, rounded breasts and gently curving hips as it whipped the black muslin gown about
her slim frame. The officer's hot, cocoa-colored
eyes above the neatly clipped mustache ran over the

delineated contours. Too slim for his appetite . . .
Still . . .

He moistened his fleshy lips with the tip of his
tongue, finding himself unaccountably attracted to
the girl. It wasn't just the unusual coloring, or the
still childish but provocative shape of her lips, that
promised untold delights. Nor was it the sensuously
shaped eyes that smoldered like violet embers behind the thick spectacles. But what was it?

And what was she doing there on the beach
alone? A runaway indentured servant, possibly?

Lieutenant Alejandro Aguila made a quick decision then. Why tell her that the mission accom-
modated travelers?—which, in truth, it did. But
only for the dignitaries and grandees and those
blessed by wealth. There was no room for such as
he—a Castilian of high birth but little money,
forced to accept an officer's post at some stinking
command in the middle of nowhere.

Yes, he would keep this girl for a while—a
week, a month. Then she could strike out on her
own. *Por Dios,* she should thank him! Only her
coloring saved her from being sold off by some en-
terprising mind to one of the waterfront whore-
houses.

3

Standing stiffly, Kathleen tried not to betray how uncomfortable she felt under the appraising gaze from the unblinking eyes, but dutifully thanked the lieutenant when he offered to escort her to La Palacia Posada.

"Whomever you are waiting on would know to find you there," he assured her.

Ordering his men to proceed without him, Aguila assisted Kathleen up the grass-worn slope, although she abruptly withdrew her elbow from his grasp once they reached the main dirt road.

"Are you visiting relatives here, señorita?" he

asked, detaining a carriage and tying his horse to the carriage's rear.

Kathleen grimaced at the thought of riding in close contact with the man. "No," she replied tersely, turning away from the officer's hooded eyes to look instead at Santa Barbara's outskirts of brown, box-shaped houses with low, flat roofs.

How far could she trust the supercilious officer? What if this ranchero, Señor Reyes, didn't find her at La Palacia? What would she do? How stupid she had been to set out blindly for the Mexican province!

But then, in truth, there hadn't been time to make any arrangements. Only time to hurriedly pack the valise with several of Amanda's dresses—how the scraggly hag would screech when she found them missing—and, of course, the derringer from her father's small arsenal. How soon before her father would miss the prized pistol given him by Edmund, who had even gone to the expense of engraving the Whatley name on it?

The carriage rolled into the plaza, where stood the Commandante's Palace, with its graceful architecture of the Spanish renaissance, and the two-story shops, their long white arcades of shaded stone *portales* protecting mud sidewalks. Here Kathleen saw strolling women whose eyes were half hidden by the colorful *rebozos* and men whose faces were barbarously mustached beneath glazed sombreros heavy with metal ornamentation.

Looking around at the sleepy, impoverished town that was such a stark contrast to the bustling prosperity of Boston, Kathleen knew she would need every ounce of fortitude she could muster to exist there. She, who was accustomed to being waited on, would now have to wait on others; accustomed to having everything, she would have to survive on little. Yet she could do it . . . she *would* do it before she would return to Edmund.

La Palacia Posada, a two-story adobe building lavishly ornamented in the churrigueresque style, ran the entire block on one side of the plaza. Inside, sparkling chandeliers of thousands of candles radiated their light, creating an intimate atmosphere over the plush mulberry-red sofas and the Brussels carpets spread on plank floors.

Even though it was still early in the evening, Kathleen saw, in the gambling room that opened off one end of the main *sala,* men richly dressed in dark boleros and tight trousers, crowded around the monte tables, testing their skills against the golden goddess of chance. At the other end of the *sala* there appeared to be a ballroom, now empty.

But it was toward a door at the rear of the establishment that Aguila led Kathleen.

"Gemma will see to it that you have a room," he said.

Kathleen noticed the taut nervousness of the man's voice, and a warning bell rang in the back of her mind. Something was awry. Or perhaps it was her own nervousness.

"The owner?"

Aguila nodded. "And, to a greater degree, the real authority over Santa Barbara—through her influence over Micheltorena, the new governor." The tone of Aguila's voice changed. "Other girls have found it profitable to emulate her. It's said that Gemma Chavez was born a ragged *peón* in Mexico and came here as a comely young girl. That her reputation as the best monte dealer helped her to lay away a fortune."

Kathleen neither missed the lieutenant's implication nor the reptilian eyes that slithered over her. Warily, she moved on ahead of him.

Watching her straight, proud back, Aguila permitted himself a smile. He could also tell the girl that Gemma had an uncanny knack for intrigue. He hoped he could persuade Gemma to aid him in his plans for this naïve girl. A mistress as golden as a field of sunflowers could carry prestige and perhaps draw the governor's attention, remedying the stagnation of his own military career.

As Kathleen entered the office, she saw the chocolate-brown eyes of the proprietress look her over shrewdly before flickering past her to Aguila. Kathleen had expected a hard, painted woman of advancing years, but the female who sat on the edge of the pine-paneled desk could not have been more than thirty. Her auburn hair was swept back from

the magnolia-white face into a demure chignon at
the nape of her neck. And a soft yellow gown of
chenille tightly hugged the curvaceous figure before
flaring at the hem in flounced ruffles. A picture of
devastating femininity—but for the thin cigarillo she
held between long, tapering fingers.

However, it was the other in the room who drew
Kathleen's attention. He sprawled negligently in a
chair, his long legs, stretched out before him, en-
cased in leather leggings. From the right legging
protruded a long, wicked-looking knife.

Slowly Kathleen's eyes raised past the soiled gray
poncho, upward to the spare, swarthy face, which
was nearly concealed by the handlebar mustache
and short, stubbled beard. Narrowed eyes regarded
her from the shadow of the stained sombrero. It
was a rough, not at all handsome face. Totally in
keeping with the one copper earring that gleamed
ominously in the left earlobe. He looked more like
a Mediterranean corsair than a common vaquero,
she thought, unconsciously moving a step backwards.

Gemma arched one delicately plucked brow.
"Sí?" she asked of Aguila, although she continued
to openly appraise Kathleen.

"A room." Aguila went on to explain about a
room he would need for—the light brows raised
meaningfully—his friend here. But Kathleen paid
little heed to the exchange between the lieutenant

and the proprietress of La Palacia, so uneasy was she under the vaquero's relentless glare.

It was with relief that she escaped Gemma's office to follow Aguila up the main staircase and along a maze of corridors to her room. To her surprise, she found the room was little more than a narrow bed and a notched bureau. Quite drab in contrast to the plushness below. Only the terrace door that opened out onto the small balcony saved the room from resembling a cell.

As she turned back to the door, she realized for certain what Aguila had in mind. She waited as he closed the door, adroitly tucking the room's key into the high pocket of his short braided jacket. When he faced her, his desire showed plainly in the bulge of his pants. Coolly, Kathleen produced her father's pistol from the folds of her skirt.

Noting Aguila's startled expression, which was swiftly replaced by barely controlled fury, she said, "I seriously doubt, Lieutenant Aguila, that your intentions are honorable. No, *es la verdad?*"

"*Puta!*"   . .

He took a step toward her, and she raised the pistol so that it was only inches from his chest.

"The derringer does not miss at close range. Now unlock the door, drop the key on the floor, and get out!"

He hesitated only a moment before doing as she instructed. But after the key clanked on the plank floor, he said between gritted teeth, "No one treats a member of the Aguila family like dirt beneath their feet—especially not a *gringa*—without reason to regret it later."

He whirled from the doorway and was gone. Kathleen sighed, the tension of the day escaping in the delayed trembling of her hands. Carefully she replaced the pistol in her valise. She could not stay there. Aguila could easily obtain another key from Gemma.

But where could she go? Even if she managed to find her way out through the labyrinth of hallways, it was already dark outside. She would only be inviting more trouble.

No, better to stay the night. With the pistol, she would be comparatively safe. However, as a precautionary measure, she would abandon the room. Surely one of the rooms in that wing of the establishment was unoccupied. After knocking tentatively on one of the doors farther down the hall and receiving no response, she tried the knob. It was unlocked.

Her heart beat like Thor's hammer in her ears as she slipped inside the room, which was much the same as the previous one. When she had ascertained that it was indeed vacant, she dragged the one chair in the room across the floor and propped its back beneath the knob.

Dizzy now with fatigue and hunger and fright, she discarded the idea of rummaging through her valise for the flannel nightgown. Instead, after sliding the derringer beneath her pillow, she stripped down to her flimsy satin chemise and fell across the bed in an exhausted stupor . . . certain that she was safe, at least for the night.

A hand clamped across her mouth much later, proving how wrong she was.

4

"Is there some reason why you're anxious to share my bed?" a low, slightly slurred voice asked in Spanish at her ear.

Kathleen's eyes flew open. Above her, scant inches away, loomed a dark face. The odor of tobacco and leather mingled with mescal to envelop her in a pungent cocoon.

Half drugged with sleep, she frantically began to fight the stranger, but his free hand caught her two hammering fists in an iron grip, yanking her hands ruthlessly above her head. The heavy, muscular body rolled across her tossing one, so that she was locked motionless beneath the man. Desperately, Kathleen bit the hand that covered her mouth.

"Damn!" he swore beneath his breath, and released her abruptly. "So the vixen wants to play the bitch. Shall I tame you?"

He sank his teeth into her neck. Kathleen's body jolted in surprise and pain. But when she would have cried out, the man covered her mouth with a hard, brutal kiss, his rough beard abrading her skin.

Could this really be happening to her? She, who hitherto had yet to feel the touch of a man's lips on her own—to suffer such an indignity as this?

But shock after shock he dealt her as he ripped the satin chemise down the front, then half caressed, half assaulted her tender breasts, his hands demanding. Kathleen stiffened in a frightened paralysis as the man's knowing fingers traced a searing path from the rose-tipped peaks to the sunken navel . . . and even lower to the triangle of spun gold.

Her breathing came in ragged gasps wherever he touched her, electrifying her like currents of white lightning. With a frenzied lunge, she twisted the lower half of her body out of his reach, but one hand still held her wrists firmly.

"What? The woman of the night still plays hard to get? Or is it that you want your money beforehand?" He rolled to his feet in one lithe, catlike motion and dug into his pants.

Standing there in the descending moon's light that streamed through the wooden slats of the terrace doors, he looked like some grim-visaged specter, and, as a peripheral thought, Kathleen realized he had entered her room by way of the balcony, for the chair was still in its place against the door.

But even as she noted this in the distant recesses of her sleep-filled mind, he advanced on her, once again in the shadows, and she cowered against the pillow. With a start, she felt the cold, heavy coins dropping on her nude belly.

"Spanish gold for a piece of gold!" he laughed lowly.

It was then that she glimpsed the glint of copper at one ear. The vaquero! She opened her mouth to scream.

"Go ahead . . . if you want spectators."

Good God! She must be in some sort of bordello! She bit her lips until she tasted blood. Stark fright mingled with helpless rage as she heard more than saw the man unbuckle his belt, dropping the leather *chaparreras* carelessly on the floor.

There was one hope! Kathleen's mind soared like a bird, released at the thought that all was not yet lost. Furtively, she slid one hand beneath her pillow. The pistol—it was gone!

His laughter was low and harsh. "Your derringer—if it is yours, *bebé*—is on the bureau. Without the shells."

Inexorably then, he moved towards the bed and

lowered himself atop her. In spite of her fierce struggle, he subdued her with his greater strength. And finally his sinewy body posed above her, for what seemed an eternal moment that would be forever engraved on her memory, before ripping into her flesh.

Again and again his rigid organ drove in her, burning her like a cattle brand, marking her his possession. And with each thrust her own body arched upwards, as if riding on a tidal wave of pain before ebbing downwards again into semioblivion.

Dear God, would it never end? Would that she could mercifully die! Then, with an explosion of his breath, he slumped across her.

And in the haze of the physical degradation, Kathleen's mind seemed to clearly say: "So this is it. This is what the other girls sighed over in romantic, curious giggles . . . and matrons whispered about behind dimpled hands, their attitudes ones of martyred resignation."

"Dios mío!" she heard him whisper harshly. "Why didn't you tell me?"

Her body was as limp as a rag doll's, but her mind still rebelled, still fought to keep the flickering ember of self-mastery ablaze. She would never give the cutthroat the satisfaction of knowing he had been the first!

"Tell you what?" she taunted. "That you rut like a beast of the fields? Besides," she said, her voice dropping to a listless whisper, "would it have stopped you?"

For a fraction of a second she felt the man's fathomless eyes intent on her. Then the bed creaked as he rose. Does he plan to kill me now? she wondered apathetically.

But from across the room came the sound of water swishing in the basin. Then there was the shock of the cold cloth on her face, wiping away the perspiration.

"No!" she cried hoarsely as one hand gently spread her thighs. Ignoring her pleas, he wiped the stickiness from her with the cool, damp cloth.

When he finished, he fell across the bed, prepared to sleep, already forgetting her presence. It was the final humiliation. The very touch of his arm half-flung over her in a proprietary manner revolted her almost as much as his brutal act of rape had, and she sprang from the bed out of his reach. He laughed, softly, mockingly, but did not stir from his sprawled position.

Gathering courage, Kathleen retrieved her muslin day gown and rapidly began to dress. But when she bent to button the high kid boots, a metallic gleam caught her eye. There among the vaquero's rumpled clothing strewn on the floor was the long knife she had seen earlier, tucked into his legging. Stealthily, she bent, her fingers outstretched.

The steely-hard hand locked over hers. Kathleen

looked up to meet his cold eyes. In spite of the fact that he was still sprawled on the bed, there was a tenseness in the muscles of his arm, communicating to Kathleen that he was, like a mountain cat, quite capable of springing within the blink of a lash.

"Unless you're sure as hell you could succeed, *bebé*, I wouldn't try it."

Stooped as she was, Kathleen's eyes were on a level with his. Their gazes locked. Before his compelling, unrelenting stare, her own lids dropped, the sweep of her long lashes laying like dark fans over her high cheekbones.

The knife clattered to the floor between them.

Her eyes raised in a blaze of fury to meet his steady regard. "You had best kill me now," she told him in a hissing whisper. "Because if we ever meet again, if I have the chance, I swear before God I'll kill you!"

At that moment, with her heavy hair hanging loose over one shoulder and the tantalizing tilt of her eyes no longer concealed by the thick glasses, Kathleen's beauty was fully exposed to the man before her.

His eyes ran boldly over her. "Killing you," he said in a lazy drawl, "is not what I have in mind. You sorely tempt me to forgo my sleep, the longer you stay."

She jerked erect. Grabbing up her valise, she backed toward the door, damning the vaquero with every step. But had she cursed him aloud, she

doubted that he would have heard. Already there
came the soft, steady cadence of his breathing.

It was not until she wandered down the complex
of hallways that she allowed the bitter tears to flow
freely. And yet she was still alive. That was something. She would find a way to stay alive for the
next twelve months. But how—with no prospects
for employment?

It hurt unbearably to walk, even with the slow,
unsteady steps she forced herself to take, and she
would have dropped then, uncaring of what could
further happen to her, had not the sight of light at
the far end of one hall drawn her onward.

She paused there at the railing, overlooking the
main *sala,* and blinked her eyes unbelievingly. Was
it really the muted light of sunrise that shined
through the wooden shutters to fall in slanted patterns on La Palacia's carpets?

She shrank back as two early risers—Californios—passed directly below her, engrossed in talk.
When they had moved on, Kathleen crept down the
stairs, hugging the wall. If only she could slip
through the front doors.

"Kathleen!"

She whirled, prepared to fight, to scream—whatever it took. The great purple eyes, glazed with fatigue and fear, closed in sheer relief. "Nathan." It
came as little more than a whisper.

The sea captain caught her up as she sagged, setting her gently on the nearest sofa. The violet

shadows beneath the fringe of inky lashes, the tawny curls that fell about her shoulders in abandoned disarray . . . What had happened? he asked himself grimly. What was she doing there—in the most notorious house of promiscuity on the California coast? Had the girl come looking for him? Or had he been wrong in rejecting the rumors that she was some cast-off mistress?

Kathleen's eyes opened to see the contradicting thoughts that played on Nathan's weather-lined face. What else could he think, she thought furiously, trying to sit up straight and at the same time distractedly pushing at the curling strands that laid on her shoulders. "Nathan, I've—is there somewhere else I can stay . . . until I can locate someone—a Señor Reyes?"

A startled look passed over the man's ruddy face. "I can take you to Santa Barbara Mission, Kathleen. You can stay there. This Señor Reyes—if he's in town, I'll find someone to get word to him."

By the time Nathan obtained a carriage for Kathleen, Santa Barbara was coming alive with street vendors on their way to the plaza's market, driving their produce in clumsy oxcarts or carrying their wares atop their heads.

Neither of them spoke during the few minutes it took to reach the mission. In the early morning sunlight, Kathleen thought the mission's arched roof of tiles set above the earth-plastered stone walls looked like a fiery cyclops eye, and she shuddered in spite of the sun's warmth. Only the five copper bells in the high-towered belfry ringing out the matins helped dispel her inexplicable aversion.

Nathan helped her alight from the carriage, and a plump monk in a coarse brown cassock came down the mission steps to greet them with an effusive welcome. After Nathan arranged for a room, he turned back to Kathleen, taking her hands in his larger ones.

"If you should need me, I have to sail up the coast to Monterey to report to the customs officials. But you can find me there—if—"

"Thank you, Nathan," she said, sparing him his tactful groping for words. "I'll always remember your kindness to me."

Reluctantly, she watched him go, before following the padre down a damp, musty corridor to one of several small but amply furnished cubicles kept for guests.

She did not even bother to undress as she fell across the rawhide bed, both Nathan's kindness to her and the horror of the vaquero's violation of her body temporarily forgotten in the slumber of exhaustion that claimed her.

5

Later that afternoon, after Kathleen had awakened and satisfied her hunger with fruit and a delicate onion soup served by quietly gliding Indians, she allowed the abbot to show her the mission—its peach orchard, the lavishly ornamented friary, and the flower-covered graveyard enclosed by high walls behind the mission.

She found it strange, the great number of Indian names that marked the small wooden crosses at each grave. "Ah, my daughter," Father Gaona replied to her question, "there were unfortunately more deaths than births among our converts—sanitation problems, diseases, things like that. But the

Church has accomplished much," he went on, pride beaming in his protruding eyes. "In the few decades we've been here, we've not only converted the Indians—we converted the land." The plump hand stretched out to indicate the orchards, with dozens of varieties of trees, and the acres of gardens. "With the *acequias*—irrigation ditches—the Digger Indians built, we've been able to make this into a prosperous land the Lord has given us."

Kathleen paused in the courtyard at a stone well. "I was under the impression that the land originally belonged to the Indians," she said, leaning over the well's rim to see her reflection.

"You're correct, of course," the padre said. His unlined face puckered in a flustered look. "But the Indians didn't know how to care for their land. We taught our neophytes—our converted Indians, that is—how to work the gardens, sow our crops, and tend our cattle and sheep—what's left of our herds, since Mexico began secularizing the Church. *Gracias a Dios, el gobernador*, Micheltorena, is restoring some of our lands to us—the Church, that is," he added hastily.

"And reading and writing—did the Church teach the Indians how to do these skills also?"

The usually complacent countenance frowned under Kathleen's questioning, and he looked down at the wooden crucifix his pudgy fingers continually rubbed.

"My daughter, you have to understand these

primitive children. Before, they only knew how to gather seeds and nuts for their survival. You must see that they need to know more how to cultivate the land and such trades as tanning and blacksmithing than they need to learn such unessential instructions as reading and writing."

The abbot's bovine attitude annoyed Kathleen, and she begged off touring the rest of the mission, saying she wished to change and wash up for dinner.

That evening Father Gaona and another padre, old, gaunt Father Marcos, presided over the guests at the dinner table. Besides a dashing Russian officer, Dimitri Karamazan, who all but ignored the mousy-looking Kathleen, there was a Castilian family returning to Spain after a lengthy visit with relatives. The middle-aged Doña Inez, who was much younger than her austere husband, Don Felipe Feito, kept the conversation flowing with gossip of her cousin Lucia's daughter.

"Francesca is truly a beauty," she said between samplings of the succulent chile stew. "Like her mother, Lucia. Francesca's skin is paler than a pearl—and her eyes—*Madre de Dios,* they're as black as coals! Why, 'tis said that every single male between San Diego and Yerba Buena is vying for her hand. Of course," she added with a knowing smile, "the fact that her father is one of the wealthiest rancheros about is an extra plum to the man who wins her hand."

"I believe, my dearest," Don Felipe said dryly, picking at his wooden teeth, "that your cousin's daughter has already decided who shall have that 'extra plum,' as you call it."

"Can you blame her for wanting Simon Reyes as her husband—even if his wealth doesn't quite equal her father's?"

"The young lady is still unengaged?" the Russian Karamazan asked at the same time Kathleen said, "Señor Reyes?" more sharply than she intended.

"Why, my daughter?" Father Gaona interposed. "Do you know him?"

"No." Kathleen looked around the room at the expectant faces turned on her. "I've never met the man . . . but I've heard his name . . . if it is the same man."

"It is," Don Felipe replied. "Though there's an unhealthy mystery about the man. No one seems to know for certain anything about him. Who he is— from whence he comes."

"I believe," Father Marcos said quietly, "that the man was formerly a scout in Texas. That he was taken prisoner at some place there called Goliad— by Mexico's president, Santa Anna himself."

"Then he's not a Californio?" Kathleen asked.

"Undoubtedly not!" Doña Inez said. Her eyes took on a wicked gleam. "Unlike the Californios, Simon Reyes is a man who doesn't have time for flattery and flirtation. There's something savage about him—primitive. You can imagine, my dear," she said to Kathleen, "after the excessive attentions of the Californios, how a woman could find the man's indifference extremely stimulating."

"Bah!" Don Felipe said, rejoining the conversation. "I'm quite sure Doña Delores also thought the man a savage . . . finding herself suddenly dispossessed of Hacienda del Bravo. And that Reyes arrogantly claiming the land was granted him by the Mexican government."

"He had the papers to back up his claim," Doña Inez protested. "At least, that's what Lucia says. She told me, quite confidentially you understand, that Santa Anna's wife, Maria Tosta, was rumored to be Simon's mistress—and that's how he came by his land grant."

Father Gaona made a grunt of shocked disapproval, but Kathleen caught the expression of amusement gleaming in Father Marcos's hollowed eyes.

"That's neither here nor there, my dearest," Don Felipe said. "If Spain still ruled the Californios, you could be certain something as outrageous as the dispossession of Doña Delores's land would have never occurred!"

"But Don Felipe," Kathleen said, "I thought that Spain also made land grants when it ruled the Californios. Except, in Spain's case, the grants would have been dispossessing the Indians, would they have not? So this, Señor Reyes hasn't really done anything so outrageous, has he?" Why she felt compelled to defend Simon Reyes, who wasn't even concerned enough to meet his tutor, was beyond her.

"Actually," Father Marcos said, "I understand Simon Reyes didn't dispossess Doña Delores. That when he arrived here a year ago he allowed her to continue living at del Bravo until her death, some months back."

Father Gaona's placid expression changed to a scandalized look. "How Doña Delores could have suffered the scoundrel in the very house her husband built for her can only be attributed to her fine religious upbringing."

"Doña Delores," Father Marcos explained to the guests, "was reputed to be the most beautiful girl in the California province, the daughter of an *alcalde* of pure Castilian blood."

The father nodded at Don Felipe, acknowledging the gentlemen's own Castilian blood, and continued. "Andrew King, an Englishman, came to the province on one of the whaling ships that frequented the coast before Mexico forbade it. Andrew saw Doña Delores one day in the plaza and, of course, fell instantly in love with her. I married them myself. Unfortunately, the good Lord did not bless their union with children."

"So you can imagine," Father Gaona broke in, "how upset Doña Delores must have been to have someone else own the house meant for her longed-for children. This man is a curse to our—"

"You've met this man, then?" Kathleen asked.

"No," Father Gaona admitted. "But his uncivilized actions are common knowledge. A rakehell, he's called. It's even whispered that he killed a man in a duel over a daughter of Don Juan Bandini— San Diego's former *comandante*. Simon Reyes has been a thorn in the Church's side since he arrived. A crude heathen trying to play the *caballero*—no better than the pagan Indian renegades!"

Kathleen glanced at the older padre, but Father Marcos's expression remained mild beneath the ivory brows as Father Gaona continued his diatribe:

"And the Indians! *Dios mío,* I'll wager one day they'll revolt en masse—murder every one of us in our beds! *Por Dios,* between the renegade Indians and the growing horde of bandits that ride the roads, it's unsafe to leave one's home these days. Let me tell you, more than one wealthy *hacendado* has recently been waylaid and relieved of his purse."

"I hear," Karamazan said, fingering his black goatee, "that several times lately your military has been forced to yield the wagon shipments of silver from the mines they guard."

"Quite true, my son!" Father Gaona said.

"Well, I can only say that I'm glad we're leaving this place," Don Felipe said. He stifled a yawn with the back of his veined hand and turned to his wife.

"We must sail on the tide the morrow. Shall we retire, my love?"

Kathleen would have dearly liked to learn more about Simon Reyes, but she bade the Spanish couple good evening and murmured a polite response to Dimitri Karamazan's courtly bow of farewell. When she had thanked the fathers for the dinner, she sought out her own room, just as the bells rang out their Ave Maria.

It seemed to her that night that her nerves were strung as tightly as the ropes that held the five copper bells. For months she had waged open warfare on her father—and then Edmund—fighting, then retreating, only to fight again. She felt drained mentally and physically and sought the refuge of sleep in her cell's rawhide-thonged bed.

But sleep did not come quickly that night for her. She tossed and turned as if she were still aboard the storm-besieged *Tempest*. Dreams plagued her. Sweat-drenched dreams of the vaquero's cold eyes . . . and nightmares—that her father would find her . . . and horrible visions that her employer, Señor Simon Reyes, would not.

The latter found her. And she wondered later which would have been the worse.

6

Dusty streamers of light from the single window played on the tiled floor of the abbot's study, where Father Azcona told Kathleen she would find her visitor.

The tall—well over six feet, Kathleen judged—slim-flanked man, dressed in the black, braided bolero and tight breeches of the ranchero, stood near the grilled window watching something outside. As she softly shut the door behind her, he turned to confront her.

Above the square, clean-shaven jaw line and high, jutting cheekbones, half-closed eyes ran over her lazily. Kathleen returned his bold look, noting that the powerful nose, which flared sensuously at the nostrils, looked as if it had once been broken, and that the arching line of the left brow was sharply curtailed by the white slash of an old scar.

It was a face of angles and planes, and was saved from harshness only by the startling, light green eyes, which contrasted with the sun-bronzed skin and the thick, walnut-colored hair that ended in unruly curls just below the ears.

The eyes, made to seem even lighter than they actually were by the comparative darkness of long lashes, narrowed for a moment with a flicker of—it couldn't be surprise, Kathleen thought. Surprise that she wasn't a male. Surely Nathan would have told him his new tutor was a woman.

No, she would swear it was something else that flashed like a spark in their green depths.

A slow half-smile parted the well-carved, mobile lips, displaying the ranchero's only perfect feature—even, white teeth that gleamed diabolically in the semidarkness of the musty office.

"You aren't exactly what I had in mind when I sent the passage fare—to a Robert Patton, if I remember rightly." The voice, spoken in the drawled English of the Southwest, was deep and surprisingly quiet in the hush of the room.

So this was the notorious Simon Reyes. Kathleen lifted her chin. She wouldn't be intimidated by him. "Certain circumstances forced Mr. Patton to forgo the post you offered him. But I believe I'm equally qualified to teach English and reading and writing to your children."

"There are no children of mine to be taught, Miss—"

"Summers," she lied. "Kathleen Summers." Of course there would be no children, she thought, remembering Doña Inez's gossip of Francesca's infatuation with this man.

"There are only Indians to be taught—which makes you most unsuitable for the post, ma'am."

His overbearing manner, his sarcastic attitude, irritated her. "Then may I say you are certainly not suitable for an employer? A worthwhile employer would have had the common decency to have met his employee when the brig anchored in the bay."

His hands hooked in his belt, the man walked slowly in a circle about Kathleen, his narrowed eyes raking over her as if she were a piece of merchandise. Kathleen remained standing as she was.

When he was once more before her, he looked down at her with an insolent smile. "Maybe you were expecting someone like the handsome Lieutenant Aguila? *Su amante* does seem to make easy conquests."

Kathleen gasped. "He is not my lover!" she spat without thinking, in Spanish. How did he know of Aguila? she wondered wildly. Was her name already on every tongue in Santa Barbara?

"So, you speak Spanish in addition to your other—". His gaze rested on her breasts, which heaved beneath Amanda's coarse gown. "—qualifications," he finished derisively.

"Un poco." Why tell the ill-mannered boor she had been raised in Spain? The interview was going worse than she had anticipated. Dear Lord, what if he didn't hire her? Where would she go? What kind of work could she find?

As if reading her thoughts, he said, "I'm afraid you won't do, Miss Summers—even if you do speak Spanish. If you'll excuse me . . ." He made an impatient move toward the door.

Gambling in desperation, Kathleen stepped directly in his path, planting fists on her hips. One slim, winged brow lifted in mockery as she looked up into the rough-hewn countenance.

"What?" she taunted. "Don't tell me you're afraid to deal with a woman, Señor Reyes. I wouldn't have thought it, by—"

In one rapid movement he caught her up against him, inhaling her subtle scent of jasmine while tasting the soft provocativeness of her lips.

Kathleen tried to push the man from her, to escape the hateful embrace, but he only crushed her to him the tighter. One of her hands freed itself, and she raked his cheek with her long nails. Like a buzzing in her ears, she heard his low laughter even as his hard mouth bruised hers, parting her lips in an intimate manner that made her weak, so that her struggling ceased. A strange lethargy crept over her.

"Ahhhemmm!"

Both whirled to face Father Gaona, his tonsured head shining in the lighted doorway. Kathleen could see the shock that whitened the poor man's round face.

"You'll forgive us," Simon said quite carelessly. "It's been so long since we've seen one another." He took Kathleen's flinching hand in his. "Are you ready to go, *mi vida?*"

She glared up into the cool eyes that dared her to deny she was his sweetheart. Knowing that he had intentionally placed her in the compromising situation, she could only nod her head as she straightened the eyeglasses that had been knocked askew in her struggle.

"With the *bandidos* on the roads again, Padre," Simon continued, "I carry little money. But you'll find an ample amount in your donation box this Sunday—in gratitude for accommodating *mi novia.*"

The plump abbot was servile in his thanks. *"Muchísimas gracias,* Don—"

"Señor. Señor Simon Reyes, Padre."

The padre's protruding eyes looked as if they would fall from their sockets, and, in spite of her anger, a dimple formed in Kathleen's chin, deepening the cleft.

But when her valise had been loaded into the boot of Simon's private coach and she was alone with the ranchero, she could only hiss her disgust.

"How dare you presume! *Su novia*! I'd rather be in a nunnery than engaged to you!"

Simon chuckled, lighting up the thin cigar, glad that the *Tempest* had brought him a new supply. The Virginian tobacco outranked the flaky, black Mexican tobacco any day. He exhaled slowly, savoring its flavor, before replying.

"You're not exactly levelheaded, are you, Miss Summers? Seems to me someone as badly in need of employments as you appear to be should have a more biddable nature." He smiled. "More like a docile mare, ma'am, than a spirited filly."

Kathleen bristled. "You aren't so levelheaded yourself, Señor Reyes!"

The slashed brow raised questioningly, giving him a savage look.

"Who will you find to replace me as tutor for your Indians?" she explained.

Simon frowned. Damn, what was wrong with him? . . . kissing the little minx like he hadn't seen a woman in a month. He should've known better than to drink all night at La Palacia. Of course, he might blame the last few nights' state of intoxication on the strain and tension of recent days—in addition to the little sleep he had had. Gemma had been acting like a woman possessed, demanding more, until he had left her in the early hours of the morning, finally satiated.

There was a dull throbbing at his temples, no doubt made worse by the tangle with the bespecta-

cled woman who sat across from him. One brown
hand came up to gingerly probe the fresh marks
scraped along one cheekbone. A hellcat, she was.
Well, she certainly asked for the mess she got herself in. Now, what in God's name would he do with
her?

Across from him, Kathleen saw the finely chis-
eled lips curve in a smile that did not match the
cold harshness of the green eyes; green like she had
never seen before—green like the odd vegetation
that dotted either side of El Camino Real. "Chollo
cactus," Father Marcos had called the spiny plant.

"I don't like getting something other than what I
paid for, ma'am—and I did pay for your passage
out here. However, as you've so cleverly pointed
out, I'm now without a tutor—and, for some insane
reason, you want the post. You'll therefore work
out your passage fare for me . . . until another tutor can be brought out. And I expect you to obey
me just like my other employees do, or—" He
shrugged.

"Or what, Señor Reyes?"

"I've never had to threaten my employees,
ma'am. They're smart enough to know my word is
law at del Bravo. I hope you're just as smart."

For one wild moment Kathleen repented her pre-
cipitous action in exchanging places with Robert.
Yet she was free of her father's authority and
Edmund's narcissism. And she had survived that
hideous night at La Palacia. Surely she could sur-

vive anything now. At least she would have a roof
over her head and food in her stomach. She only
needed to endure the ranchero's autocratic demeanor for a half year. Six months was little time
to wait.

"I understand you perfectly," she replied at last.
She turned away to gaze out the window, determined to say nothing as the coach hurtled on its
way south toward the next mission, a day's journey
away.

Sometimes, as the coach rounded a hairpin
curve, it seemed to Kathleen that the wheels were
only a breath away from a headlong fall to the sea-
swept rocks below. And when the coach swayed
precariously, she would have to catch the window
sash to keep from tumbling into the arms of the
man across from her. But the rough ride seemed
not to bother him in the least.

He stretched out his legs on the seat opposite, so
that beneath the *calzoneras*—the fitted trousers that
flared out when unbuttoned to lend themselves to
riding—brown leather boots rested indolently on
the plush seat of the Concord-made coach, only
inches from her.

Kathleen pretended to watch the rolling breakers
of the Pacific, which, as the coach descended once
again to the shoreline, rolled up almost to the edge
of the King's Highway. But occasionally her eyes
slid over to the arrogant man dozing across from
her.

There was something about him . . . but then, it was really difficult to say what, to judge him with the flat-brimmed, low-crowned hat pulled low over his closed eyes. Except that he was younger than she had at first supposed—perhaps nearer thirty. And there was an aura of danger about him—confirmed by the flintlock pistol thrust into the waist of the pants, gleaming as diabolically in the dimness of the coach as had his green-flecked eyes gleamed in the dimness of the abbot's study.

The long eyes opened at that moment, catching Kathleen's gaze on him. Instantly she looked away toward the coastal mountains that lay along the shoreline like some sleeping giant, dark and formidable-looking, as was the man across from her. Vexed, she bit her lower lip. It would be insufferable for the man to believe mistakenly that he interested her!

"I suppose you can ride a horse?" he asked, in a half-lazy drawl.

"Of course!" she snapped. She could also tell him that she had been told she had an excellent seat by her riding instructor, the best in Boston. Everything had been the best—for she had been a marketable commodity. Her father had been grooming her to take her place in society as Edmund's wife for nearly fourteen years. Fourteen years of suffering Edmund's malignant glances and soft hands.

"Good. Since you were foolish enough to want the post offered to a man, I'm sure you won't mind

if we skip the night's rest in San Buenaventura.
We'll leave my coach at the rancho station there
and ride on to del Bravo. I can't afford to be away
too long."

"That would suit me perfectly. Spending the
night in the same room with you would be the last
thing I want."

She saw the reckless slant of his lips and could
have bitten her tongue.

"Oh?" he drawled. "I had the distinct impression,
Miss Summers, you somehow enjoyed my presence
back there at Santa Barbara."

Kathleen's purple eyes were as frosty as chilled
grapes. "You're detestable! You're—you're no
gentleman!"

His own eyes hardened, and he said, "I never did
claim to be one, if I remember rightly. And you're
making a mistake, ma'am, if you try to play the
lady with me. Do you deny that you're running
away from a lover? That you've hardly docked and
your name's already the scandal of Santa Barbara?"

Oh, dear God, why had she ever told those two
busybodies such a tale? She had only meant to
shock them with the story that she was a politician's
mistress—to keep the old maids from prying further. But now that she was confronted by the lie,
she'd choke to death on it before she'd deny it. Let
him think the worst of her!

"I find this conversation tedious," she said, turning back again to the window and fixing her attention on the seagulls crying stridently overhead.

Simon exhaled the smoke of the cheroot, so that the smoke drifted in a mystical haze between them. "I admire your aplomb, ma'am. I just hope your performance as a tutor is as good."

Kathleen's gaze flickered to the green eyes that studied her. There was no mistaking his meaning. The ranchero would dismiss her without a qualm, should she not prove herself.

If she didn't succeed there, could she truly bear the life she would face should she be forced to return to her father . . . the revulsive pawing of a perverted husband . . . or worse, if she refused to marry Edmund, the fate her mother had suffered . . . to spend the rest of her days shut away in solitary confinement?

The vision of her mother, the last time she had been permitted to see her, rose like a specter before Kathleen's eyes. The vacant stare from eyes like marbles—eyes that had once been full of gentleness. The saliva that dribbled from lips that once must have been soft and passionate . . . passionate enough to welcome a Spanish lover as a buffer against the cold, calculated cruelty of her husband.

Involuntarily Kathleen shivered. "You'll find me quite capable, señor," she replied mechanically.

Simon frowned, his dark brows drawing together to meet in a straight line above the high bridge of his nose. Damn it! Why should he be disappointed that she hadn't risen to his bait? What had he been expecting, anyway? Certainly not that distant aloofness following on the heels of her fiery outburst. He should never have agreed to hire her.

No matter . . . she'd be on her way with the arrival of the next tutor.

7

She could not help but be piqued by Simon Reyes's indifference to her. It was a great contrast to the young men who had courted her in Boston with whispered words of adoration and confessions that they would surely die of heartbreak should she not accept their proposals.

Of course, Kathleen was shrewd enough to know that the courtships were not for herself alone. Her father's wealth and political power were added incentives. But that part of her life had ended the year before, with Edmund Woodsworth's formal request for her hand. And if she did not want Edmund to take possession of her as he lasciviously

had her father, then she would have to consign herself to whatever way Simon Reyes chose to deal
with her in the interim.

Simon napped the rest of the afternoon, his arms
crossed and his chin resting on his chest. But Kathleen found the journey too exciting, if not jolting,
for sleep. El Camino Real was packed with travelers: couriers carrying mail; padres with pack
mules, poking along beneath their burdens; heavy
wooden-wheeled *carretas* carrying hides, "leather
dollars," for illegal trade with foreign vessels.

But by the time the sun, red like a hot coal,
hovered just above the sea, and bilious black
clouds, foretelling of a seasonal storm, climbed
steadily on the eastern horizon, Kathleen earnestly
wished she could take back her retort about not
sleeping in the same room with Simon—and every
other traveler who elected to stay the night.

Her stomach growled embarrassingly with hunger, and she ached between her shoulder blades and
on the seat of her buttocks. The thought of a bed,
even if it were the way station's customary tabletop,
seemed more precious to her than water to a
bedouin. Nothing could seem worse than the prospect of mounting a horse and riding throughout the
long night.

At last the coach rolled into the dusty pueblo of
San Buenaventura, which was little more than a
motley collection of mud-brick huts and the now-

abandoned mission, its wooden-belled tower inhabited by a multitude of pigeons and swallows.

Like an excited child, Kathleen leaned her head out the coach's window as the whip drew the team of six horses to a halt outside the small adobe rancho station. On either side of the rancho's splintered wooden door were hung lanterns, already lit against the rapidly descending darkness, their pools of light roaming over the hard-baked earth with each gust of wind.

When the postillion opened the door, Kathleen turned to awaken Simon and found his steady gaze once more on her. Was he puzzled by her, or amused—or something else? she wondered, turning away quickly to descend from the coach.

Inside, the main room was hazy with smoke, and the only light came from two or three wax candles that sputtered in their wall fixtures. To one side a tin basin rested on a bench where the travelers could wash up. Eagerly Kathleen reached for the tallow soap in the side dish.

"Careful," Simon warned, beside her. "The soap'll curl the hide off a buffalo."

In spite of her tiredness, Kathleen smiled, unaware of the way the wide, gay smile subdued the sharp angles of her square jawline; or of the effect it had on others. "My skin feels like a buffalo's right now."

However, she passed up the luxury of soap and settled for splashing her face and hands clean with

the tepid water before drying them on a roller towel
that had obviously seen better days.

Finishing her toilet, Kathleen looked up to find
Simon still standing within the doorway, his narrowed eyes sweeping the room, as if by habit; taking in everything, revealing nothing. When a short
monkey-faced man hurried forward, it seemed to
her that Simon relaxed imperceptibly. But despite
the easy posture, the lean and powerful frame contained a leashed strength that made her uneasy.

"Señor Reyes!" The little owner greeted Simon
with a happy smile. "We were hoping you'd get
here. Old Carmela has even prepared your favorite
dish of *chilaquiles,* though my patrons"—he jerked
his kinky-haired head in the direction of the travelers gathered on the benches about the long
wooden tables—"they have almost devoured everything. Like vultures."

"Or *cóndores,*" Simon said, his long eyes half
closed but watching the proprietor attentively.

"Exactamente, señor."

"Well, we'll eat whatever's left, Juan—and a
little of your wine. Then we'll be on our way."

"But, señor, you're not planning on riding out
tonight? *Una grande tormenta* is brewing like a
bruja."

"There isn't time to wait, *amigo.* Can your son
saddle two of my horses? The quarter horse and the
Morgan."

"Con mucho gusto, señor. I, myself, feed and

groom your horses. They are too fine to allow my lazy *hijo* around them."

After the owner hurried away, Kathleen dropped to one of the benches at the nearest vacant table. She dearly wanted to stay the night, even if it meant sleeping on the table. But she'd drop in her tracks before she'd show feminine weakness by requesting this of Simon. And she doubted whether he would have been gentlemanly enough to accede to the request anyway.

Wearily she looked up to find his light eyes on her. "You can still change your mind."

Kathleen's shoulders straightened immediately. "I can manage."

"As you wish," he replied, and swung his long legs over the bench on the other side of the table, seating himself as Juan bustled into the main room with two platters. His son, a thin youth with a pockmarked face, set two chipped glasses before them and filled the glasses with wine, the sight of which made Kathleen's mouth dry with thirst.

Simon lifted his glass in a toast. "May the California winds sing of your beauty and the valley grasses dance for your smile."

Kathleen was not sure if he was mocking her or playing the gallant *caballero*. "Does that come from Texas or Mexico?" she asked defensively, wondering if the tale of the Mexican president's wife being his mistress was true.

Simon's lips met together in a tight line. "Neither. It's a line from a Shoshone Indian song."

"Oh," she said, somehow regretting her spitefulness. The rest of the meal was eaten in silence broken only by the intermittent conversations of the other travelers, mostly rancheros on their way to Santa Barbara or Monterey, the capital of the province.

But she was well aware of Simon's intent regard, and at last boldly met his gaze, which had come to rest at the high neckline of her black dress, now coated with dust from the day's journey.

"Is there something about me you find fault with?" she asked icily.

Simon crossed one booted leg over the other and took his time lighting up another *cigarro*. "Since I didn't expect a female tutor, you'll have to be content without a sidesaddle. I take it you didn't bring anything suitable for riding astride?"

Reluctantly Kathleen shook her head. It was just one more opportunity for him to prove how inadequate she was for the job.

Simon grimaced but motioned to Juan. "Can you spare a pair of your son's *calzones*—and a *camisa?*"

"*Sí*, Señor Reyes. *Un momento, por favor.*"

Simon turned back to her and said brusquely, "You can change in the back room."

Kathleen's square chin shot up. "I'll not dress like a boy!"

Simon's voice was cool and detached, so that the other travelers knew nothing of the tension that hung over the table where the ranchero and the fair-haired woman sat. "You'll do what I tell you, ma'am . . . unless, that is, you care to find work here on the coast. I'm sure the *soldados* would be most appreciative of your charms. Maybe you could even try La Palacia. Or, if you want, you could return to wherever you came from . . ." He shrugged and let his voice dwindle off insinuatingly as Juan's son came into the room with an armful of clothing.

"Well?" he asked, raising one dark brow questioningly. "What's it to be?"

She put out her hand for the clothing. "You don't give me any choice, do you?" Hadn't she once said the same to her father?

Simon's laugh was as bitter as her voice had been. "Few people get choices out here, ma'am. You take what life deals you and play the hand the best you can . . . as I'm sure you'll learn to do. I've no time to pamper some lady of the evening. If you can't handle the post, I'll ship you back." He ground out the *cigarro* in his empty plate. "Now get dressed while I see to the horses."

Furious, Kathleen took the clothing and, whirling, went to the room Simon indicated. Other than the silver-mounted saddle hung on a peg and a striped *serape* rolled up against one wall, there was only a bed with a mattress of "prairie feathers"

—grass ticking. Then Kathleen spotted beneath the bed the one luxury she had been hoping for, a porcelain chamber pot.

Fumbling with her skirts, she dropped the lace-edged pantalettes and at last relieved her aching bladder, before hurrying to change. She yanked at the buttons of her bodice, detesting the ranchero even as she obeyed his command to don boy's clothing.

The loose *camisa* fitted her more like a short dress than a shirt, and the baggy pants she had to roll around her ankles. A *riata* served as a belt for her narrow waist, and *huaraches* hugged the slim feet. When she was dressed, she rolled the kid slippers and pantalettes in her dress.

Hesitantly she opened the door and slipped along the wall, hoping she would not attract the attention of the others in the outer room.

Once outside, in the swaying light of the lanterns, she saw a sardonic smile curve the long line of Simon's lips. "It looks like my tutor has now changed to *un muchacho*."

"Let's hope you can remember I'm your tutor—and that's all."

Simon laughed. "If you could see yourself, you'd know you have no worry in that direction. Now let's get going before the storm breaks."

At the corral Juan stood waiting, holding in one hand the reins of a stocky but powerful quarter horse and a sturdy black Morgan. Simon took the yellow slicker strapped to the cantle of the quarter horse. "Put it on."

"No!" Kathleen said, rebelling at wearing the hot, sticky garment.

"Suit yourself," he said, and swung the large cape over his wide shoulders like a greatcoat.

She noticed that her valise was slung over the saddle of the Morgan. But rather than delay Simon, who now wore an impatient frown, by hauling down the valise and repacking her dress, she turned to Juan and handed him her clothing.

"Señor, I can't take these with me," she told him. "Perhaps the woman in the kitchen—Carmela— maybe she could use them."

"Muchísimas gracias, señorita," he replied with a shy smile, taking the clothing.

There was a peculiar look in Simon's eyes, but it vanished quickly as he assisted her up into the saddle, his hands easily encircling her waist.

Leaving the rancho station behind them in the blackening night, Simon turned the quarter horse, Salvaje—and Kathleen thought the great beast truly resembled some savage animal—east in the direction of the Santa Clara River, which followed the foothills of the Topotopo Mountains.

The pueblo of San Buenaventura was far behind them, only a huddle of lights, when the first sprinkling began, growing steadily into a torrential downpour. Hours later the pelting rain plastered

Kathleen's hair to her face, and her clothes clung to her shivering frame like a transparent second skin.

Simon looked back at her once, laughing as if he were enjoying himself in nature's lashing elements. The wind filled his giant yellow slicker, making him look like some apparition. His voice came to her in a shout over the roar of the storm. "Chupu—the god of the channel coast—he must be angry to bring the rainy season this early!"

That Simon should know so much of the Indian folklore of the California province surprised Kathleen. But then, she was beginning to realize that this was a resourceful man she worked for. Then, as a hurricane of wind swept down out of the heavens, she was too occupied handling her mare, Estrellita, to give Simon Reyes further thought.

The *arroyos* that cut deeply into the hills, forming *barrancas*, raced with rainwater. Overhead, lightning danced across the spiraling tops of the *piñon* trees. Several times thunder rumbled down the canyons, exploding in earthshaking claps, and Kathleen's mare would shy, rearing perilously and snorting its terror.

As experienced a rider as she was, Kathleen was too exhausted and drenched to control the frightened horse. When Estrellita next reared, Simon wheeled about, sawing on Salvaje's reins with exasperation. Moving in close to Kathleen, he grabbed the bridle of the wildly dancing mare.

"*Dulce! Dulce!*" he called gently. And as the

animal's terror ebbed, Kathleen found herself swept up in one sinewy arm and transferred, like a bag of potatoes, to Salvaje, so that she was held tightly before Simon.

"I thought you said you could ride."

"I can! But I'm tired! And wet!"

"Well, if you're going to take on the responsibilities of a man, you can damn well endure the hardships!"

"But Estrellita, she'll—"

"Estrellita'll follow. She's more docile than you."

Gritting her teeth, Kathleen subsided in apathetic indifference, too tired to care what happened. She was unwillingly grateful when Simon enfolded her within the dry folds of the slicker. The heat of his body enveloped her, making her drowsy.

When next she awoke, she was dimly aware of the spare, angular face above her; of arms that cradled her, lowering her to a bed of incense-cedar boughs and soft animal skins.

8

Kathleen stirred, not wishing to awaken from the languorous feeling which drugged every muscle and nerve in her body. But little by little she grew dimly aware of hands that tore away her sopping shirt, revealing the taut, cold breasts barely concealed beneath the chemise.

Drowsily she protested as the hands pulled at the *riata* that held her *calzones* in place. But the soaked pants clung to her thighs. When Simon rolled her over on her stomach, yanking roughly till the pants slipped about her ankles, she cried out suddenly in fear.

He laughed softly—evilly, it seemed to her. His

hands crushed against the small of her back, almost encircling her waist. "What? The *muchacho*'s afraid? Shall I take you as the *soldados* did each time an Indian boy escaped from the mission compound? Or maybe I first ought to whip you into submission? I don't think you'd like either."

His hands crept up her rib cage to cup the small, perfectly shaped breasts. "Or maybe you would enjoy it," he taunted, as he lowered his body atop her buttocks, so that, even through the tight, wet breeches, she could feel his manhood pressed hard against her.

"No—no," she begged in a whisper, hating herself for pleading. She twisted beneath his weight, but it was useless. His ironlike grasp tightened about her, cutting off her breath.

"Maybe you prefer the Castilian class . . . like your Lieutenant Aguila—to the lowly *cholo?*"

Kathleen began struggling again, but to her dismay she found herself abruptly released. Simon rose, standing astride her like some Grecian statue. Forgetting her nudity, she turned on one elbow and glared up into the face that mocked her.

"You're no more than an animal," she spat.

The teeth gleamed in the darkness of the cabin. "You'd do well to remember that, Kathleen. Like an animal, I don't waste time on the usual preliminaries of your gallant *caballeros*, but take what I want."

His eyes, cold as chips of green ice, raked over

her slowly. "But you, my tutor, are hardly what I want. You look like a half-drowned cat."

"Here," he said, tossing her a shirt of deerhide he had taken from a row of pegs on the wall. "Get into that while I tend the horses."

He stalked outside, letting in a blast of rain before closing the door sharply behind him. Kathleen hurried to slip the heavy, warm shirt over her head before he could come back. It was far too large for her, its fringed hem reaching almost to her knees.

In the stillness that enclosed the cabin room she became aware of the faint sound of running water. By straining her eyes, she could make out in the darkness a small ditch that cut through the cabin floor, bringing the melodious tones of a swift flowing mountain creek. She could barely discern ferns growing in various spots through the pine-board floor and climbing up about the shuttered window.

Apparently someone had trained the ferns. A feminine hand, no doubt. Kathleen wondered with piqued curiosity what other woman (or women?) Simon had brought there . . . and what the woman was to him.

The door came open with the wind, and she quickly dropped to the bed of cedar boughs as Simon entered. He did not even glance in her direction, but shrugged out of his own wet shirt and pants and crossed to the fireplace. His rich walnut-colored hair glistened with raindrops, so that when he shook his head and the drops splattered, he looked like some great wolf shaking his wet coat.

Covertly she watched him as he knelt on the stone hearth and began working with the tinder and flint. When the small sticks took flame, his polished bronze skin glinted eerily, throwing into relief the angles of his face and shadowing the expressionless eyes. Squatting there before the growing flame, he could have been some ferocious Indian rather than a civilized ranchero.

When he rose, tall and lean, Kathleen crouched back in the shadows. His nude body outlined by the firelight, he advanced on her. She shuddered, scooting back until she ran up against the wall.

"You've got nothing to fear," he said evenly. "I'm too tired to count coup on you tonight."

She felt the bed give slightly under his weight. When some moments had passed and he made no move to take her, she eased herself into a prone position. But the bed was scarcely large enough for one, and she was forced to endure the intimacy of his bare skin against hers.

For a while she huddled at the bed's far edge. At length, realizing from the deep, even breathing that he was asleep, Kathleen moved closer, seeking his warmth. There was the odor of the shirt's worn leather and Simon's rain-dampened skin in her nostrils. As the fire's warmth spread throughout the small room, she felt her lids grow heavy with sleep again.

In the early hours of the morning she awoke to find herself pinioned beneath one of Simon's muscle-corded arms. One long leg, shadowed with fine hair, was thrown across the lower half of her body. She stirred, trying to ease herself from him.

"Were you seeking my embrace, Catalina?" he murmured against her ear.

The Spanish use of her name affected Kathleen strangely. She turned her head to look up into the dark face so near her own. A man shouldn't have eyelashes that long, she thought.

Then she was suddenly aware of the length of their bodies touching, of his leather shirt bunched up about her thighs.

What in the name of all that was holy could she be thinking about, lying in bed with the man—and not at all distraught? Had that one night at La Palacia brought her to this? No shame? No qualms?

"Your embraces are the last thing I want, Simon Reyes," she told him fiercely. The amused smirk on his face made her want to scratch his eyes out. "I want only the job. Or do both necessarily come together?"

Simon raised on one elbow and looked down at the girl beneath him, all golden in the early morning light, with her hair fanned out around her like spilled champagne. He laughed even as his eyes swept over her wickedly. "You're safe from me, Catalina. I prefer my women warm and willing."

Rising, he gave her a swat on the hips. "Your clothes are drying by the fire. Get dressed. We've got a lot of ground to cover today."

It seemed to Kathleen that she was always undressing or dressing for him. Averting her eyes from his nakedness, she padded on bare feet across the plank floor, stepping carefully over the narrow ditch of running water. For some seconds she stood in front of the fireplace, letting the dying embers warm her chilled skin, before reluctantly picking up the *camisa* and *calzones*.

"Would it be too much to ask you to turn your head while—"

Simon's hand came over her mouth like a vise, shutting off her last words. Pulling her with him, he backed toward the heap of clothing he had deposited on the floor the previous night.

Kathleen found herself pushed into the corner as Simon swiftly scooped up the flintlock pistol, which lay on top of the clothing. They were standing in the shadows when the cabin's door slowly opened.

A man of medium height with sandy brown shoulder-length hair stood there, a muzzle-loader cradled in his arms. He was dressed in fringed buckskin, and a powder horn was slung about his neck. The keen gray eyes took in Simon and the small figure behind him, and he smiled.

"You haven't lost that sixth sense of yours, have you, Simon?"

Simon chuckled and stepped forward. "Frémont,

you've no respect for a man's privacy." He began pulling on his pants. "Where's the uniform?"

The man called Frémont moved into the room. "My father-in-law felt it should be left behind on this expedition."

"So Senator Benton thinks the Mexican officials might not take too kindly to a soldier of the U.S. Army wandering through California?"

"More than that. He's pressuring Polk—as soon as the man takes office—to make Mexico an offer. But my orders are for the Oregon Territory. I was afraid I'd missed you yesterday."

"I got held up—on business." Simon nodded in the direction where Kathleen waited in the shadows.

She saw the other man's eyes ease over her with a look of—pity? Oh, dear Lord, that would be the last straw. What must the man think of her—half naked there with Simon?

"I'd like to dress," she said stiffly. "If you two wouldn't mind."

"Captain John Frémont," Simon said, "you are beholding the first female tutor in the California province—Miss Kathleen Summers."

Frémont's sun-squinched eyes were sympathetic. "Pleased to meet you, Miss Summers," he said softly, dropping his backpack on the floor.

Kathleen lowered her lids and nodded, too embarrassed to speak.

"Turn your head, Frémont, before her maidenly modesty gets the best of her. Had your coffee yet?"

"No, and I'm hungrier than a family of buzzards."

The man leaned the long rifle against the wall and turned to open the shutters while Simon took a battered tin coffeepot from the crude hutch that stood in one corner. Mountain air, fresh from the night's rain, filled the room.

"What about the man Polk's named as his Secretary of the Navy?" Simon asked. "Did you get a chance to corner him—what's his name?"

"Bancroft—George Bancroft," Kathleen answered automatically, without thinking, as she quickly pulled the now-dry cotton shirt and pants on.

Both men whirled on her, startled. "Do you know him?" Simon demanded.

"I do read the newspapers." How shocked Simon would be if she told him his lowly employee had danced with the historian at President Harrison's inaugural ball.

She saw Frémont's gaze jump to Simon questioningly. And the almost imperceptible shake of Simon's dark head. Feeling something like an intruder, Kathleen turned away, busying herself with the tangled mass of her hair, pulling it once more into the severe knot at her neck and donning the bothersome glasses.

As the coffee perked over the coals in the fireplace, the two men turned their talk to affairs in California instead. "Then it's true," Frémont asked, "that the missions have at last been taken out of the hands of the religious authorities?"

"Secularized." Simon's voice was scornful. "Oh, yes. The Indians that Mexico freed were supposed to get a portion of the mission lands. But most of them were either cheated of their shares or forced to sell them for little in order to survive. For several years now the Indians have been drifting into the ranchos. Looking for any kind of work."

"We hear that the bandits are rife again—and the revolutionists."

Simon smiled. "Much to Mexico's irritation."

"It's what the senator's been waiting to hear."

Simon nodded curtly before his face closed over. Pouring the parching coffee into tin cups, he handed one first to Kathleen, who sat on the hearth. She tried to make her face as much of a blank as she dared, but she was interested in the conversation. However, nothing more was said.

Frémont pulled out hardtack biscuits from his backpack and passed them around. When the meager breakfast was finished and the clutter had been cleared away, Frémont said good-bye to Simon and Kathleen outside the cabin. "Hope to see you again, Miss Summers. On my next trip back."

"If she hasn't deserted for a more rewarding job," Simon said, his eyes flickering from Frémont to Kathleen.

Kathleen knew all too well what Simon was think-ing—that she might once again find it more prof-itable to be the paramour of a highborn Castilian soldier. And she found it ludicrous that instead she had been for one night the whore of some lowborn *cholo.*

But that would be one thing she would never let the arrogant ranchero know. She could imagine the contemptuous curl of Simon's thin lips if he should learn she had been taken by a common vaquero. It was one satisfaction she wouldn't give him.

Frémont swung up onto a cantankerous-looking pack mule, and the two men shook hands. Kathleen watched with a feeling of dejection while the soldier rode away. She was once again at the mercy of Si-mon's vacillating whim.

After Frémont disappeared over a rise, Simon abruptly grasped Kathleen about the waist and lifted her onto Estrellita's back, before mounting his own horse. He wheeled Salvaje around, setting off in the opposite direction, and Kathleen's mare meekly followed.

It seemed to her as the afternoon passed they climbed ever higher, passing windfallen pines and sheer cliffs broken in places by massive rounded domes and spectacular waterfalls.

As they began a gradual descent, her attention turned to the great herds of cattle grazing in alpine gardens. And far below in the valley she could see the gleam of white adobe and red tile. Amidst the tropical vegetation, so green it hurt the eyes, she made out a hacienda. Sprawling in all directions, it had to have at least thirty rooms. About it were smaller ranch houses, huts, and corrals.

Noting her interest, Simon said, "We've been on land belonging to Valle del Bravo for some time now."

"Then all these cattle are yours—and the sheep and goats?"

"Everything in this valley is mine."

Kathleen glanced sharply across at Simon. Did he imply she was included in that inventory? But his face was as impassive as ever.

The remainder of the descent was broken only once—when Kathleen questioned Simón about the great bird circling overhead; swooping, then soaring. A bird of prey, Simon told her. The vulture— *el cóndor*. If Kathleen had been superstitious, she would have believed the condor to be an ill omen.

9

How does one mark the passage of days, weeks? For Kathleen it was a time of respite. The sunny days passed to the drumming of hooves, the squeak of saddle leather, the jangle of spurs' rowels; and the evenings to the melody of soft voices and the strum of guitars shining in the moonlight.

Only in the deep hush of night did she still suffer. Few nights passed that she was not plagued by the same nightmare. The same lithe body to crush her, to possess her, to smother the last breath from her. And when the earring gleamed in her dreams like a coiling copper snake, Kathleen would awake with screams of horror trembling on her lips and perspiration running in rivulets down her body.

But with the dawn her nightmares dispersed, ushering in another perfect Mediterranean-like day at the hacienda. Hidden away in the Valle del Bravo—Valley of the Brave—the hacienda kept the world at bay. The sun-dried adobe house with its encircling veranda and red-tiled roof was nestled among wild orange trees, scented peach orchards, lime groves, and date palms. And everywhere grew the fragrant hibiscus, oleander, and bougainvillea.

Though more than a hundred people lived on the rancho—including cousins, aunts, and nephews of the workers—there was never the frenzied rushing that Kathleen associated with Boston. Rather there pervaded an atmosphere of indolent tranquility.

In spite of the people who came for their lessons each afternoon at the grape arbor—carpenters, tanners, house servants, and vaqueros—Kathleen felt a loneliness that sometimes pierced her through. For those Mexicans and Indians who could neither read nor write held the *maestra,* or tutor, in awe. Hidden behind the thick spectacles, she appeared to the students who sat at her feet, beneath the shade of the grapevines, more a person of neuter gender than a woman.

Only Diego, an old leather-jacket soldier, saw Kathleen for what she really was—a lonely young woman. As majordomo of the hacienda since the death of Andrew King some twenty years earlier, he saw and knew everything. He spent the long, warm days sitting on a hard bench on the veranda. The bench stood next to the kitchen door, and, amidst the clucking of the chickens and the barking of the yard dogs, Diego listened to the gossip of the household servants. The brown, wrinkled face beneath the thatch of white hair would smile in secret amusement as the cook, Maria Jesus, chased her grandson from the pies cooling in the kitchen or would grow nostalgic as he overheard the vaquero Julio whisper flirtatious words to plump Amelia, one of the house servants.

So it was Diego's bench Kathleen naturally sought, after her teaching duties were completed. Sometimes they talked of days past; sometimes they only sat in companionable silence. But many times Kathleen wished to ask bony Diego what he knew of Simon Reyes.

Yet a perverse reluctance kept her from doing so. She rarely saw the haughty *patrón* of Valle del Bravo, but when she did, there was something about him that never failed to infuriate her. Maybe it was the sardonic curve of the lean lips. Or the way the slashed brow raised in mocking amusement whenever their eyes happened to meet.

She was therefore glad that Simon rode out every day, dressed in leather britches and a worn cotton shirt like the other vaqueros; she was glad to be rid of his unsettling presence.

However, this ended with the advent of the

spring festivities. These gay celebrations sometimes went on for a week at a time, often moving from one rancho to the next. Each family competed to display the most bountiful table, the most gracious hospitality. Peace, gaiety, harmony—a pastoral paradise.

And Kathleen was introduced to this idyllic life through the avid curiosity of the Southern California populace.

"*Qué?* A woman tutor?" cried Doña Arcadia, the wife of the richest man in California—and the ugliest—the horse-faced Don Abel Stearns. "You must bring her, Simon!"

"*Una mujer norteamericana, mi amigo?*" Don Pio Pico, the ex-*gobernador* exclaimed. "I have to see the young woman," he told Simon, his fierce gray mustache quivering beneath his large, aristocratic nose.

"So you see," Simon explained to Kathleen in the privacy of his study, "good manners require that I present you at the next fiesta."

Kathleen tore her gaze from the shelves of bound volumes—*Don Quixote* . . . *Laws of the Indies* . . . *Gil Blas*—confused to find that the Texas scout should have such an education. But then perhaps the books had belonged to the previous owner of Valle del Bravo, Doña Delores. Yet somehow she doubted it.

Returning her attention to Simon, who stood

looking out the grilled window, his hands jammed in his pants pockets, Kathleen said crisply, "I was somehow under the impression that you were not one to bother with good manners."

Simon turned with a laugh of pure amusement. "You got to permit an uncouth ranchero his black moods, Kathleen," he said with a wry grin. "But no, it's very important that the good manners of Valle del Bravo never be questioned."

Kathleen was tempted to inquire further, but Simon went on, his relaxed attitude once more replaced by cool, clipped words:

"You'll need something more . . . oh, festive."

He nodded at the heavy woolen gown she wore, one of the few gowns she had. It was formerly the cook Amanda's, and was more suitable to New England's cold climate than the semitropical weather of California.

"I'm afraid I've nothing fitting for a party, Señor Reyes."

"Simon," he said with exasperation. "Well then, have one of the Indian girls make something up for you. Show them what you want. You know more about that than I do," he said impatiently.

It was one of black silk and ivory lace. And when the gown was finished, it accomplished just the opposite of what Kathleen had planned—attracting the attentive eye of every person at the fiesta of Don Pedro and Doña Lucia Escandón, the relatives the Castilian couple at the mission had spoken of to Kathleen.

Kathleen had meant to appear matronly, but the lovely apricot skin and shimmering gold tresses against the background of the brilliant black gown had just the reverse effect. Only the thick, distorting spectacles spoiled the perfection of Kathleen's appearance.

The fiesta, which was to begin before noon and last for two days, drew neighboring families separated by distances of hundreds of miles or more. In that Mexican province which revered the horse, no one came by buckboard or buggy. Corpulent duennas, sober matrons, flippant belles—they all rode sidesaddle. And the men, from youths to grandfathers, proudly rode in advance of the women.

Kathleen, dressed in a russet riding habit, rode astride Estrellita, with fat Maria Jesus at her side, weighting down a bony burro. The cook, whose flat, dour face made her the perfect duenna for Kathleen, was one of the few Californios who did not take to the four-footed animal as a means of transportation. In one hand she clutched the burro's reins while with the other she told her rosary, mumbling beseechments with each obsidian bead.

The Escandón rancho was some twenty-five miles from Valle del Bravo. Twenty-five miles of juniper and chaparral, mountain creeks and lily-pad-filled lagoons. Twenty-five miles that passed quickly, as Simon talked casually of the Californios Kathleen would meet.

He told her of old Juan Bandini, whose performance of the decorous fandango was the high point of any fiesta; and of the American, Henry Fitch, who had run off with Josefa Carrillo to Chile.

"The most dramatic elopement in California," Simon said, smiling.

"Why?"

"It seems the flinty American had been courting Josefa for three years. There they were at the altar, when there's brought an edict banning their marriage. Issued by none other than the governor, Echeandia—Josefa's spurned suitor."

Kathleen was delighted with the story—and at the same time somewhat amazed at the unseen humorous side of Simon. "Tell me more," she prompted.

"You may meet another American—Cave Johnson Couts. His wife Ysidora, a daughter of Bandini, fell into her husband-to-be's arms when she was watching his column of cavalry from her roof and the railing gave way."

Then he told Kathleen of the leading merchant in Monterey, Thomas Larkin, whose wife would soon give birth to the first fully American baby born in the California province and would therefore be unable to attend the fiesta. "An American woman," he said, "is as rare here as the white buffalo. There are only *yanqui* husbands seeking Mexico's daughters."

"All the more reason why you should keep me as your tutor," Kathleen told him. "I'm an oddity."

Simon laughed aloud. "That's something I've found out for myself!"

The hours flew by with Simon's stories of the Californios who would be at the fiesta. But never did he once speak of the host and hostess's beauteous daughter, Francesca.

By the time they arrived, the guests were having their midday feast at tables set out in the gardens or on blankets spread beneath the trees. Kathleen's mind spun with the long, difficult names of those she was presented to, many of them requiring the Castilian lisp to pronounce correctly.

Simon seemed to find it amusing when Doña Lucia at once cornered her, demanding to know of the latest fashion in the United States.

"Not nearly so feminine as your lace mantillas and high-backed Spanish combs," she told the pompous matron politely.

But when Kathleen turned back to Simon, she found he had abandoned her to talk with a gentleman who still wore his graying hair clubbed at his neck with a ribbon, a style that had gone out a decade earlier.

"That's the Lord of the North, Mariano Vallejo," a woman with warm brown eyes and a friendly smile said, joining Kathleen. "All his daughters are married to American men."

"Which is all the more reason for Vallejo to join us, Doña Arcadia," the man at her side said, his heavy jowls quivering with anger. "If Vallejo listens much longer to that damned Sutter, we won't stand a chance against Micheltorena!"

"José!" Doña Arcadia said warningly, and hastened to present Kathleen to the ex-general of California, José Castro.

"Well, you can't ignore the fact," the man said indignantly, after the introductions were made. "The Californios are suffering under Micheltorena—Santa Anna's puppet!"

Warming up to his subject, the general rocked back and forth on his heels as he continued his tirade. "And Micheltorena knows we want him removed. It's no secret. What's more, if there were a separation of the political and military commands, there wouldn't be such discontent among the Californios!"

His diatribe on California politics would have continued indefinitely had not Doña Arcadia rescued Kathleen, saying it was time for the siesta. "A voluble man, but a brilliant general," she said with a smile as she led Kathleen to the room that had been assigned her.

Kathleen had not yet become accustomed to the siesta, the hour which promised to make a young woman's eyes more brilliant by candlelight but unfortunately also brought about matronliness. During this hour the women gathered in the spacious *recameras*, the bedrooms, which were cool and dim after the hours of untempered sunlight, and gossiped of the day's flirtations.

For a while Kathleen talked with the woman she shared the bedroom with, Anita de la Guerra, who, although only twenty-five, had been married for eleven years to the American shipping agent at Santa Barbara, Alfred Robinson. But after a while, Anita grew drowsy and dozed off.

Unable to sleep, Kathleen used the hour to freshen herself. She was sitting before the marble-topped bureau, repairing her wilted hairdo, when a girl of no more than sixteen or seventeen years entered. Small in height, she was elegantly dressed in black lace and yellow silk, with a high-backed comb of black pearls securing the heavy ebony tresses.

Her jet eyes flashed at Kathleen. *"Perdóneme,"* she said. "I have the wrong bedroom."

"That's quite all right," Kathleen replied to the girl's image in the mirror, an image that was both seductive and innocent—one that Kathleen imagined would lose its appeal with age.

"I am Doñanita Francesca Escandón," the girl announced imperiously.

"My name is Kathleen Summers." What did the girl want?

"You are Simon's little tutor?"

"I work for him."

Francesca stood in the doorway a moment longer, her curiosity clearly not satisfied, unable to think of any further excuse for remaining. *"Con su permiso,"* she said finally, with pouting lips, and closed the door.

Kathleen breathed a sigh of relief with Francesca's departure, knowing instinctively that the girl disliked her sharing the same household with Simon.

She smiled faintly at the girl's naïveté. If Francesca could but know of the contemptuous indifference with which Simon held his tutoress . . .

That evening, as the stars came out, fires were lit and the guests dined on barbequed beef, corn griddle-cakes, a thick soup with meatballs and red peppers in it, and the *vino del país*. Later the older guests retired to the benches to tell stories while the younger ones danced to the gay music of guitars and violins.

Feeling, as a tutor, not quite a part of the grandee class, Kathleen remained in the shadows watching, observing. During the intervals between the dances she saw Francesca flirting with the admiring *caballeros*, tapping one on the shoulder reprovingly with her jeweled fan or laughing gaily at another's whispered words.

Tiring of them, she danced more and more with a handsome black-haired man who seemed to have eyes only for her. Kathleen thought she recognized the man from the mission.

"That's Dimitri Karamazan, isn't it?" she asked Doña Arcadia.

"*Sí*. It is said that he decided to remain in California when his countrymen gave up their settlement at Fort Ross."

But apparently Francesca grew weary of trying her newly found feminine powers on Dimitri, for Kathleen watched the girl's eyes rove longingly in the direction of Simon, who had been engaged in deep conversation with various men the entire evening.

"You can't really blame Francesca for preferring Simon Reyes over the Russian officer," Doña Arcadia said.

"Why do you say that?" Kathleen asked, with an inflection of casual interest.

Doña Arcadia's dark brown eyes regarded Kathleen wisely. "Well, you must admit that Simon is not as handsome, but—"

The woman's eyes took on a speculative look as Simon turned to find Francesca at his side. He seemed to give the girl his full attention, and a slight smile hovered at the ends of his long lips.

"There's something about him," Doña Arcadia resumed. "His tough defiance—and his genuine interest in women . . . when he asserts himself . . . that makes his rough masculine looks undenyingly attractive."

Kathleen arched a sceptical brow.

"Well, never mind," the other woman said. "You'll find out."

Kathleen's gaze strayed to Simon. Dressed in a jacket of black silk, a richly embroidered waistcoat, short breeches with white stockings, and deerskin shoes made by his Indian workers, his lean, tall physique did indeed cut an impressive figure.

But, unlike Francesca, Kathleen had no intention of succumbing to the ranchero's rugged attractions.

10

Amelia brushed out the golden hair of her young mistress. The lovely *maestra* had already, in one short month, captured the affection of all of Valle del Bravo.

Everyone, that is, thought the plump, brown girl, except *el patrón*. A pity, she mused. For though Señor Simon looked as ferocious as Satan himself, he had been more than fair in his dealings with the servants since he came to Valle del Bravo.

And the *maestra*—Amelia looked in the mirror at the reflection of the young lady who sat dispassionately before her. Although the *maestra* was gentleness itself, and very patient in the hours she spent teaching them, there was something about her—a fierceness that matched *el patrón*'s.

Perhaps it was the way the violet eyes slanted—or the tawny mane that framed the golden face. *La señorita* reminded Amelia of some cat that would come down from the mountains to drink from the ponds . . . never to be tamed, only subdued by a mate of equal spirit. Yes, she was glad that *el patrón*, on his return from the Escandón fiesta, had told her to care for the *maestra* during the long months of fiestas ahead.

Simon Reyes occupied Kathleen's thoughts too. Why did she feel so uneasy around him? Not since that rainy night at his cabin had he been anything but polite to her, though in an almost mocking way. True, he had probably heard the gossip spread by those two spinsters—and had seen her on the beach with the detestable Aguila. But was that any reason to judge her—when his own past seemed just as open to speculation?

And believing her to be a woman of easy virtue—or worse—what could Simon have been told by Nathan Plummer to make him change his mind and return to interview her?

However, Simon's poor opinion of her was little to worry about, since she rarely saw him anyway. He was always gone, often for days at a time. And, fortunately for her, on the days he did spend on the rancho, he would ride out early in the morning with his vaqueros to hunt wild horses or round up stray cattle, the *cimarrones*, and not return until late at night.

And that was another thing. Kathleen noticed that in spite of his Spanish surname, Simon did not adhere to many of the Latin customs, such as taking the heaviest meal in the middle of the day. Rather, after his return, he would bathe, then dine alone at the long, heavy table of oak.

But that night, after Amelia left Kathleen, things were to be different. There was a timid knock at Kathleen's door as she brushed her teeth before the pine-framed mirror over the bureau. She pulled the lawn wrapper about her. "*Sí?*" she asked.

"*Perdóneme,*" Amelia said, opening the door slightly and sticking her round, pigtailed head through the aperture. "*El patrón* would like to see you in the dining room."

"At this hour? It's almost ten, Amelia. Can't it wait until tomorrow?"

Amelia's eyes widened, and she opened her mouth, then closed it. Of course, thought Kathleen, no one keeps *el patrón* waiting. "Tell Señor Reyes I'll be there in five minutes, *por favor.*"

Amelia bobbed her head in relief. "*Sí,* Señorita Catalina."

Kathleen put on one of three day-dresses Amelia had made up for her in the weeks since the fiesta, a lilac batiste with ribbon sashes, and pinned her hair up in a chignon, but did not bother with the spectacles, in her haste to dress.

She realized it would be the first time Simon had seen her without the disguising glasses, but in the dimness of the scented candlelight she doubted whether Simon would notice. Yet from the far end of the table she saw the scarred brow raise in mild amusement.

"Yes?" she asked, ignoring the twitch of his lips. "You wanted me?"

"Take a seat, Kathleen. Maria Jesus'll bring you something to eat."

"No, thank you. I've already eaten."

Kathleen noticed that he looked tired; the lines around his mouth seemed harsher, deeper. And against the whiteness of the linen shirt, his face, normally as bronzed as an Indian's, looked pale.

"I asked you to sit," he said evenly. The green eyes, as fathomless as mirrors, watched her, waiting.

"Very well." Kathleen took the seat at the end opposite Simon, remaining silent as Maria Jesus brought in another plate. Kathleen took a few tentative bites, noticing that Simon did not eat much either, though he consumed a great deal of the sangría from the decanter Maria Jesus had left on the table.

When the strain of the silence began to grate on Kathleen's nerves, Simon spoke. "The workers—

what have you taught them so far? Are they willing to learn?"

Kathleen put down her fork. "At first they were hesitant. Especially the older servants. The first week Maria Jesus refused to come to the arbor. Declared she was too old. But she comes now and listens, though she still won't participate."

"And Diego?"

"Diego's quick, you know. He and Amelia seem the most promising. He's picked up English remarkably fast. And since he's started coming, I've found that after the *comida* some of your shepherds and vaqueros steal into the arbor during the siesta hour instead of resting."

Kathleen leaned forward, her great purple eyes shining with pleasure. "They sit quietly, like Maria Jesus, not saying anything. But I know they're assimilating most of what I say. Do you realize, Simon," she went on eagerly, "what could be accomplished if only ten of the Indians who work for you learn to read and write? Think of it! With an education they could raise themselves out of the squalid—"

Kathleen broke off, aware of the inscrutable expression in the eyes that watched her so closely.

"You're a surprising woman."

Kathleen was unsure how to take the statement. "I . . . Thank you," she concluded awkwardly, putting her napkin on the table. "If you'll excuse me—if that's all, I'd like to—"

"No, it isn't. I want to talk with you about your job."

"You're not satisfied?" she asked, perplexed.

"As tutor—sure. But I want you to take on an added task—mistress of the hacienda."

Simon nodded at the portrait of Doña Delores that hung on the far wall. Kathleen had never liked the portrait and found it hard to believe that the heavyset woman with the faint shadow of a mustache over the bitter line of the lips was the famed beauty Father Marcos had mentioned.

"I'd hoped Doña Delores would stay on as mistress here, but she died shortly after I arrived." His face grim, he went on. "Since everyone seems quite enchanted with your . . . charms, I'd like for you to be responsible for the household—to see that all runs smoothly at the fiestas that'll be held here."

"Until another tutor can be brought out?" Kathleen lifted one slim brow.

The corners of Simon's lips curved in a lopsided grin. "So you're reminding me of the nasty behavior I displayed at the mission? Yes, until another tutor can be brought out."

Kathleen rose. "Then I'll bid you good night."

Simon nodded, and she left the room, savoring the fleeting moment of triumph.

Once in bed, Kathleen found she was too excited to sleep. Her impulsive flight from her father and

Edmund was working out far better than she could have hoped for. She was actually enjoying the simple life of the rancho and even found Simon pleasant to work for at times.

Hours later she still lay awake, wide-eyed and restless. She had long since discarded the thin coverlet as the heat seeped through the thick adobe walls. The moon splattered slanted patterns on the tile floor, beckoning her outside.

Once more Kathleen slipped into the wrapper at the foot of the bed and, softly throwing open the veranda doors, followed the silvery path of moonlight outside, across the cool tiles to the wrought iron railing.

There was not the smallest breeze, and her tangled curls lay damply against her neck, hanging heavily to her waist. With a movement as graceful as the mountain cat Amelia had compared her to, she stretched, lifting the mass of spun-gold hair over her arms, high off her back.

Something made her turn, made her aware of another's presence. In the shadows she saw only the red glare of a cigar tip, but she knew it was Simon who silently watched her.

"I—I didn't know anyone else was about," she murmured to the darker shadow. She pulled the wrapper tighter about her. "I couldn't sleep. The heat. I'm not used to it."

"It's the still before the Santa Ana," Simon said,

getting up from where he sat on the wooden bench. He came to her side and tossed the cigar over the railing so that the red tip arced in the blackness of the night like a shooting star. "The desert winds— the Santa Anas—they come the last of May. The ocean breezes suddenly halt, and the hot, dry winds come whirling down the canyons, through the passes, and rush out into the valleys."

"You talk like you've been in quite a few of these Santa Anas."

Simon glanced at her sharply. "Once is enough. The winds are harsh and burning. They rip off palm leaves, snap branches, and topple over eucalyptus trees. They bring so much dust and heat that no one dares make a light—even a stove."

Intrigued and drawn by the low, even cadence of his voice, Kathleen unconsciously leaned on the railing close to Simon.

"How long do these winds last?"

"A few days. After the winds stop, there's a celebration to coincide with the roundup. During the day, there are rodeos and the branding of the calves. And at night, barbeques and dancing."

"It must all be quite exciting," she said softly.

"You'll find out for yourself," Simon said, rising from the railing. "Unless you decide to run away again."

Kathleen looked up quickly. How much did he know? But the rough-cast face in the moonlight was enigmatic. The heavy-lidded eyes held hers, as if calmly waiting.

"I'd better go back inside," she said in a husky whisper, feeling more like a silly schoolgirl than a grown woman. "It's late."

"Come here, Kathleen."

She froze in the act of turning away. His hands were warm on her shoulders as he came up behind her, pulling her against him. "Are you afraid?" he whispered at her ear.

Kathleen's breath was as bellows in her lungs. *Yes!* she wanted to cry out. *I'm afraid to submit to the demand of your kisses . . . to the power man holds over woman . . . and the pain.* But the words never reached her lips.

Simon turned her to face him, and his mouth closed over hers. For a long moment Kathleen stood immobile against him. There was the heavy, sweet smell of sangría on his breath.

Then, as his lips left hers and roamed over her face, lightly tracing a trail that came to rest at her ear, Kathleen's legs began to tremble. She felt a warmth spread throughout her belly. To keep from sagging, she caught at his shoulders and felt him wince.

Instantly she drew away. "What is it, Simon?"

"It's nothing. I was hurt riding herd today. Diego tended to it this evening."

But Kathleen's left hand came away damp and sticky. "Your wound needs to be rebandaged."

Simon chuckled in the darkness. "I'm kissing you, and all you can think of is tending a wound?"

But he submitted and let her lead him to the kitchen. While he removed his shirt, Kathleen lit a candle and searched through the shelves for a clean cloth. When she turned around, Simon was sprawled in the rickety chair at the table. In the light of the candle the hair that matted the wide expanse of chest shone like the glossy pelt of some forest creature. She colored faintly as she realized she was staring at his naked torso with fascination.

Briskly she moved to him, laying the cloth and scissors on the table. "It won't take long," she said in a businesslike voice.

Kathleen still trembled from Simon's kiss. She was angry—at Simon for taking advantage of the fact she was hired help, at herself for letting her emotions get out of control. It could be disastrous for her if she should be forced to leave the sheltering hideaway of the hacienda.

Ignoring the lips that curled in faint amusement, she gently pulled at the old bandage, clotted with blood. Once, when the cloth adhered to the skin, she quickly stripped it away, knowing it must hurt. But Simon said nothing, only watched her.

"Simon, you've been grazed by a bullet!"

"One of the vaqueros' guns went off."

Kathleen picked up the candle, holding it close so that she could see while she deftly stanched the slow trickle of blood. As she finished, her gaze involuntarily strayed to the muscled column of Simon's neck. For the first time she marveled at the beauty in the masculine physique.

Then the candle began to shake in her hand as she stared unbelievingly at Simon's earlobe. *Dear God, no! It couldn't be!* But yes, there it was. In the light of the quivering candle could be seen the slight indentation in the lobe. A pierced ear.

"You!" The single word came out as hot and blistering as the Santa Ana. "You're the vaquero at La Palacia!"

She would have killed him then; would have buried the scissors in his heart. But Simon was swifter. In one liquid, quick movement he caught her wrist in a steel grasp as she lunged for the scissors.

The candle fluttered out on the floor.

"I'll kill you, I swear!" Tears of anger coursed down her cheeks. "I'll make you pay for what you did to me, Simon Reyes! You're a loathsome, bestial savage!"

Simon laughed softly as he jerked her against him so that the scissors fell to the floor with a clang. "I seriously doubt that you'll kill me, Catalina. For, where would you run next? Or don't you know that rewards were posted today in every town on the California coast"—one side of the lean lips lifted in a cruel smile—"for information leading to the whereabouts of a Miss Kathleen Whatley."

He shoved her from him. "Yes, I'm your vaquero, and you, *mi vida*, are Kathleen Whatley, are
you not? What crime are *you* running from?"

11

Gone were Kathleen's sweat-soaked nightmares. But they were replaced by hate-induced daydreams of revenge. There would yet be some way she could wreak her vengeance!

If Simon did not hand her over to the Mexican authorities first. But since that night three days ago, he had done nothing to indicate what his intentions were. If he did not intend to turn her in (and he certainly did not need the reward money), then did he plan to use her as he had that night at La Palacia?

Just let him try, Kathleen thought. The kitchen

knife she kept beneath her bodice would at least make the rogue think twice. Unconsciously she crumpled in her hand a paper one of her students had copied from a religious tract.

Dear God, how long could she continue to play this cat-and-mouse game, careful to always keep within earshot of one of the house servants during the day, laying awake at night, her ears straining to catch the fall of footsteps?

Her nerves were near to snapping, and in the tumultuous days that were to follow there was only the one moment of peace—like the calm before the storm.

That moment of calm came the same afternoon, as Kathleen sat on the veranda going over the students' papers. There came the sound of a horse cantering down the palm-tree-lined road toward the hacienda. But the hot, dry desert winds had begun to pick up, and the swirling dust concealed the rider's identity. However, Kathleen could tell, by the inexperienced way the rider sat the horse, that it was not one of the *vaqueros*—nor was it Simon.

She laid her papers aside and crossed to the railing, calling out in surprise as the rider approached and dismounted. "Nathan!"

Her hands gripped the railing in a paralysis of fear. Had Nathan, too, learned of her identity? Had he come to bring her back?

Nathan climbed the veranda's shallow steps in

one stride. "Kathleen," he said warmly, taking one of her hands. "How nice to see you again!"

"You know—you're a friend of Simon's?"

The sea-blue eyes were solemn. "Simon and I met a year ago. When the *Tempest* took him on, off San Blas, Mexico."

"Then why didn't you tell me in—"

"You didn't tell me your employer was Simon Reyes until the morning I left you at the mission."

Kathleen nodded, with a wan smile. "Of course. You visit Simon often?"

"Simon and I are partners in a trading venture. I buy his hides and tallow, and he buys silks, furniture, farm implements, and the like from me."

"Oh," she said, her breath easing from her lungs in relief. That explained the visit. And if Nathan didn't know her true identity, maybe no one else did either.

At once she felt lighter-hearted, tremendously glad that Nathan had come. His presence would soften her loneliness, would serve as a buffer against the hostility that existed between herself and Simon.

Like a schoolgirl, she tugged at the hand that held hers. "Come along, Nathan. We'll stable your horse. There's something I have to show you."

Unaware that the blue eyes rested on her with thoughtfulness, she led Nathan toward the rear of the hacienda. Near the stables was a small arena where the bulls were run. "Look," she said, climbing on the slats of one of the stalls.

A great bear, of perhaps nine hundred pounds or more, lumbered restlessly about the arena. His cinnamon-colored coat shone with a deep luster in the late afternoon sun.

"Diego said it's a grizzly bear, Nathan. Isn't it a beautiful creature? The vaqueros brought him in yesterday."

Standing on the slat, Kathleen was nearly the same height as Nathan, and when he looked back to her, she saw the sadness in his eyes.

"Within the month he may be dead."

Kathleen's own eyes widened. "Why?"

"When the roundup comes, lass, the vaqueros have a bear-bait. They match the grizzly in a fight with a bull, goading them until one of the animals kills the other. It's not a pretty sight."

"No! They can't do that!" In her indignation, Kathleen lost her balance and toppled from her perch on the slat. Immediately Nathan caught her in his arms.

It was this intimate-appearing scene that Simon first saw when he rode up, reining in sharply. Simultaneously, Kathleen and Nathan looked up into the dark, unfathomable face.

"There were rumors that a garrison of soldiers was attacked last week," Nathan said, swallowing the last bite of wine pudding. "And that the customshouse in Monterey was razed . . . caught fire, they say."

Simon set his wine glass down. "Probably because of the dry season. Or do the officials think otherwise?"

Kathleen saw Nathan glance in her direction. Did he think her silence rude? But then, he could not know about Simon—about the rape. How could he guess that the dashing, wealthy ranchero found his amusement by masquerading as a common vaquero, taking his pleasures regardless of what his victims suffered? As she suffered now, gracing the dining table—at Simon's command.

"The officials think it's the work of Indian renegades," Nathan said, turning back to Simon. "Posters are already being nailed around. Offering rewards to anyone that can give information."

Simon shrugged and pulled out a cigar. "If it isn't the Indians, it'd be the Californios revolting again. Though, obviously, nothing ever comes of it."

"Then you think the time is ripe for another revolt?" Nathan asked, leaning closer over the table.

"I doubt that the Californios will stand much longer for Mexico's high revenue laws—or being excluded from sending representatives to the Mexican Congress. I think one day the Californios will successfully revolt against Mexico—like your American colonies did against Great Britain. And then the cargoes you bring me will be in even greater demand."

"And, in turn, we'll turn a pretty profit," Nathan said, lifting his wine glass to Simon in tribute.

Kathleen stood up. Her hands held the table's edge to steady her trembling legs. "Excuse me, please, gentlemen," she said stiffly. "I'm rather tired. I'll leave you to your conversation."

She dearly wanted to tell the two men she found their avarice disgusting. But she found her own lack of courage even more so.

It had taken only one mention of reward posters, and she had gone as weak as a prisoner facing a firing squad.

Dear God, would she always feel haunted—followed—trapped? How long would she have to wait before her father died? Before she was free of Edmund Woodsworth?

And what if her father lived another ten years?

"Why'd you force her to sup with us, Simon?" Nathan asked after Kathleen had fled the room. "Especially when you knew there were plans to discuss. You realize you humiliate her, don't you?"

"What's it to you, Nathan . . . or do you hold some special feeling for the girl?" The icy green eyes held the sea-blue ones.

"Good God, Simon! Did you have to rape her? Is no woman safe from you?"

Simon's eyes narrowed. "Did she tell you that?"

"Do you think that's the kind of thing she could tell someone? Hell, all you have to do is look at her, Simon, and you can see the wariness creep into her eyes. . . . Nay, it wasn't the lass who told me. When I returned from Monterey, Gemma was fit to be tied. The girl's torn undergarment was found in your room. If the girl had been there, Gemma probably would have tried to tear her eyes out. It was the pistol with the Whatley name engraved on it that told me who your night-of-love was. You already know, I suppose, that the posters are everywhere for information about her."

"Saw them on my last trip in. Who-all suspects Kathleen's identity?"

Nathan produced the pistol from a pocket in the denim jacket. "As far as I know, only the two of us. Now I'll ask you—is she something to you? With your scorn for women, this will certainly be a change."

Simon took the pistol and pocketed it. "You might say we tolerate each other. She detests me . . . and I find her no different than the other women I've known."

"There's no comparison, Simon! You know it as well as I do."

"You're fooling yourself, my romantic friend, if you think that. The fact that she slept with our fine

Castilian lieutenant the same night merely proves my point. Or did she neglect to tell you that when you found her in the lobby that morning?" Simon asked, with a contemptuous sneer.

12

The desert winds at last arrived—and with them
the end of Kathleen's respite. The Santa Ana was
even worse than Simon had described. Day and
night there was the clashing and clattering of the
palm fronds as the wind played them like cymbals.
Each time Kathleen ventured outdoors her throat
and eyes burned as if exposed to the open blast of a
furnace, and her skirts lashed about her frame like
the sails against a ship's masts in a hurricane.

Yet that day the sting of the wind did not bother
her as she braved its blast in search of Simon.
When Diego informed her earlier that morning that
Simon had suspended her teaching duties, her cau-

tion was overcome by a wrath as fierce as the winds.

She found him as he strode toward the corrals. "Simon!" she yelled, grabbing at his sleeve to get his attention. He turned, and Kathleen was petrified. The harsh wind whirled about them, isolating the two of them from everything but their own thoughts.

And Kathleen remembered with terror—the mouth that had brutally possessed her, the hands that had ravaged her, the mocking words that had tormented her.

"Simon," she said, gathering courage, "you can't suspend the classes! If it's the wind, the classes could be held indoors. But the students, they have a right to—"

The slashed eyebrow lifted in the mocking way she so detested. "One would think you actually are a tutor . . . instead of a—what is it—murderess, thief . . . or prostitute?"

Kathleen's hand swung upward in an angry arc. But Simon was quicker and caught her wrist in a cruel grip.

"Careful, Kathleen. Don't try my patience. Or I'll be tempted to forget my need for a tutor—and remember the posters offering a reward for a fairhaired woman of twenty years."

"I hate you, Simon Reyes! And I'll make you sorry you ever—"

Kathleen broke off with a start as the long fingers

of one buckskin-gloved hand reached toward her and caught a thick strand of sunlit curls that the wind had whipped about her neck.

"You've already told me how you feel about me, and I'm tired of listening to your tirades," he said softly as he tugged on the curling strand of hair so that Kathleen was forced to move nearer.

She looked up into the green eyes that blazed as hotly as the wind about them. Her skirts swept around Simon's long legs. From a distance the two appeared to be lovers in a tryst.

"Maybe I should make you change your mind."

Kathleen pulled away with a wild laugh. "Hell'd go up in smoke first, Simon Reyes!"

Simon's lips tightened in a thin line. "You'll get your students back." He pulled his hat low over his eyes. "After spring roundup. Every hand is going to be needed till then." He swung away, and then turned back. "And get rid of those spectacles. If you can spot a pierced ear, *bebé*, you sure don't need glasses."

With a wry grin at her indignant "Ohh!" he left her, heading toward the corral, where several vaqueros were gathered to watch the breaking of the penned mustangs.

Kathleen should have returned to the house, but she stood rooted by her hate as she watched Simon swing easily over the top bar of the corral. And while he gently cornered one of the wilder horses, which snorted and reared at his approach, she weaved vicious plots of revenge.

She could wait until the servants had retired and then shoot the man outright—if she had her pistol. Of course, she could always use the knife she carried. But as lightly as Simon slept, he would probably turn the blade on her first. And even if she did succeed, she would only be a hunted animal once again. No, better to suffer his taunts and hope he did not find another tutor before her father died.

When Simon finally mounted the nervous horse, all the while whispering calm words she could not hear, Kathleen thought how it would solve everything if the mustang threw Simon, pounding the man to death beneath flailing hooves.

But even in that, Simon defeated her. One sure hand gripped the animal's mane, and gleaming spurs drove into the heaving, sweaty flanks each time the great animal reared, viciously bucking and twisting in an attempt to throw the rider. Dust swirled about the man and the beast as they dueled for supremacy. Then it was over. At last, spent and frothy at the mouth, the mustang hung its head. It had been mastered.

And when Simon gently stroked the horse, Kathleen abruptly turned away. Simon would never master her. No man would master her. If she had to run for the rest of her life!

Her purple eyes as stormy as California seas during a sou'easter, Kathleen stalked back to the hacienda. She might be deprived of giving her lessons, but she would at least ride during her enforced idleness.

Quickly she changed into the *calzones* and *camisa* that Simon had once forced her to wear. She would have dearly liked to flout Simon's orders and continue to wear the glasses, but they were a nuisance. On her way out, she dropped them in the chest at the foot of her bed, glad to be rid of them.

At the kitchen door, she stopped at the bench where Diego sat napping. Even the hot wind racing down the *portales* did not disturb him. She hesitated there, hating to awaken him. But one rheumy old eye opened in a squint.

"Qué quieres, hija?"

She stooped to his side. "Diego," she shouted above the wind. "I'd like to go riding. May I borrow your sombrero, *por favor?*"

"Simon has said it would be all right to ride out in the Santa Ana?" Only Diego had the audacity to use Simon's given name.

"No!" she said more sharply to the old man than she intended. "But I'm sure what I do or where I go is of little concern to *el patrón* as long as his tutor is available when he decides the lessons may resume."

"Do not judge him harshly, *hija*," Diego said, and handed her his sombrero before closing his eyes again. "There are things even a tutor does not know."

The brown, wrinkled face wore an inscrutable expression, and when Kathleen would have touched the stooped shoulder to ask Diego what he meant, she realized he was already asleep again.

Both puzzled and offended, she pulled on the gray, floppy hat with its worn braids of silver ornamentation and made her way, leaning against the wind, to the stables.

"Have you missed me riding you, Estrellita?" Kathleen asked as she heaved the saddle over the mare's back. "Then take me somewhere, little star, where I can ride free and fast—like California's wild winds."

Obeying her mistress's request, Estrellita galloped from the hacienda grounds, unrestrained and frisky, down the tree-lined road and out through a field of wild, rank mustard. Its thick stalks were bright with wispy yellow flowers, the only color in the parched landscape. All about Kathleen, the hills were as brown as umber, and up along one ridge a brush fire burned.

Kathleen let Estrellita have her lead, and the mare followed a path that led through the pasturelands, where a Durham calf ran bellowing after its mother at Kathleen's approach. Kathleen laughed aloud at the mother's indignant brown-eyed glare and spurred Estrellita away from the milling herd up into the foothills of the Pine Mountains. There the wind was not as harsh or fierce. Kathleen threw back her sombrero so that it dangled from her neck by its cords, and let the breeze rumple her damp curls.

Pausing beneath the black shade of a live oak, she savored the moment of peace. Across the valley from her she spotted a line of trudging figures, shrouded and shapeless, that she knew must be Indian women. It made her feel suppressed just to look at them, to contrast them to herself.

She wondered what kind of lives they led, if they ever rebelled against the drudgery and restraints, if they ever yearned for the freedom that was now hers. Or were their traditions so strong that those women had no idea that anything existed other than the confining life they led?

The very thought of leading that kind of life repulsed Kathleen. The image of what marriage constituted—submission to the debasing intimacy, fettered to the will of one man, a mere servant of his passion—made her tremble with revulsion so that she swung her hand forcefully across Estrellita's rump.

The mare reared and sprang forward along the foothills. Dejectedly, Kathleen turned the animal back toward the hacienda. When she once again encountered the road that wound its way like a snake toward the hacienda, Kathleen found she was not the only traveler using the track.

Apparently Simon had had visitors in her absence, for a black carriage pulled by a bay rumbled slowly down the road toward Kathleen. At the carriage's side cantered a lone horse whose rider sat like a giant in the saddle. At first, Kathleen thought the man whose face was shadowed by the wide brim was Simon, and her breathing quickened.

But the man, a battered-faced Mexican, was presumably a guard, with a pistol strapped to his hip and a rifle sheathed at the saddle.

Kathleen reined Estrellita to the side of the road as the carriage drew near. She was curious to see the occupant, who obviously disdained riding horseback. However, instead of continuing, the woman in the carriage pulled the bay to a halt.

Chocolate-brown eyes looked Kathleen over with condescending amusement, and Kathleen's lips tightened with chagrin, realizing how unappealing she must look at the moment, with her hair tangled in a mass about her shoulders and her boy's clothing clinging to her body, wet with perspiration that even the wind, which was dying somewhat with the end of the day, did not dry.

The finely plucked brows in the magnolia-white face arched. "So you're working for Simon now?" Gemma asked.

Kathleen stiffened in the saddle. La Palacia's proprietress recognized her—from the brief meeting at the bordello, or from the reward posters? Kathleen inclined her head as royally as an empress. "I'm the tutor for Valle del Bravo."

Gemma smiled coldly. "Oh, then the bed is not the only place you earn your livelihood, señorita?"

Kathleen heard the guard's snort of laughter, but she continued to gaze evenly at the woman. "How one earns a living is no measure of good manners. And I must say yours are an excellent example of the manners of a *puta*."

She saw the woman's eyes blaze and heard the hissing intake of her breath and knew she now faced an enemy. But she did not cower.

"No wonder Simon prefers to bed another woman," Kathleen added, with a contemptuous smile. "A lady of quality."

The guard's uproarious laughter was cut short by the woman's sharp command of *"Cállate!"*

Calmly, Kathleen urged Estrellita past the furious woman, towards the hacienda. *Lady of quality!* she thought bitterly.

She certainly had not behaved like one. Her gentle-bred mother would have blushed with shame at her daughter's brazen conduct. She could not imagine what had prompted her to act so rudely. Unless it was just to dent the woman's haughty self-assuredness. She wondered what Gemma had been doing there. And if Simon learned of her own atrocious behavior—would he dismiss her?

As Kathleen dismounted, she realized that her hands trembled with anger. And she knew her anger was not for Gemma—for she herself was no better than the proprietress, now that Simon had had his way with her. No, her anger, her hatred, was reserved for Simon Reyes. May God damn his black soul!

13

The Santa Ana blew itself out, and the indolence of the hacienda gave way to industrious work as the spring roundup progressed. The vaqueros stayed busy counting the cattle, branding the calves, and corraling the older cattle for the rodeo that would climax the roundup.

The household servants swept, dusted, and scrubbed every inch of the whitewashed walls and terra-cotta floors—under Kathleen's watchful eye. If she could not perform her duties as tutor, she certainly would not give Simon any reason to complain about her duties as mistress of the hacienda.

Diligently she saw to it that the bed linens in

each of the nine bedrooms were fresh, that vases of columbines graced each room with their honeyed scents, and that Maria Jesus began preparations for the many meals that were to be cooked during the fiesta. As the day of the fiesta approached, even Diego roused himself from the sunny place on his bench to help oversee the decorating of the courtyard.

In every sense of the word—but one—Kathleen was mistress of Valle del Bravo.

At night she thought she would be too tired to do anything but collapse in her bed, but she felt more than ever driven to work so there would be no time to think. Restlessly she would pace the room, brushing her hair, checking her list for last-minute preparations.

Seeing her mistress so distracted, Amelia smiled pityingly to herself. She could tell the proud, young *maestra* what was needed to cure her ailment, but she doubted that the *maestra* would believe her. A man like Julio could wipe away that look of discontent that haunted the plum-colored eyes.

Qué suerte that Julio couldn't see the *maestra* now without those ugly glasses and with her hair hanging loose like an Indian woman's! But then, Julio had been too busy with the roundup to come around the hacienda. Hopefully she would see more of Julio when the roundup was over. Perhaps when Padre Marcos came for the rodeo festivities she could even persuade Julio to seek the good father's blessing in marriage.

Amelia crossed herself quickly in hopeful prayer.

Kathleen's thoughts were not tender ones of romance. At the moment she was cursing Simon Reyes with every vile word she had ever heard the vaqueros use, wishing him as dead as the long-deceased Father Serra, the founder of the California mission system.

The confrontation between her and Simon earlier that afternoon still stung her thoughts, simmering within her like Maria Jesus's tallow for candles.

The confrontation had occurred shortly after the siesta hour, when Simon worked in his study while the others rested. Diego had summoned her from the kitchen with the message that *el patrón* wished to see her.

Kathleen rapped on the study door, and Simon's low voice bade her enter. From behind his desk he looked up as Kathleen crossed the room. He was dressed in dusty denim pants and a worn red baize shirt.

"You wanted to see me?"

"I've just learned you were out riding last week—alone, dressed as a *muchacho*."

"Are you trying to tell me I'm a prisoner here, that I'm forbidden to do as I wish with my own time?"

"Enough, Kathleén!" Simon's bronzed hand slammed down on the oak desk, and he came to his feet, his stern face only inches from hers. "I'll not have my men so inflamed by the sight of a woman in pants that they're incapable of working."

His hard eyes moved past her throat to where the small mounds of breasts rose in agitation. A flush of heat spread over Kathleen's cheeks as she remained unmoving under his sneering regard.

"Unless you happen to enjoy being raped," he finished. "And in that case, I'm sure my vaqueros could provide—"

"Ohh!" Kathleen's hand came up to deliver an intended blow. But the memory of another time she had struck him and Simon's resulting anger halted her. Abruptly she swung her hand across his desk, scattering the papers on the floor.

"You bastard!" she hissed.

Simon's green eyes narrowed dangerously, and a cold shiver rippled Kathleen's spine at the intensity of the anger she saw there.

He stretched out a hand, and Kathleen flinched. Lightly tracing the scar that ran along her cheek with one finger, he laughed softly. "And you, Catalina, are no lady. We're rogues, both of us."

At his touch that seared like a hot iron, Kathleen's mouth parched. "Don't!" she croaked.

Simon's gaze ran over her face, as if baffled by something. "You're right," he said. "What we are is neither here nor there. We both understand how we feel about one another."

He reached into a drawer and handed her a sheaf

of papers. "There's a list of names included. Make out invitations to the families for the fiesta next week. When you've finished, Diego will see that the invitations are delivered."

Kathleen glanced at some of the names on the list, names of the most prominent families in the California province. Many she had met at the Escandón fiesta: Carrillo, Bandini, Pico—liberals who favored secularization and separation of political and military commands; Vallejo, Alvarado, and Castro—conservatives who supported the rule of militarism.

Kathleen looked up at Simon. "I'd not thought you the type of man to pretend interest in politics."

Simon quirked a brow. "You, yourself, ought to understand the benefits of pretense."

"No better than you, vaquero!" she retorted, whirling from him and slamming the door behind her.

The first guests began arriving early that morning, in time for the horse races and the games of chance, such as monte and *chuza*, which resembled roulette, and the games of skill, the most popular being the *carrera de gallo*.

In the *carrera*, Diego told Kathleen, the horseman would ride at top speed toward a line of roosters, buried neck-high in the sand fifty feet apart, and grab at the roosters' heads. The rider who unearthed the most roosters won the contest. Later in the afternoon a barbeque was to be held, followed by the bear-baiting and rodeo.

None of these games did Kathleen watch. Not only because she was busy seeing that everything ran smoothly, but also because she found the sports of the *caballeros* cruel. It was bad enough when Amelia told her that the magnificent brown bear had been defeated, had been gored to death by a great black bull.

However, as Kathleen helped Maria Jesus in the kitchen, the flat faced old woman gently shoved at Kathleen's back. "*Vaya*, Señorita Catalina. You're young—enjoy yourself!"

Kathleen would have protested, but the cook practically pushed her out onto the veranda. From the arena came the musical calls of the vaqueros: "*Hooch, hooch, hooch! Who-hah! Who-hah!*"

With a sign of resignation, Kathleen wiped her hands on her black broadcloth skirt and made her way to the crowd gathered about the arena. Rather than join the guests in the stands, she found a vacant spot near one of the stalls, where she had a much better view anyway.

Inside the corralled area the cows bellowed and puffed and tossed their heads at the vaqueros. Dressed in a Mexican beaded vest of porcupine quills and in concho-ornamented *chaparejos*, Simon looked impressive as his Spanish cow pony cut first to the left and then the right, finally cornering a monstrous Andalusian bull. With a swish of the

slender rawhide riata, Simon lassoed the bull's rear
legs, bringing the animal to the ground in a whirl-
pool of dust.

Any moment Kathleen expected one of the
sharp-horned bulls to gore a vaquero. But there occurred in the following minutes a mishap of a different nature. Amelia's *novio*, Julio, had just
lassoed a calf, when the turn of his *delavuelta* about
the saddle horn hopped, pinching off the first joint
of his thumb. He half-slid, half-fell from his horse,
and before anyone realized what had happened,
Kathleen, who was nearest the vaquero, slipped
through the slats and ran to him.

Within seconds Simon was there also, whipping
his black handkerchief from his neck and tying it
about the wrist of the doubled-up vaquero.

"I'll see to him," Kathleen said. "Get back to the
rodeo."

Simon gave her a peculiar look, but allowed her
to lead the young man away.

It was a gory sight, with the bone gleaming
through the jagged rim of flesh, but Kathleen managed to clean it before Amelia rushed into the
kitchen, her brown face ashen with fear.

"Quítate!" Maria Jesus told Amelia, pointing
her finger at the door. "You'll only make matters
worse! Get out!"

Amelia hesitated, looked to Julio, whose acorn-
colored eyes were glazed with shock, then to Maria

Jesus. The frown on the cook's face won out, and Amelia retreated from the kitchen.

Clucking like a hen, Maria Jesus dragged out a tin from the cupboard—balsam of myrrh the tin contained, she told Kathleen—and set about applying the ointment to the mangled hand.

After Kathleen bound the thumb with strips of cloth, the dazed Julio thanked them before heading for the door, determined to ride again in the rodeo.

Kathleen leaned in the kitchen doorway, watching the youth lope back to the arena. And the vision came to her mind of Simon deftly applying his handkerchief as a tourniquet to Julio's wrist. She saw again Simon's swiftly moving hands. Hands that were as sure at lovemaking as riding, shooting, and gambling.

14

Kathleen reclined in the rose-scented water, letting its sensuous warmth soothe her aching muscles. The fiesta day had been a long one and still was not over.

But all in all, it had run smoothly so far—which was what Simon had wanted, and expected, when he had put her in charge of the hacienda. If only she could get through the evening's festivities without incurring one of his black looks. What was it about her and Simon that made them seem like two wary cocks—ever ready to fight but restraining themselves for the moment?

Would that moment come? God help her then,

for Simon Reyes would be a foe to reckon with. But then, so was she, and she would yet have her revenge on the man. *Patience . . . patience,* a voice inside her whispered. *Your chance to vindicate that night will come.*

The sounds of guitars and trumpets and violins tuning up floated through the hacienda, and Kathleen realized she would have to hurry. Quickly she stepped from the hip tub and, taking the large towel Amelia handed her, dried her peach-hued skin before slipping into a satin chemise. Over this she pulled a white satin gown with puffed sleeves and a scooped neckline. Spangled satin slippers and a lace fan completed the startling white attire.

As Amelia swept Kathleen's silken mane up into a crown of curls atop her head, tying the abundant hair with a white ribbon, Kathleen applied a light touch of rose salve to her lips and pinched her cheeks for color.

When she was ready, she cast only a cursory glance in the mirror, not realizing the beautiful young woman reflected there was such a great contrast to the woman who had arrived on the shores of California wearing thick spectacles and a severe hairdo.

So, naturally, she did not interpret the strange look that flickered in Simon's eyes when she entered the *salu*. Nor the sidelong glances of envy thrown by the female guests or the admiring ones openly bestowed by the men.

She paused there in the *sala*'s double doorway, hoping to see Nathan's familiar face. In the light of the gleaming candles the mixture of iridescent white cloth and golden skin and hair was a stark contrast to the sober, dark colors worn by the guests. Her radiance eclipsed all there but that of Simon, whose tall, sinewy frame was clad completely in black, with only the ruffles of white silk at his wrists and throat to serve as relief.

As he moved toward Kathleen, more than a few pair of eyes noted how the tutoress and the ranchero seemed to complement one another—like the brightest star against the black velvet of night.

Among those watchful stares Kathleen saw the black-eyed glare of Francesca and was glad she had been able to avoid the petulant-looking girl the whole day, leaving it to Amelia to show Francesca and her mother the bedroom they were to share with Doña Modeste and to see to it that they were comfortable.

Francesca's eyes hungered after the broad back of Simon Reyes, unaware of Dimitri's whispered words of flattery to her. Just as Kathleen was unaware of Simon's appraising gaze until he was at her side, handing her one of the two glasses of wine he held.

"You're a *bruja,* Catalina," he said in words meant for her ears alone. "Like a witch, you cast your spell, changing yourself from a gray mouse to a fairy queen." He raised his glass in an intimate gesture of toasting. "To Calafia, the golden amazon queen for whom California was named."

Kathleen could scarcely believe she heard right. She looked up into the harsh features, searching for a sign of his usual mockery. She saw instead the dark flickering of desire in the green depths of his eyes.

Her lips curled scornfully over the rim of her glass. "You dare believe your honeyed words could win from me what your body has so savagely taken? Have done with your ridicule, Simon. I'll be out of your life within the year. And, *gracias a Dios,* you'll be out of mine!"

Simon's eyes crinkled in laughter. "Already you've turned back into a *bruja.* Maybe the warmth of a man's kisses would change the witch into a fairy queen again."

"That's an opportunity you'll never have!"

She turned from him, her dress swirling about her ankles, and made her way through the crowded room with the intent of talking with Don Pio Pico, when she saw Diego admit a brawny man dressed in the sailor's garb of navy-blue duck trousers and jacket and a thin blue tie.

She deposited her untouched glass on a nearby table and hurried to the entrance. "Nathan," she said pleasurably.

His big, rough hands closed over Kathleen's. "How've you fared, lass?" He looked over her head, his blue eyes questioning the tall man who approached them.

Simon nodded. "How are you, Nathan?"

"Touchy as a porcupine at the moment, with the customs officials on my heels." His gaze roamed over the guests. "I see the cream of California are gathered here. By the end of the fiesta there should be no doubt as to your patriotism."

Simon smiled thinly but made no reply. Instead he turned to Kathleen. "I think the gentleman over there in blue—Señor Martínez—is boring Father Marcos. Would you rescue the good padre, Kathleen?"

"Of course," she answered. "I'll leave you two gentlemen to discuss your nefarious enterprise."

As she made her way across the room, Nathan said, "I made a mistake in telling you about her, Simon."

"I won't discuss it—not even with you, Nathan."

"She's gentle-bred," the sea-captain persisted. "It's obvious, isn't it, by her manner?"

"And you think my base-born manners too coarse for the girl?"

"You're asking for trouble, Simon. Gemma's screeching her ire at every turn. I'd tread warily on your next visit to Santa Barbara."

"That may be sooner than planned. Gemma's been here once already. On the pretext of visiting the Castro rancho for the weekend. She brought word that Santa Anna has ordered our illustrious *deputado*—Martínez there—to see to it that Micheltorena expells Frémont and his men from California—by force, if necessary."

The gaze of the two men returned to where Kathleen stood in conversation with Martínez and Father Marcos. At that moment Francesca and Dimitri joined Kathleen and the men with her.

"I met you, did I not, at the Santa Barbara Mission?" Dimitri asked, as if he did not quite believe his eyes. "It is the same lady, isn't it, Father Marcos?"

The brown-robed padre laughed, and Kathleen said, "I'd begun to think you had a poor memory, Dimitri. I was also at the Escandón fiesta, but you didn't seem to recognize me then."

"You are right to chide me, señorita," Dimitri said. A flirtatious smile erupted beneath the thin black mustache. "A thousand pardons."

As if she did not like being left out of the conversation, Francesca said sweetly, "Are you trying to make a convert of our little tutoress, Father Marcos?"

Martínez raised startled, bushy brows. "Señorita, you do not share the Faith?"

"Señor Martínez," Father Marcos explained, "is Monterey's *deputado* to Mexico, and, as such, feels strongly about the obligations of the people."

The corners of Kathleen's lips curved upwards. "I'm afraid I don't share the Faith. I'm as gentile as the renegade Indians you were denouncing."

The *deputado* looked at Kathleen askance. "Have care, señorita. The Faith is not a thing to be taken lightly. You realize, do you not, that the Protestants have no legal rights in California."

Kathleen paled slightly. "But, Señor Martínez, why should I have concern over legal rights? I'm only here for a temporary period of time."

"The *deputado* doesn't mean for his words to frighten you," Father Marcos said gently. "But there are those who wish to overthrow the Mexican rule, and one can never be too careful. However, my daughter, your intentions would never be questioned, working as you do under the roof of such an esteemed gentleman as Señor Reyes. Am I not right, Señor Martínez?"

"Oh, quite, Father. But tell me, señorita, how is it Señor Reyes was fortunate enough to employ a woman as a tutor?"

"Yes, do tell us," Francesca said, fanning herself fiercely. "I'm sure it makes an interesting story."

"Indeed," Dimitri added, his dark eyes roaming over Kathleen with the same speculative gaze she had seen in the eyes of Boston's fortune hunters. "The sight of an American woman is rare here. And one as beautiful as you—and a tutor, besides, well . . ." The black eyes flashed appreciatively, unaware of Francesca's pouting lips.

"I'm here because—" Kathleen broke off, not knowing what to say next. Perspiration broke out on her temples. Could any of those about her relate the reward posters to herself?

"Miss Summers's job as tutoress is quite easily explained," a voice said behind her. Simon came to her side, tall and self-assured.

"Miss Summers and I met briefly in Europe, where women teachers are more readily accepted." Simon glanced down at her with a polite smile. "I was persuaded by her delightful combination of charm and intelligence that she'd make an excellent employee. And when I settled here, I immediately made plans to hire her."

"But, Simon, you never told me you had been to Europe," Francesca said.

Simon smiled engagingly down at Francesca's sullen face. "There are a lot of things I haven't told anyone." Simon looked around at those about him. "For fear the *deputado* here would report me for being such a rakehell!"

Martínez's laughter boomed throughout the room. "Impossible, Señor Reyes. I'd have to report all of us, then!"

There was a general eruption of laughter, and when it died down, Simon said, "Now if you'll excuse us, we should attend our other guests."

Simon took Kathleen's arm and guided her among the few guests, mostly older ones, who still remained within doors. From outside, the refrains of a violin's haunting melody drifted through the open veranda doors. The sweet night air enveloped

Kathleen, as she and Simon made their way out onto the veranda, restoring some courage to her shaking limbs.

The words of gratitude came uneasily to her lips as she and Simon paused beneath one of the lanterns hung from a camphor tree. "Thank you, Simon. For sparing me, in there." She kept her eyes on the couples who danced sedately to a Spanish ballad.

"Your thanks aren't what I want, Kathleen."

Her eyes met his. "You'll receive nothing else from me—freely given."

"Careful, *bebé*. You tempt the hands of Fate."

Then, before she could protest, he drew her within the circle of his arms and whirled her out into the center of the patio to join the other dancing couples.

"Stop this, Simon! Do you want a scene?"

He pulled her against him, holding her firmly as they moved as one. "Why? I thought all women liked to dance." His mocking words fanned the curls against her temple where his lips rested.

"Can't you understand? I hate the touch of your hands on me! I hate you!"

"Oh? Then I'm not good enough for you?"

"Ha! You have the audacity to ask me that? A profiteer? A gigolo? Or do you deny that you used Santa Anna's wife to gain del Bravo? No, don't bother. You're a man without loyalties, principles. I find your kind despicable."

"And what kind are you, Catalina?" His smile was a sneer. "A woman that'll go to bed with a man for the right price or rank?—a Castilian soldier can buy your charms, but not a *cholo* vaquero."

Kathleen stiffened in outrage. But the fury that rose like bile in her throat was choked back by sudden fear. Her knees grew weak as she stared past Simon to the dark figure on the veranda.

Edmund Woodsworth's lipless smile was like the malevolent grin of a skull.

15

Like some ghoulish fiend in a nightmare, Edmund moved down the veranda steps toward Kathleen. The dolorous strains of "Ojos Negros" died away. One by one the guests turned toward the stranger.

Kathleen wondered abstractedly, even as she cringed unknowingly against Simon, whether curiosity about the stranger had interrupted the fiesta or if the guests felt, as she did, the subtle presence of something malignant.

Simon took her arm to steady her. "What is it, Kathleen?" In the wide burgundy-colored eyes he saw a fear that had not been there even on the night he so brutally took her.

Kathleen's head shook wordlessly, and Simon, following her glazed look, saw the thin, elegantly dressed man moving languidly toward them. But it was the soldier beyond, who stood menacingly on the veranda, that caught Simon's attention. What mischief was Aguila bent on now? Simon wondered.

The stranger, dressed in nankeen pantaloons and a claret coat, which did not conceal the gleam of the sword at the waist, brought Simon's thoughtful gaze back to the moment at hand.

Edmund bowed low before Kathleen. "My heart has been slowly dying since the moment you left," he said with a chilling smile.

She would have laughed at the affected words of endearment had not stark fear gripped her. "You don't have a heart, Edmund!" she whispered hoarsely, struggling to retain some semblance of composure.

Edmund drew himself up in feigned righteousness. "How can you accuse me so unjustly? Have I not followed you halfway across the globe . . . just to be at your side again?"

"Don't pretend with me. You know I don't want you as my husband!" Her words tumbled on in a rush. "I wouldn't have you near me for all the money in the world! Your touch is repulsive—as slimy as a viper's!"

Kathleen's hands clenched the delicate lace fan,

and it broke with a brittle snap in the silence of the courtyard.

Edmund's eyes glittered with rage. He said, in a silky, soft voice full of threat, "I'm afraid you've no choice, my dearest. You are my fiancée, are you not?"

"I don't believe you understood the lady." Simon's voice was just as soft and low, but its very lack of emotion lent a lethal tone to it.

Edmund turned pale blue eyes on Simon. "And what business, my dear sir, is this matter of yours?"

Simon's eyes narrowed, their color changing like a chameleon's from the cactus-hued green to a deadly gunmetal gray. "I'm the owner of the land on which you presently stand—without an invitation."

The guests shuffled about uneasily, and from the edge of the crowd Kathleen saw Don Pio Pico, followed by Aguila, push his way through the crowd toward her and the two men who faced each other like duelists.

"What's going on here, gentlemen?" Don Pico asked in his troll-like voice.

Edmund looked at the leathery ranchero. "And you are?" he asked with a disdainful lift of fair brows.

Simon's lips curved in a mirthless smile. "A former representative of the Mexican government—Don Pio Pico."

Edmund sketched an elegant bow. "In that case, Don Pio, I shall address myself to you."

He withdrew wrinkled papers from his waistcoat and handed them to the older man. "I'm Edmund Woodsworth, Don Pio. Miss Whatley, my intended"—he smiled thinly at Kathleen—"decided to leave Boston prior to our wedding. Through the passenger list of one of the ships I traced her to Santa Barbara, but was unable to find her."

Edmund's slim white finger pointed at the top sheaf. "I had this reward posted"—he looked directly at Simon—"and an informant told me I could find my fiancée here."

Kathleen whirled on Simon. "You! You—*Judas!* You turned me in!"

Dear God, and she had almost turned to Simon for protection! His concern for her, his anger at Edmund, had been so convincing. But it had all been a charade. A trick.

Kathleen's hands came up as if to claw Simon's eyes. But his betrayal, coming on the heels of Edmund's arrival, so numbed her that her attack resembled more a beseechment as she swayed in helpless fury toward him.

"Come along, Kathleen," Edmund said, and he moved as if to take her.

"No!" she cried, shrinking back against Simon.

"I would not do that if I were you," Simon said with a deceptive softness.

Edmund's hand fell to his side to grasp the hilt of his sword.

Nathan stepped forward. "Just a moment here, Woodsworth. You can't just walk in, claiming the lass is your intended, and whisk her away."

"If you'll look at the other papers, Don Pio," Edmund said imperiously, "you'll find documents from James Whatley, making me his daughter's legal guardian and requesting that I escort her back to Boston."

As Pico held the papers up to catch the light of the lanterns, his somber expression changing to a frown as he read, Nathan moved to Simon's side, and Kathleen heard Simon whisper briefly to the sea-captain before Pico handed the papers back to Edmund.

"The documents look in order, Simon. And Miss Summers—Whatley—is not of legal age yet. So I see no other—"

"Gentlemen," Simon said, "as you can see, my wife is weak with shock. If—"

"Your wife?" Edmund snarled with disbelief.

"If you'll be so good as to excuse us," Simon continued with exaggerated patience, "I'll take my wife to our room—and return to clear up this unpleasant matter."

Kathleen's lips parted in dismay. "You can't be—"

Simon's iron grasp about her waist crushed off

her words in a gasp even as startled whispers at his revelation passed among the group gathered there.

Aguila stepped in front of Simon as if to block his way. Simon growled low, "Move aside, Aguila."

As if for acknowledgement, the lieutenant looked to Edmund, but Pico interrupted. "Get out of the way, damn you, Aguila! Can't you see the lady's ill?"

Edmund nodded his head with a slight motion, and the officer stepped back as Simon swept Kathleen up in his arms and moved forward. There was a confused rush of talk when the ranchero and the woman he carried in his arms and called his wife disappeared within.

But Kathleen was unaware of the words that leapt from tongue to tongue of the guests outside. "Are you insane?" she demanded. "Do you think I'd marry you either? You're as despicable as—"

Simon kicked open the bedroom door with one booted foot and unceremoniously dropped Kathleen on the four-poster bed. At the same moment that Kathleen gasped in outrage, she heard smothered words from the other side of the room and turned to see Nathan frowning and behind him Padre Marcos.

Padre Marcos moved past Nathan. "Are you ready, my children?" he asked Simon. "We must hurry with the ceremony!"

"The ceremony?" Kathleen asked.

"I had Nathan tell the father that we wished to be united in holy matrimony."

Kathleen bounded to her feet. Her eyes blazed as hotly as mountain brush fires. "I'll not be wed with you!"

Simon folded his arms akimbo. "As I see it, Kathleen, you only have one choice . . . Edmund Woodsworth or myself. Which is it going to be?"

"That's no choice. Either way, it's a sentence of living death!"

Simon shrugged. "Do as you wish, then."

Kathleen's eyes narrowed to purple slits. "I don't trust you, Simon! You dislike me as heartily as I do you. Why are you doing this?"

"That's my business," Simon replied. He took her wrist and pulled her toward the padre. "If you will, Father Marcos, we are ready to be wed. Nathan, you'll be our witness."

"Even for you, my son," Father Marcos said, "I cannot bless this marriage before God without her freely given consent."

"Well?" Simon asked, facing Kathleen with his fists at his hips. "What's it to be?"

16

Kathleen looked to Nathan. His ruddy face was bland. Numbed, she nodded with a submissive inclination of her head.

"Do you have a ring?" Father Marcos asked Simon.

"You should know, after all this time, Father, that I wear no jewelry. Nathan, you've a ring?"

Nathan shook his head. "Nay, Simon."

The whole situation seemed ludicrous to Kathleen but for the sudden smile of irony that curved Simon's long lips.

He crossed to the *trastero* that sat on the bureau. Opening the cupboard's door, he reached into a small drawer. When he returned, there lay in the palm of his hand a ring-shaped object.

As he passed it to Nathan, the gleam of copper caught Kathleen's eye. The earring Simon had worn that night at La Palacia!

"No!" she spat. But Simon was already taking her hand, his skin warm against Kathleen's frozen fingers. *This can't be happening,* she kept thinking. *This can't be happening!*

But it did, the simple ceremony being short— with only one pause, when Father Marcos asked her, "Do you, Kathleen Whatley, take Simon Reyes for your husband . . . forever?"—and the word "forever" rang in her mind like the repetitive call of the mission bells.

As Father Marcos went to the bureau to write out the marriage papers, Simon's hands grasped her by the shoulders, and his dark head bent low over hers. "No!" she whispered fiercely and turned her face away so that his lips lightly brushed her ear instead.

"My blushing bride is unduly modest."

Her head swept upwards, her gaze as intense as his. "I'll make you sorry you ever took me as your wife!"

"So you're always threatening me—Señora Reyes," he replied with a wicked grin.

"Ohhh!" Kathleen stamped a satin-slippered foot, feeling as helpless as a child.

Nathan cleared his throat. "They're waiting outside, Simon."

Father Marcos sanded the papers and held out a pen freshly dipped in ink. "If you'll sign these papers, my children."

Simon took the pen and affixed his signature before handing the pen to her. "Kathleen?"

Kathleen hesitated for a moment, looked to Father Marcos. The compassion she saw on the gaunt face told her what she already knew. She had no recourse. Silently she took the pen and wrote her name beneath the heavy scrawl of her husband's. A drop of ink fell from the pen and splotched the parchment. She stared at it, wondering if, like the marriage paper, her life would be splotched from that moment forward.

Simon took the documents and slid them inside one of the bureau drawers. "I'll convey to our guests," he told Kathleen with a thin smile, "your regrets at missing the rest of the fiesta."

"No," she said, as he opened the bedroom door to leave.

She did not trust Simon. Nor Edmund and him together. The curtain, she was certain, had yet to fall on the final act of the night's performance.

"I'll come with you," she said, crossing to him.

"Have it your way," he said with a shrug, though his eyes watched her closely as he stepped back, allowing her to precede him.

When the two of them, followed by Nathan and

Father Marcos, reached the *sala*, they found that all the guests had gathered there as if anticipating something unexpected. The atmosphere was electric with the tension that ushers in a storm.

Edmund and Aguila stood in the foreground together, talking with intensity. Behind them Kathleen saw Dimitri and Francesca. The Spanish beauty's face mirrored both disbelief and bitterness, and Kathleen thought with her own bitter resentment how gladly she would change places with Francesca.

Kathleen looked up into Simon's expressionless face as he came to stand beside her, resting one arm lightly about her waist in such a way that clearly proclaimed she belonged to him.

"My wife is feeling somewhat better," he told the crowd, "and insists the fiesta continue."

Edmund's lipless mouth stretched downward in a sneer. "I don't believe Kathleen's your wife, Reyes. Why else did no one know of your wedding?"

"That's really no longer your business, Woodsworth," Simon replied coolly.

He turned to the crowd of expectant faces. "But, for the benefit of my guests," he told them, "this was to be a double celebration tonight. Kathleen and I were married in secret by Padre Marcos some time ago. We planned to make the announcement tonight."

Simon's smile was tender as, pulling Kathleen closer to his side, he gazed down at her. But she alone saw the mockery in his eyes. "Our love," Simon said, addressing the guests again, "was too great to wait for the roundup fiesta."

"Do you have any proof of this so-called marriage?" Edmund snarled.

"Do you think I'd be so careless?" Simon's lids lowered lazily, as if he were bored by the discussion. "However, if your curiosity is not satisfied, Woodsworth, I'll have my majordomo bring the marriage documents."

"That shouldn't be necessary," Don Pio Pico told Edmund, his hooked nose wrinkling in disgust. "Padre Marcos can easily confirm our host's statement and clear up this boorish matter. Can you not, Father?"

The padre nodded at Don Pio with a twinkle in his eye that faded to a benign gaze as he turned to Edmund. "What Simon says is the truth."

"There," Don Pio said. "As an ex-*gobernador*, I find this untidy matter settled from a legal standpoint—and that should satisfy all concerned." His hawklike eyes beneath the great bushy brows looked pointedly at Edmund before coming to rest on Simon. "Shall we go on with the celebration, Simon?"

"Not yet," Aguila said, stepping forward. "There are other matters to see to first."

"I was wondering what the Mexican military was doing in my home uninvited," Simon said dryly. "I'm sure you'll soon enlighten me, Lieutenant."

"My pleasure, Señor Reyes," Aguila snapped. "My men and I are here to search for a band of insurrectionists." His scorning smile turned on Simon. "And in particular their leader—the renegade Indian known as El Cóndor."

There were gasps of fear from several of the guests. The wife of General Castro, Doña Modeste, looked as if she would swoon. "You think that murderous band is near here?" she cried.

"You want to tell us what makes you believe this El Cóndor is at del Bravo?" Simon asked in a soft, lazy voice that did not match the watchful glint in the narrowed eyes.

"Merely that several weeks ago one of my men wounded the band's leader in the shoulder. We're inspecting every hacienda in the vicinity."

There was a sharp intake of breath, and Aguila's scrutiny switched to Kathleen, whose hand clutched at her throat. "What is it, señora?" he asked, stressing the proper form of address with a sneer. "Do you know of this man's presence?"

Kathleen's eyes flickered upwards to meet Simon's hard green gaze. She saw something there she had never seen before. A purpose—a single purpose—that would brook no interference, that would let nothing stand in its way. She shuddered. And by her silence acknowledged the precedence of that steely purpose—as the tree acknowledges the precedence of the wind.

Aguila watched the silent exchange between the

two. "Reyes is El Cóndor, isn't he?" he said with a triumphant grin.

Simon laughed lightly, taking Kathleen's hand in his, in an affectionate gesture. But Kathleen knew the slight pressure of his fingertips was not a sign of husbandly adoration but one of clear warning. "You should know, Lieutenant, that even if your preposterous claim were true, a wife can't give evidence against her husband."

"You go too far, Reyes!" Aguila thundered, his confidence gone.

"No, Lieutenant. You do. To enter my house without a warrant may be permissible under our Mexican government. But to accuse me without proof is another matter . . . a personal one—which I shall be more than glad to answer at another time. Nathan Plummer will serve as my second. Choose your weapon and send him word of the time and place."

Edmund's eyes glittered with the opportunity presented him. "If I may," he said smoothly, "I shall be more than glad to represent Lieutenant Aguila in the duel—my choice of weapons, of course, being the sword."

"Gentlemen, gentlemen!" Don Pio Pico cried. "You know that dueling is forbidden." He fixed Aguila and Edmund with a reproachful look. "This is a party, señores. Certainly you can conduct your business at a later time!"

Aguila's jaw clenched in impotent fury, and he

wheeled about to leave. But Edmund's pale gaze claimed Kathleen. "My business is not finished with you," he said in an icy calm that Kathleen did not doubt.

17

The fiesta was at last over. Kathleen slammed the door of her bedroom. Wringing her hands in restless thought, she began to pace the floor. The fury in her built to a boiling rage.

To think that even for a brief moment she had credited Simon with an impeccable act of unselfish consideration! Knowing with how little esteem he held her, she had been more than justified in her suspicions of Simon's noble sacrifice to protect her by giving her his name. It was she who had been sacrificed! Simon Reyes had wedded with her in order to protect *himself*.

So engrossed was she in her loathing contemplation of the man that she did not hear him enter the room in that lithe, animal-like way of his. His hands gripped her shoulders from behind and spun her around to face him.

"All right, you little schemer, you've got my name to protect you now from whatever crimes you're involved in with this Woodsworth. Now I want to know what your game is! And I want a straight answer—if you can manage the truth."

"Your name to protect *me!*" she raged.

Her feelings of fear and anger had accumulated that night to the point where she could no longer contain them, and she frenziedly beat her fists against him. "To protect *yourself*, you mean, Simon Reyes! Ohh! How dare you call *me* a schemer. You'd out-finesse Machiavelli himself. You married me to protect yourself. So that I couldn't give testimony against you—whoever you are. Whatever you are—Indian, vaquero, ranchero—you're contemptible!"

Simon waited until her anger was spent, his square jawline rigid with tightly curbed impatience. Then he caught her wrists in his hands. "I've business to discuss with Nathan, my dear wife. But when I return . . ." He looked at Kathleen with a mocking curve to his lips and the burning light of desire in his eyes, and a shiver of apprehension rippled up Kathleen's spine. "When I return, I plan to claim the rights due a husband."

He thrust her from him and stalked to the door,

and Kathleen cried out, "Damn your heathen soul to Hell!"

But when the door shut, she threw herself on the bed and pounded the mattress with determined strokes, like a judge pounding his gavel. No! It couldn't have happened to her. Not Kathleen Whatley, who had sworn she'd never be a slave of the passions of a man—unconsidered and ignored, lowered to the level of an animal. And here she was—married to a man who was little better than an animal himself.

Dear God, she was wed to an Indian; a dirty native, as her father had called the peons of Spain . . . as he had called her mother's lover. "Like mother, like daughter," she could imagine him saying with a distasteful grimace.

She had escaped one trap only to be ensnared in another. Trapped—powerless and defenseless in the same house with the man, waiting to claim what he had brutally taken once before. The thought of his touch, hands stained with the blood of countless victims, made her nauseated with disgust.

Kathleen rolled to her back, stuffing her fist in her mouth, not believing that this one man could break the courage that had brought her through dangers without the merest flinch. Yet it was inevitable. She had experienced his crushing strength, his callous disregard. She could fight and struggle, but it would make little difference. She was alone against him. And outside there were a hundred vaqueros to obey the snap of his fingers. How few seconds were left before he would come to claim his rights?

But all power of action was not gone. She had escaped once, and she would do it again. She bounded from the bed and yanked out a bureau drawer, where she found the *camisa* and *calzones*. The white satin gown slipped down about her ankles, and Kathleen stood poised for a moment as the irony of the situation struck her. Tonight she had wedded—dressed as any elegant bride—all in white satin. But it was not a handsome knight from *Ivanhoe* that would take her in his arms with a gentle kiss, but a disfigured savage that with a grunt would satisfy his lust.

Spurred by fear, she kicked the satin gown across the tiles and quickly donned the peon clothing. She paused only long enough to braid her hair before quietly slipping out through her terrace doors onto the veranda. She glanced down its empty corridors. No one watched. The guests had long since gone, and apparently old Diego had already deserted his bench for the rawhide bed. In the distance she could see the campfires of the vaqueros and hear their plaintive songs.

From the veranda it was only a quick dash in the inky blackness of the night to the stables around back of the hacienda. Still, at the stable door, Kathleen paused to look behind her, to ascertain no one had followed her flight. And she listened. But no sounds came from within the stable except the occasional whinny of one of the horses. Her heart pounded so loudly she thought it would surely betray her, but when no one raised a hand to halt her escape, she entered the stable. The smell of dusty hay filled her nostrils. She felt blindly along the rough boards until she came to the tack room. When she found a saddle, she half carried, half dragged it to Estrellita's stall.

"It's only me," she told the mare, as she shoved the silver-worked saddle on the horse's back.

Those next few minutes, as she cautiously walked the mare from the stables and out of the hacienda grounds, seemed like hours. Only when she was safely down the road, and out of sight and sound of the flickering campfires, did Kathleen feel free to mount the nervous horse.

Then she was on her way. Where, she did not know. But it was enough to feel the wind against her face, streaming her braids behind her; to feel the touch of the powerful horse between her knees; to feel the delicious taste of absolute freedom rush through her veins.

It was an exhilarating feeling. For it was not just an abhorrent marriage she was escaping. It was also the constant threat of life incarceration in some place for lunatics, which had hung over her head since that first glimpse of her mother slumped listlessly in the corner of an asylum cell.

For a good while Kathleen let Estrellita follow

the faint depressions grooved by wagons and buck-boards. But she knew the Indian in Simon—or El Cóndor—would easily follow her trail. She looked up at the gray clouds that scurried like frightened rabbits across the sliver of a moon. No, there wasn't enough rain in the clouds to wash away her tracks. She would have to cover her trail another way.

At the point where the wagon path paralleled a shallow creek, Kathleen reined the horse off through the buffalo grass and into the stream, leav-ing it several hundred yards further east at a stony creek bed. From there she headed south along a rocky path that climbed upward to what she hoped was a pass in the mountain.

The thought of Simon's harsh face, his mocking lips and bold eyes, pursued her through the night, so that as each hour passed Kathleen mercilessly urged Estrellita to a faster pace along the perilous ridges. The howling wind laughed at her, and the thick, twisted chaparral tore with gnarled hands at her clothing.

Lightning streaked the sky, illuminating the dras-tic change of landscape that had occurred in the span of one night. As she neared the backbone of the mountain, the barren ridges gave way to dense forests of juniper and pine. But the promise of the thunderstorm rushed onward to the west, and in the east the purple streaks of a new day threatened. What new horrors would it bring? As if in answer to her black thoughts, a coyote yipped its lonesome cry on the plains somewhere far below, and Estrellita danced nervously in response. Kathleen's knees hugged the mare's sides reassuringly. "It's all right, Estrellita," she whispered. "Everything's all right."

But in the growing light of day Kathleen could see, beyond the cactus-dotted plains, the white expanse of desert looming like a gigantic furnace. When she had ridden out so precipitously, she had not given thought to where she would go, what she would do. Now she faced scorching sands that it was rumored men had died trying to cross.

Yet the idea of the Mojave desert appealed to her. If she could elude Simon, she knew the dandified Edmund would never think of, nor want to search for her in, that burning wilderness. Surely, if she kept to the desert's rim, she could leave its edge farther south and turn west again in the direction of the coastal town of Los Angeles. From there her own whim would dictate where she would go.

But she had to get there first. And Estrellita was spent. "Only a little farther," she told the animal as it scrambled down a narrow path. "We'll rest when we're out of the foothills."

But was there time to stop? she wondered. And was it safe? And what about food for herself? Silently she cursed her foolishness at not planning her escape but fleeing headlong into the night. When faced with the prospect of marriage with Edmund, she had been cunning and patient. What was wrong with her now, that she would behave so stupidly?

As if aware of Kathleen's indecision, Estrellita paused near an alkali mudhole rimmed by scraggly mesquite trees and sagebrush, awaiting her mistress's bidding. But Kathleen was as weary as the horse, too weary to make a decision now. She slid from the saddle and tied the reins to the nearest mesquite. Dropping to the ground beneath the sparse protection of its straggly branches, she closed her eyes just as the sun scattered the last patches of pink and gray from the horizon.

It was a restless dream, as Simon's face relentlessly pursued her. Simon . . . the vaquero; El Cóndor . . . the Indian; Simon . . . the *hacendado*. But she awakened to find another face peering down at her. A horrifying face with one eye seamed closed by scars, and yellowed, misshapen teeth grinning in an ugly leer.

18

"Ha! *Amigos,* it's not a *muchacho,* but a *mujer.*"
His small eyes ran over her. "*Por Dios,* what a
mujer!"

Kathleen cringed against the ground as the man's
foul-smelling breath assailed her, and he laughed
even louder.

"*La mujer* does not find me handsome. Maybe I
should show her I have a way with women. Eh,
amigos?"

By then six or seven others, some dressed as vaqueros in what looked like blankets but most
clothed only in the breechcloth of the Indian,

gathered about Kathleen and the ugly man who crouched over her.

"You must share whatever you find, Angel," one laughed. "And since I'm the oldest, I get her first."

There was a lump of nausea in Kathleen's throat as the realization of their intentions seeped through her still-drowsy mind. The men seemed to press around her, stifling her, and a hand was already at her shirt, pulling, fondling, when a voice burst out: "No!"

Above the heads of those hovering over her, Kathleen saw a young, beardless man with a scarlet scarf tied behind his head in the Gypsy fashion she had often seen in Spain. The young man's high brow bespoke of the only hope for intelligence in the motley group.

The others looked up also, irritation at his interference showing plainly on their faces. "Do you want to fight us for her yourself?" the one called Angel asked with a contemptuous snigger.

"Come on, Renaldo," another said. "You're nothing but a boy. Let us show you what men can do."

"No!" Renaldo cried out, grabbing the shoulder of one man even as Kathleen felt the *camisa* rip open. Quickly she covered herself as Renaldo said, "*El jefe* should know about this first."

There was a perceptible stiffening among the men.

"But the leader is not in camp," Angel pointed out.

"Then you had better wait," Renaldo warned. His thin, aesthetic face wore a grim expression.

Deprived of the appeasement of their lust, the men were rougher with Kathleen than they would have been had they had their own way. Under Renaldo's angry eyes, they bound her wrists and ankles with a leather riata and tossed her crosswise over Estrellita. Kathleen grunted with the pain. Before one of the grubbier looking men tied a dirty handkerchief about her eyes, she looked to the young Renaldo for aid. But it was obvious from the helpless look in his liquid brown eyes that, other than his intervention against the mass rape that would have occurred, there was little else he could do for her at the moment. She would just have to suffer the present discomfort and hope she could escape once the band reached the camp they spoke of.

But it was several hours, more than half the day, of torturous jogging on the horse, over what seemed to her to be shifting sand dunes, before she was even allowed to rest. Hands pulled her roughly from the horse's back and dropped her to the ground. After a moment, the handkerchief, now wet with her own perspiration, was gently removed, and Kathleen looked up into Renaldo's concerned eyes. He held a tin cup to her lips. Greedily she drank the stale water.

"Not so fast," Renaldo cautioned her.

"Where are they taking me?" she asked between gulps. "Can you help me? Please!"

Renaldo looked to the other men, who had squatted a little ways off to themselves. He shook his head mutely. "I can't tell you anything, señorita. Only do as they say—and try not to draw attention to yourself."

The men were rising again, and Renaldo hastily retied the handkerchief about her head before she could ask further. Once more she was thrown across Estrellita on her stomach, and the ride resumed. When the boiling sun finally dropped behind the mountains, Renaldo was allowed to remove the handkerchief and the riata at her ankles so that she could ride astride. The coursing of blood back to her feet shot waves of pain up her legs, and she reeled dizzily in the saddle as she sat in an upright position for the first time in hours.

In the evening twilight, Kathleen noticed that they traveled in a westerly direction, steadily upward through narrow passes. In the sandstone cliffs of the canyon walls she glimpsed jumbles of caves carved by winds and rain.

"Robbers' Roost," Renaldo said, nodding at the faint outline of the caves as he dropped back to ride alongside of her.

"How much farther?" she asked. She had never felt so tired in all her life. It was an effort just to straighten her sagging shoulders.

"Only a few more hours. Just beyond Acton Pass. Then there will be rest and food."

The rocking-chair moon hung high in the heavens when the party passed through a rocky enclosure that opened into a hidden Alpine-like valley. Below, nestled among the chestnut oaks and sycamores, Kathleen saw the *rancheria*, a crude assortment of beehive-shaped tule windbreakers that Renaldo told her were called wickiups. Their many campfires looked like lightning bugs, lending a paradoxical tranquility, Kathleen thought, to the camp of cutthroats.

As the party rode into the camp, Kathleen was surprised at the populace. Everywhere there seemed to be people, mostly men—Mexicans wearing dirt-stained sombreros and packing horse pistols at their hips, or Indians in breechcloth and leggings, with tomahawks belted to their waists.

Occasionally a woman was to be seen, usually dressed in white cotton blouse and brightly colored peasant skirt, though a few wore tunics of deerskin that reached to their knees. Here and there a few children played in front of open doorways while the women cooked over the open fires and the men cleaned their rifles or groomed their horses.

When the bandits came to a halt, Angel yanked Kathleen from the saddle. Renaldo stepped between her and the hulking man.

"*La mujer* will stay in the wickiup of *el jefe.*"

Angel's massive hand went to the butt of his pistol. "She's mine, Renaldo. I spotted her first."

The slim young man did not back down. "I do not think *el jefe* will be pleased."

For a split second Angel's veined eyes glared their hostility, but wavered as Renaldo's warning sunk in. He whirled and lumbered off, and Kathleen breathed a sigh of relief. Before further objections could be raised, Renaldo hustled her inside one wickiup that looked to be slightly larger than the rest.

Inside, part of the dirt-packed floor was below ground level, with a black-and-white *tiruta*, a woven blanket, laying in one corner. About the walls was a raised platform of willow wands, which was covered with pine needles and soft tanned skins. In the wickiup's center was the blackened earth of a firepit neatly lined with stones, and around the walls Kathleen saw baskets hung, in which were domestic utensils, clothing, and dried food.

"I'll see that hot food is sent to you," Renaldo told her in his soft, cultured voice. "Try and rest. I'll sleep outside."

"What will happen?" she asked, turning back to him as he lifted aside the curtain that hung in the doorway. Her large purple eyes glittered like a night creature's in the darkness. "What will they do to me?"

"I don't know, señorita. I honestly don't know. It will be up to *el jefe* what will be done with you."

Kathleen shrank further back into the darkness. "They'll—he'll have me killed?"

Renaldo shrugged. The pity showed in his eyes. "The knowledge you have of us could be used to betray us. Please don't ask me what I can't tell you. *Buenas noches, señorita.*"

Kathleen sank to the platform with a feeling of dread as the doorway's curtain swished closed behind Renaldo. Good God, was this what it had come to? All her planning, the months of running and hiding—only to be executed by some renegade band of outlaws? Her fingers rubbed her temples in disbelief, in incredulity that she should find her early death here in a remote valley at the end of the world, when she had planned returning one day to the comforts of Boston to live fully an independent life, eventually dying in contentment of old age.

A middle-aged woman with dark, tousled hair and lively eyes brought in a bowl of savory food. "Stew," she said, handing the bowl to Kathleen. "I make the best in camp."

Kathleen took a tentative taste of the stew while the woman lit an oil lamp. She set the oil lamp down and turned to face Kathleen with her hands planted at her thick waist. "My name's Concha, *niña*. I'm Armand's woman."

"Armand?" Kathleen asked, bewildered by the turn of events that had culminated in her imprisonment in a wickiup and being waited on by this garrulous woman.

"Armand Devier. He's one of the mountain men. But you're new here. Tomorrow you'll understand more."

Kathleen wanted to ask more, but the feisty woman was gone before she could swallow her mouthful of stew.

How long before this leader returned? And what then? She looked around the wickiup but saw nothing with which to defend herself. Nothing except the wooden spoon. She put it in the bowl and set the bowl away from her. Her appetite was gone. Anger, mixed with anxiety at her helplessness, churned inside her.

She would not give in meekly to this scurvy band of men. If nothing else, her tongue would serve as a weapon. She would wait for the leader's arrival and cut the vile wretch to shreds, hurling every abuse upon him she had ever heard. She would scratch his eyes, tear his face to ribbons.

The oil-dip burned low as Kathleen wove plots that she knew were nothing more than foolish fantasies, but nevertheless, the inventive workings of her mind kept her fear at bay. Yet even as she planned how she would meet her foe, her haughty demeanor reducing the beggar to abject humility, her eyes closed in weary slumber.

19

She should have known! Why hadn't it occurred to her that he was the leader of the band of renegades?—insurrectionists, Aguila had called them. El Cóndor, the vaquero, *el jefe*. They were all one . . . Simon.

For all her good intentions to remain awake, he had come upon her as silent as the Indian he looked now, staring fiercely down at her, his burnished skin glinting in the early morning sun that streamed through the curtained doorway. From outside came the faint stirrings of the awakening *ranchería*.

"You!" she hissed with all the venom that

coursed through her as she jerked to a sitting position.

Simon grinned a sudden lopsided smile, looking almost boyish with wet hair that glistened as if he had just bathed. The breechcloth barely covered his nakedness. Kathleen's gaze fell to the rigid muscular thighs as he dropped the curtain back in its place and moved further into the wickiup. Embarrassed, she quickly raised her eyes to his face and saw the amusement displayed there.

"I hope my wife has rested well."

"Your wife?" she sputtered. "I'll never be your wife, Simon Reyes! You're the lowest, the vilest human being—no, I take that back. You're not even human. You're an animal that—"

"You mean, *mi vida,* those tender words you swore before God, and the marriage papers you signed, meant nothing?"

"Don't call me that—*mi vida!*" she shouted. "I'm not 'your life.' Or your wife either! I'm nothing of yours!"

A sarcastic grin curved Simon's lips. "I'm under the impression, from Renaldo's report, that you're my prisoner."

"How did you find me? I was careful—Estrellita didn't leave tracks. And when are you going to make them let me go?"

"Your horse didn't leave tracks. You did." He held up a torn strip of white cotton material. "On a sumac shrub."

He tossed it to her and crossed to the far corner, where he dropped the saddlebags that were slung across one shoulder. Kathleen looked up from the ragged patch she held and warily watched as he haunched over the saddlebags and drew out a razor. He rose and faced her.

"And as for when I'm going to let you go—I'm not. You're my wife, Kathleen . . . and you'll pay the price for using my name—your wifely submission."

"I won't."

The slashed brow raised in mock surprise as his long, brown fingers rubbed the beard-stubbled jaw. "Where will you run to next? Back to Woodsworth? How long do you think a lone female would survive in California? Don't you know the only other American woman in the California territory is Larkin's wife? Yesterday should've proved to you what your chances are alone out here."

"I'll take that chance any day against staying with you."

"Oh? My men'll be glad to hear that. Women are scarce here—and an American woman, well . . ."

Kathleen gasped. "You wouldn't let them!"

Simon crossed to her and stood above her. "Wouldn't I?" he asked softly. "Do you dare test me?"

The image of the wild mustang she had watched him break flashed through her mind. She saw again the frothing mouth, the broken spirit. Kathleen's head dropped to her chest with the realization of the power the man held over her.

As if recognizing her submission, he said, "I'll send Concha to you with some breakfast—and clothing. When I return this afternoon, I want you dressed as a woman—as befitting my wife. Do you understand me?"

Kathleen's head swung up. Simon waited. She looked away. "I understand you," she said stiffly.

The green eyes, as ever startlingly light against his bronzed face, studied her for a moment more. He nodded slightly, as if satisfied, then abruptly left the wickiup.

Kathleen slumped back against the wall, shaken, but grateful for the reprieve of even one day. Much could happen in the span of a few hours. A careless guard. A sympathetic heart swayed. She had only to stay alert. And something to eat would certainly help her strength.

The rumblings of her famished stomach had grown to audible dimensions when Concha entered with a cup of steaming coffee and a plate of *carne asada*, a thin steak the Indians broiled on a *parilla*. Following behind Concha was a little girl of maybe three years with straight black hair and the largest brown eyes Kathleen had ever seen. In her pudgy arms she held a mound of clothing as carefully as if she were carrying fine china.

"*Buenas dias, niña,*" Concha said. "*Dormes bien?*"

"I slept all right," Kathleen replied, resenting the woman's cheerfulness. After all, the woman was there by her own volition. Concha hadn't been roped and tied like a calf and dragged half way across California to have a cutthroat burn his brand into her—as Simon would do that evening.

Kathleen shuddered at the thought of the horror that awaited her. Better to be executed—quickly—than to be slowly, bit by bit, degraded in body and spirit. And when Simon had used her, what then?

With a woman's intuition, Concha placed a roughened hand on Kathleen's shoulder and said softly, "Don't be afraid, *niña*. El Cóndor, he's a good man. He's like all men. And," she added as an afterthought, "he's like none other. But if you do as he says, he'll be kind to you."

Kathleen picked dully at her food and wondered how many other women Simon had kept there. And if they had stayed of their own accord or, like herself, been forced to stay by Simon's sheer strength of will. And it chagrined her that he had yet to use physical force on her. Her memories alone of that one night in La Palacia were sufficient to reduce her to a cringing heap at his feet, and she detested herself, even more than him, for her weakness.

The food that had smelled so appetizing settled like a lump of cold mush in her stomach, and she put it from her. Concha had taken the clothing from the toddler and, depositing it in one of the baskets on the wall, was about to depart. Not wanting to be alone with her thoughts, Kathleen detained the woman.

"The child, Concha—is she your daughter?"

"*Sí, niña*. Chela, tell the lovely lady *hola*."

The little girl stared solemnly at Kathleen, blinked, and then shyly stuck out one small hand.

"Hello, Chela," Kathleen said, charmed by the tiny creature. "Her father—is Armand?"

"*Sí*, but she has all my looks," Concha said. "I hoped so much she'd have Armand's red hair."

"She's beautiful as she is, Concha." Kathleen released the child's hand and turned to Chela's mother. "How did you come to be here? With these—these *bandidos*?"

Concha looked at the American girl evenly. "You mean how did I get to be a camp follower, little one? And we are not *bandidos*. We are revolutionaries."

The woman moved to the doorway and, pushing aside the curtain, stood looking out at the camp's activity. "I'm here because I'm half-Indian and was separated from my parents—like all Indian children—at eight years to be trained in the mission. I was to be taught the domestic duties so that I could serve in some Castilian household. Hellhole! Bah!" she spat, slinging closed the curtain and whirling to face Kathleen. "Instead—at ten—I was taught how to please the mission's *soldados*. My sister Hermelinda was more fortunate. She died of the disease the white men brought—the smallpox."

"I'm sorry," Kathleen murmured, knowing her words were of no comfort to the woman.

"I survived," Concha said stoically. "And that was enough. Armand found me and took me away."

"Your mountain man?"

"*Sí*. His parents were French. He was born in the Klamath mountains of Alta California. All his life he's trapped for furs. Until the officials in Mexico City proclaimed that foreigners were unwelcome in California—only those of Spanish blood."

Concha snapped her fingers. "So, Armand rebelled—like many others—to fight for freedom. And me . . . I fight alongside *mi hombre*."

"Freedom." Kathleen half-muttered the word to herself. She had not realized what a precious commodity the abstract word was. Until twenty-four hours ago.

Kathleen rose to tread the earthen floor, feeling suddenly as restless as the caged cat. "You speak of freedom, Concha, and yet—"

"Don't ask that of me, *niña*. Don't ask me to help you escape. I'm pledged to our cause. Give yourself time. It won't be as bad as you think."

"That's easy for you to say. You're here because you want to be. You're here with the man you love. You're not held against your will by someone whose very nearness you abhor!"

Concha's dark eyes opened wide. "You are still a child then. Or else you would see—"

"See what?" Kathleen snapped. "That he is a mercenary man that takes what he wants with no consideration for any but himself—that will stop at nothing to gain his ends . . . even forcing me into marriage to protect himself? No, you're wrong, Concha. I see that Simon—for that is the name I know him by—is a cold, callous brute. With a total disregard for anyone else's feelings. He knows nothing of the higher form of love, but will rut like the beasts of the fields."

Concha shrugged her strong, peasant shoulder and threw back her head and laughed. "I think, *niña*, it is you who knows nothing of love."

Kathleen turned on Concha. "If being raped and mauled by him is a demonstration of love, then I want nothing to do with it!"

"We shall see," the woman replied. "We shall see."

20

As the morning lengthened, the air grew stifling within the wickiup. At last Kathleen could bear no more and cautiously stepped outside the doorway. Surprisingly, she found no guards to bar her exit.

She paused to survey the *rancheria*. It looked much as it did the day before. Children laughed and chased each other through the fields of riotous wildflowers. The women busied themselves in basket-weaving with their nimble hands working the bundles of tule reeds at their feet. Only the men were missing except for the few mostly hoary Indians, who sat beneath the shade of the scrub oaks and talked of olden days, better days.

No one paid her heed. There was no one to hamper an escape.

With an idle saunter, Kathleen moved past the doorway and down a slight incline that sloped away to the back of the wickiup. Less than fifteen yards ahead of her lay the protection of a grove of madroña evergreens. And from just beyond came the sound of some tumbling mountain stream. She had only to follow it as it snaked to the west, and she would eventually make her way back to the coast. Kathleen looked about her, seeing the forest's red, edible berries and wild oranges and plums. Surely these would sustain her.

But what most sustained her was the thought that she had the rest of the day before Simon would come looking for her. Time enough for a good head start.

The near taste of freedom was as heavenly as water to a man lost on the Mojave. So when the red-haired guard with a double belt of bullets crisscrossed about his torso and a fearsome-looking Hawke plains rifle resting in the crook of his arms stepped forward, Kathleen could have attacked him out of sheer frustration.

"*Madame* is looking for something?" the guard asked, a polite look of genuine concern wrinkling the mustachioed face.

"I only wished a bath," she said, trying hard to control the fury that seethed just beneath her stilted manner even as she noted the guard had addressed her by the title reserved for a married woman. So, Simon had already let it be known she was his wife.

Suddenly the guard's hand moved to the rifle's trigger as his eyes shifted from Kathleen to something behind her.

"It's all right, Armand," Renaldo said, stepping forward.

Kathleen turned on the young man. "Am I allowed no privacy for a bath?" she demanded.

"But of course, señora. When you are ready, I'll have one of the women bring you soap and your fresh clothes from the wickiup."

She searched the thin face for any sign of ridicule, but there was only kindness in his steady gaze. Kathleen could but nod her head curtly. Brushing past the guard, whom she supposed was Concha's lover, she flounced off in the direction of the rushing water.

In a glade rimmed by scented firs she came upon the stream. It plummeted down from the mountains over a multitude of miniature rocky falls, surging in foaming eddies into a crystal-clear pool. The sunlight filtered like gold dust through the high branches. There was a peaceful quiet, broken only by the ouzel, a water thrush which flitted about in the spray and chirped his song of joy.

Kathleen stood there, transfixed by the untouched beauty of the scene; awed, after the brick-civilization of Boston, by the pristine work of nature.

If it were not for the scurrilous savage that called himself her husband, thereby imprisoning her, she would have sought to remain forever in that glorious shelter. But, as it was—Kathleen shrugged, not wanting to think beyond the moment.

She shed the dusty pants and shirt and cautiously tested the water with one dirt-streaked foot. The water was cold but refreshing. Slowly she began to wade in, letting her skin adjust to the chill. But as the sound of someone approaching reached her, she quickly slid under the water. When she surfaced, strands of hair plastered to her cheeks, a young girl, obviously very pregnant, stood on the mossy bank. Her dark brown hair was caught Indian fashion in a single braid at the nape of her neck.

The girl smiled shyly. "I'm Margarita, *señora*."

Because the girl's Spanish was poor, Kathleen answered uncertainly, "My name is Kathleen."

Margarita, whose high cheekbones were tinted with the dusky hint of Indian beauty, set the clothes down within Kathleen's reach and handed her the bar of soap. "I know who you are, señora. My brother, Temcal, told me your name. He says you are like the first golden moments of spring."

She turned to leave and Kathleen called out, "The men—when will they return to camp?"

Margarita's bright eyes, reminding Kathleen of a squirrel's, looked at Kathleen curiously. "Near dusk ... if all goes well."

Were the men away on some raid? Kathleen wondered. Oh, God, that Simon would be killed!

When the young girl had disappeared among the trees once more, Kathleen busily scrubbed the accumulated dirt from her hair. How long it seemed since she had last had the luxury of curling tongs. And from there, her mind drifted to other comforts of civilization—to once more idly muse over the pages of one of *Godey's Lady's Books* . . .

Reluctantly she put the nostalgic memories from her and finished her bath. It was already afternoon. By the time she dressed and dried her hair, it would be time for Simon's return.

And she meant to be ready for him. No, she could not yet escape him. The guard had proved she was better watched than she supposed. But she would fight Simon with the very weapon he threatened her with—sex. She would gain the advantage on him. And when she had lulled his suspicions, then would be the time to escape. No matter how long it might take. She would wait.

Her hands balled beneath her chin, one hand rubbing the tightened knuckles of the other. How long would he keep her waiting?

She rose from where she sat with her legs tucked beneath her and crossed to the doorway, her skirts swishing about her bare ankles. In the rapidly dimming twilight she could just make out Simon's form, taller than the others, standing near one of the flickering campfires. She returned to the blanket and drew her knees up under her chin, hugging her ankles against the evening's approaching chill. The waiting was torture. What would Simon do to her? What demands would he make of her?

Suddenly he was there. She had not heard him enter. But his presence in the small room was overpowering. Slowly she raised her eyes, following the magnificent male torso, naked but for the leggings and breechcloth, until her brandy-colored eyes locked with the green ones.

"Come here, Catalina."

As ever, his familiar use of her name in Spanish infuriated her. She bounded to her feet, forgetting all her plans of feigned submission. Her clefted chin jutted forward with indignation. "You have no right to—"

In two strides Simon stood before her, so close she could smell the campfire wood smoke that still clung to his bronzed skin. In his hair was the black tailfeather of the condor.

"Must I remind you that you're no longer entertaining a gentlemanly caller in your Boston parlor? That you're my wife—and under Mexican law you have no rights."

Her eyes fell under the relentless flame in his. "You had best kill me, then," she whispered faintly.

"No," he said, taking her shoulders between his hands. "I'd be admitting defeat then, Kathleen. I want your willing submission."

Icy perspiration congealed in every pore, but she faced him boldly. "Never!"

He laughed softly, and his laugh unnerved her more than anything he could have said. One hand, stained with fresh blood, came up to cup her chin, forcing her eyes to meet his. Kathleen shuddered. The desire she saw flaming in their steely depths turned her weak with disgust. Each separate nerve in her body tingled with an awareness that appalled her, that sickened her with the knowledge of his intentions.

She tried to turn away, but his ironlike grip held her immobile. His lips lowered slowly, leisurely over hers, and she writhed with horror in his arms as his tongue thrust inside her mouth and took its pleasure.

She twisted her head free with a sob. "No!"

"I could almost believe you were a virgin that night," he whispered huskily, and lifted her trembling body in his arms. His lips scorched hers as he lowered her onto the blanket. His fierce embrace that joined the length of her body with his own warm, strong one drained her of all power of resistance.

Her clothes fell away easily beneath the sureness of his demanding hands. She shrank under the ardent gaze that traveled over her nude body like a consuming fire.

Then his hot mouth pressed on hers, drugging

her like an opiate. But as his dark head slipped lower to bury itself between the rose-tipped peaks of her breasts, Kathleen cried out—only that once.

"I'll never forgive you, Simon! Never!"

21

Had it really been three weeks? Twenty-one days since that ruinous night she had wedded with Simon? *Simon!* The very name lingered on her tongue like a bad taste.

Kathleen straightened from where she knelt on the stream's bank and rubbed her work-reddened hand along the small of her back. She arched her spine with contentment as some of the ache slipped away. At least there was one ache that she did not have to deal with that day—the piercing abdominal pain that had come with each month's menstrual.

Kathleen grimaced. She supposed she had Simon's nightly ravaging of her body to thank for that. Thank God, the telltale red that morning had also released her from her fears of pregnancy.

The other women were busy chattering over the laundry they spread on the grass to dry. But Kathleen, embarrassed by her position at the *ranchería*—a white woman, a prisoner, in spite of the fact that they regarded her as Simon's wife— could not bring herself to be spontaneously friendly in response to the polite overtures of the women, even to the thirteen-year-old Imelda who, in her pigeon-toed Indian gait, followed adoringly in Kathleen's footsteps.

Each time Kathleen washed a leather shirt of Simon's, or the disgusting breechcloth, it brought home hard to her that she was nothing more than a servant . . . a slave by day and an odalisque by night. She was lower than the women about her. For at least they were there by their own free will, while she was reduced to obey like an animal at Simon's beckoning.

Kathleen went back to scrubbing the soiled clothing on the rocks, enjoying the feeling of the warm sunlight on her skin. In the three weeks she had been at the camp, her skin had darkened, had taken on the hue of warm honey, as Simon had told her one afternoon.

She bit her lip at the unwelcome memory. Simon had come in hot and sweaty from drilling the men and, taking her by the hand, practically dragged her down to the glade she had come upon that first evening in camp. "A loving wife washes her husband's back," he said, the roguish grin making him seem years younger.

"I'll never be your loving wife, Simon Reyes!"

"Oh, but you will, Kathleen. You will."

He had stripped before her then, unbuttoning the faded blue shirt, unbuckling his belt, and removing the knee-high leather leggings. Kathleen turned from him, her hands covering her crimson face, when he shucked the worn denim pants. He came up behind her so that she could feel the searing heat of his naked skin against her and took her hands from her face, turning her around to face him.

"Now, *mi esposa*, you will wash my back."

Kathleen threw the bar of tallow soap he handed her on the bank. "You wash it yourself!" she spat, defiantly planting her fists on her hips.

One dark brow cocked. "Would you rather I wash you? You know, you look like a peasant woman with your dusty feet and braided hair. Maybe a good washing will restore the breathtaking beauty that graced my home and married me all in the same night."

Kathleen understood the threat. "Get in the water," she told him, her voice as icy as the mountain stream.

He laughed lightly. "I thought so."

Like a powerful, sleek otter, he dived beneath the surface of the water, and Kathleen retrieved the soap, biting back the thousand curses that trembled on her tongue. She lifted her skirts and tucked them into her waistband as she had seen the other women of the *rancheria* do.

When Simon broke water near the bank, she saw the kindling flame of desire in his eyes as his gaze fixed on her long, slim legs, and she knew her first real taste of a woman's triumph over a man. She promised it would be her first of many small revenges against the man that had raped her, had betrayed her with her own reward poster, had used her to protect himself, and who now degraded and humiliated her each night that he took her, laughing softly at her silent struggles that would inevitably end in her passive yielding.

But this time it would be different. Simon would not have the opportunity to dominate her.

Gingerly she stepped into the current. When she halted, the water swirling about her knees, Simon rose from the water and waded to meet her. Kathleen kept her eyes on the distant tree-shaded bank until he was at her side. Then her heavily lashed lids raised to the watchful face. A slow smile eased his harsh countenance.

"I'm ready, *mi esposa*. Are you?"

"Sit down," she ordered. When he dropped to his haunches, she knelt beside him and, dipping the soap in the water, began to lather the broad, sundarkened back. She had meant only to tease him with her nearness, but the intimate task was pleasurable. As her hand glided over his back, she marveled at the muscles that rippled just below the warm skin.

The tenseness eased from the muscles beneath the gentle prodding of her fingers, and Simon grunted a sigh of relaxation. His head turned to look back at her. "Then you *can* make yourself useful," he said with a grin. "You're not just another pretty face."

An image of herself, looking like a toil-worn squaw, flashed through her mind, and she had to laugh in spite of herself. "You're a rogue!" she said and, without thinking, playfully shoved his head under water.

He came up laughing and sputtering water, his wet curls glistening in the sun. "So, you dare to challenge your husband, woman?" With a whoop, he tackled her as she staggered ashore, bringing her down among the willowy tules.

Without understanding it, it seemed to Kathleen that a magical hush overtook the secluded forest glade. There was the sensuous scent of the tropical flowers, the erotic play of the water's current about her legs—and her acute awareness of Simon next to her. She heard the quickening of her own breath. Her eyes slid upwards to encounter Simon's intense gaze, to see the nostrils that flared passionately. The smiles faded from both of their faces.

Inexorably the arms that enfolded her about her

hips moved up along her back to pull her against
him so that his wet body soaked her thin clothing,
burning her skin with the heat of his desire.

Kathleen closed her eyes against the inundating
passion that seethed like molten lead in the fiery
green depths of Simon's eyes. A liquid warmth
fanned out from the pit of her belly as his lips
traced a searing path to the base of her neck, end-
ing in the softest brush at her nape. A weakness she
could not believe claimed her. She clutched blindly
at the sinewy shoulders.

Intertwined with the ragged intake of his breath,
she heard her own whispered moan. "No, Simon.
Please, no."

The brutal grip that dug into the soft skin of her
arms jerked Kathleen back to reality. She trembled
with absolute fear, knowing Simon capable of
breaking her apart and crushing her as easily as he
would a matchstick.

There was a wintry gleam in his eyes. "You try
my patience, Kathleen!"

He shoved her from him then, and stalked from
the lagoon while she floundered helplessly in the
reeds. When she had regained her footing, she saw
Simon squatting calmly on the bank. Casually he
took a sheet of cornhusk paper and tobacco from
the tin in his shirt pocket and rolled a cigarette. All
the while his eyes studied her with an intentness
that disconcerted her.

"I get tired of reminding you of your marital obligation—namely, a warm response." His eyes suddenly narrowed to mere slits. "Or is there another that can thaw your Yankee coldness?"

Kathleen waded from the water and occupied herself by wringing the water from her skirt. "There isn't anybody else," she said tersely. "It's just that I—I don't feel like that."

Simon took the cigarette from between his lips and tossed it into the water. "Kathleen, you're a little hypocrite."

"I'm not a hypocrite! I'm not!" Kathleen told herself as she wrung the water from the laundry with agitated motions. "He's so sure of his persuasive power over other women! He just can't imagine that I wouldn't feel the same as those others."

And she wondered again as she carried the laundry back to the camp just how many others there had been in Simon's life. How many others had shared his wickiup with him.

It was with a lightened mind she recalled that that night she would not have to share the wickiup with Simon. "I'll be leaving," he had told her early that morning.

She had looked up quickly from the shirt she was mending. "Why? Where?"

Simon stopped at the doorway. "Do I detect curiosity—or concern—in that lovely voice of yours?"

"Neither," she said bluntly. "What you detect is sheer relief."

Her head bent low over the material, and she did not see the hand that tightened about the curtain in angry ridges. But his voice was even. "Then it should please you to know I'll be gone several days."

"Why? To put in your cursory appearance as the civilized ranchero? To woo the beauteous—and wealthy—Francesca Escandón? Or will your time be spent in the guise of the bandit vaquero—profitably victimizing innocent citizens? How can you keep from despising yourself?" she asked him scathingly.

"I won't defend my actions to you or anyone, Kathleen," he said, his voice taut with the anger she knew he kept barely in check.

Still, she felt driven to provoke him that morning, why she could not understand. So when Simon said, "I've requested Renaldo to stay close by while I'm gone—should you need him," she threw the mending down and bounded to her feet.

"To watch me, isn't that it? To keep me from escaping?" She flung herself against him with a cry of frustrated rage, beating with small clenched fists on his chest. "How long, Simon? How long will you keep me like this?"

He caught her hands in his, a feigned look of surprise on the rugged face. "Why, beloved, you know we vowed before God it would be for the rest of our lives—'till death do us part.' Wasn't that the way it went?"

"Then may God make your life mercifully short," she declared, her voice vibrating with a passionate loathing.

22

"He's despicable! A—an abominable, mercenary beast!"

Kathleen changed the direction of her pacing and continued her tirade. "I loathe him, Concha! What kind of low animal is he to force—to have his way with me and then leave me all this time at the mercy of these—these brigands?"

Concha set the dinner plate on the wickiup's platform and, folding her arms, faced *el jefe*'s *amante*, his golden mistress, his lovely wife. The young woman was suffering one of those dark moods that seemed to have gripped her since *el jefe* left.

"He's been gone little more than a week," she told Kathleen placatingly. "And those people you call brigands, I might remind you, are friends— *your* friends, if you'd give them a chance."

"I'm sorry, Concha," Kathleen said contritely. "I—I guess it's the weather."

"*No te preocuparás, niña.* Armand says everyone gets that way just before a storm breaks. Now eat your dinner. Else you'll be as thin as the old woman of the village. And *el jefe*'ll turn his eye elsewhere."

"God that he would!" Kathleen snapped. "And leave me in peace!"

Concha shrugged fatalistically and muttered, "*Quién entiende los modos de amor?*" before leaving Kathleen to her dinner.

Reproaching herself for her rudeness, Kathleen put out a tentative hand to detain the woman, but decided against it. She would probably only say something else ungracious, and she certainly didn't want to anger the only friend she had in the camp.

That was untrue, of course. There was Imelda. And Margarita and her brother Temcal. Kathleen had to smile, remembering how the youth, who was famed for his skill at silversmithing, had ducked his receding chin until it touched his bobbing Adam's apple the morning he presented her with a silver arm bracelet.

And then there was Renaldo. Dear Renaldo, who every night in Simon's absence slept outside her doorway. But Renaldo's Old World politeness kept the friendship between them on a more formal plane.

Kathleen toyed with the *refrijoles* and *cabrito,* but could not bring herself to eat. What *was* wrong with her? An aching, oppressive loneliness gnawed inside her, matching the gloomy clouds that had overcast the skies the last several days.

And then there was the boredom. At least when Simon had been there, there had been the challenge of sharp words, the duel of honed wits to lend excitement to the days. And then there had been the nights. The whispered words of sex in both English and Spanish to stir her senses; the knowing fingers, the burning lips that roused her to frenzied heights.

Damn it! Why must she torment herself with memories of the man who ravaged her body, despoiled her spirit, and ravished her very thoughts? She looked down at the ring on her third finger. She would never remove it! It would serve to remind her of the revenge she would one day take on Simon.

Resolutely she put the man's mocking face from her and went to the doorway, moving aside the curtain. Yes, there was the faithful Renaldo. The way he sat on his blanket—with his back against the wickiup, his arms crossed at his knees, and the sombrero pulled low over his scarfed head—reminded Kathleen of her original conception of the Mexican people.

It had been a political cartoon run in the Boston *Times Herald* at the end of Texas's war for independence against Mexico. It pictured the Mexican as indolent and lazy, believing that everything should wait on the morrow. But the men of the *ranchería* didn't fit that description. They were forever occupied with something—their horses, their guns, and—yes—their women.

And Renaldo most certainly didn't fit that misconception. He seemed more educated than most of the men, more cultured. What was he doing living like a bandit? But then, what was Simon doing living like a bandit? she asked herself. Why did he run goods with Nathan when he obviously didn't need the money? Or was he indeed involved in an insurrection?

"Renaldo," she whispered.

"*Sí, señora?*"

Then Renaldo had been awake after all. He must have known she had come outside, but, in that polite manner of his, was merely waiting for her to break the silence. She slid down opposite him on the other side of the doorway.

"Who are you really, Renaldo?" She gestured at the multitude of forms huddled at the various campfires that dotted the valley, taking their evening meal. "Why are you living a life like this?"

In the darkness she could barely make out his face, and she was not sure whether he had heard her, but after a minute he said, in that soft, precise voice of his, "I was born on a rancho. My father was a blacksmith there. Before that he was a soldier, coming from Mexico to serve under Lieutenant Luis Argüello. The company was posted at the then-new presidio of Santa Barbara. When my father had saved enough earnings, he sent to Tepic for his sweetheart, and he and my mother were married at Santa Barbara's mission.

"My father had great hopes that things would be different here; that a man would be reckoned by his accomplishments—not by his class. But he found it was not to be so. He and my mother were not of pure Spanish blood, but a mixture—*cholos* they are called here."

Renaldo paused, and his sigh, a mixture of bitterness and wistfulness, was lost in the groan of the rising wind. Chilled, Kathleen wrapped her arms about her, patiently waiting for Renaldo to continue.

"When those hopes were dimmed," Renaldo said finally, "they set their dreams on me. Every *real* they earned went to pay the rancho's padre for my lessons. And so I became a misfit—too educated for those of my own class but too lowly bred for the Californios . . . I, who can read and write, when less than a hundred of the grandees in all of California can even sign their name."

For some minutes the two of them sat wrapped in their own thoughts while the distant sky flickered with streaks of lightning and the nearby campfires burned lower.

But at last Kathleen could no longer contain her curiosity about the man who had bound her to him. "And Simon?" she asked in a voice that could just be heard above the rush of the wind through the tossing tree limbs. "Is his the same story?"

"That I couldn't tell you."

"Couldn't or wouldn't?"

"Both. Probably old Diego, *el viejo*, is the only one that knows the whole story. Maybe Father Marcos. I can only tell you that if it weren't for El Cóndor, the man you call Simon, I'd still be sitting feeling sorry for myself and those like me instead of doing something about it."

"Do you really think Simon's way is better?" Kathleen asked, not trying to hide the caustic bite in her voice.

"If you've ever been kept in one of the mission's compounds, then you could answer that fairly. There comes a time when rationalization and compromises won't reform injustice. I believe one of your own countrymen, Thomas Paine, put it much more succinctly than I."

"And where do you draw the line between the revolutionary—the hero—and the traitor—the villain?"

"History draws that line. History and, in the final analysis, your own personal evaluation of the man, señora."

Overhead the lightning crackled. The first drops of rain pelted the Indian who sat bareback on the quarter horse. The animal danced each time the lightning zigzagged across the heavens, and the man bent forward, stroking the great beast's neck. "Gently, Salvaje," he whispered. "Home is just below."

From his lookout atop the glaciered butte, the *ranchería* could barely be distinguished. Only the smoldering ashes of the campfires betrayed its existence, and then only to the keenest eye.

"Home," he repeated to himself, with a mockery that contorted his face so that, had any God-fearing person seen his countenance at that moment, one would have sworn he was Satan wandering the earth that night and loosing the thunderstorm upon his chosen victims.

Had there ever been a home? Simon wondered. No, that was the irony of it all. There had been a home—one he had known as a small child. The security, the love, that had abounded in that mountain cabin.

What in God's holy name had made him take Kathleen there that first night? He remembered feeling as if it had been a desecration, allowing her in the cabin that had been his mother's. And his father's whenever the man could escape the responsibilities of the rancho—and the eagle eye of his wife.

And now Simon had his own wife—Kathleen.

What kind of welcome would she give him tonight? Would she quiver with fear when those moments of bitterness assailed him? Would her great, wine-colored eyes flash disdainfully, displaying the hatred for him that overflowed her heart? Or would she be in one of those rare moods when the pure pleasure of delight would erupt in her bubbling laughter?

His lips stretched in a grim line, and he heeled Salvaje forward, holding the horse to a slow canter, delaying his return. Regardless of her moods, he told himself, when they came together at night, the outcome was always the same. Her resistance, which he could but admire even while he strove to break it, and which always ended in her passive yielding to him as his will finally dominated.

And this angered him the greatest. Because there was a warm-blooded—no, hot-blooded—woman beneath that cold exterior. Dammit, he knew with every nerve in his body that there were moments when the real woman in Kathleen was just below the surface. Her passion, if released, would match his. But maybe it was to be another man that would taste the honey of her love, that would devour the pleasures she would willingly give.

The thought of her beautiful, tantalizing body spread-eagled for some other man to sample, to delight in, drove Simon at times to a feverish pitch. And he would turn it on Kathleen in perverse forms of mental cruelty—and yes, wasn't his rapturous ravishing of her golden body a physical cruelty?

So what drove him to possess Kathleen? It was sheer foolishness to continue to keep her. Gemma was twenty times the lover Kathleen was. And Gemma knew all sorts of tricks to drive a man wild. And yet, didn't the mere mental image of Kathleen beneath him, her heavy tresses spread out like a feathered fan, drive him wild?

It was madness to keep Kathleen. And even crazier to try to trace this Edmund Woodsworth. To risk his life looking for a man who was nothing to him. But he, himself, must hold some interest for Woodsworth—or else Gemma wouldn't have sent word that Kathleen's fiancé had been asking questions, had even wired for a detective out of New Orleans.

The trip had proved worthless. Woodsworth had disappeared by the time Simon reached Santa Barbara. Still, he felt instinctively that he had not seen the last of the man.

So much the better, he thought. For it would be just one more severed tie that bound Kathleen to her old life. And at the thought of her, Simon's hand came down hard on Salvaje's flanks, urging the quarter horse homeward.

23

The sudden white flash of lightning illuminated the wickiup. But it was neither the lightning nor the rolling bombardment of thunder which followed that awoke Kathleen. Her heavy-lidded eyes opened to the dim vision of the dark face hovering over hers.

"Simon." It was a faint whisper, a half sigh.

The warm lips closed over hers, and the muscle-corded body slanted across her own. Even though each time before she had fought him with all her strength, her drugged-like sleep now weakened her resistance, and her arms came up unwittingly around his shoulders. Her fingers tangled in his rain-wet hair.

Startled at this unexpected display of passion, Simon raised his head to probe the deep purple eyes, but the thickly fringed lids fluttered closed to hide whatever secrets were to be found there. "Catalina," he murmured wonderingly as his forefinger lightly brushed the cleft of her chin.

And his lean lips once more claimed her own, but this time with a gentleness that caught the woman beneath him by surprise. Like the touch of butterfly wings, his kisses skimmed her lids, her cheeks, to linger at her ear.

Then, as another explosion of lightning flooded the wickiup, so were the tender moments exploded by the suddenness of white-hot passion. Simon's hand slipped downward to caress the taut, turgid crowns of her breasts, straining beneath her chemise to break free. Kathleen gasped.

His mouth silenced her low moans of pleasure before deserting her lips and burning a path along her slim-columned neck, nipping the delicate hollow of her throat. Kathleen's hands clutched at Simon's back, pulling him against her even as her nails dug into his skin.

But when he rose and shucked the breechcloth, she stiffened in remembrance of the pain and degradation and, as his body again lowered over hers, tried to draw away from his embrace.

"Kathleen." The husky whisper of his voice

against her ear crackled like the thunder in the heavens. "I'm not an ogre. I'm only a man. Here, feel me." His hand caught hers and firmly guided it downward along his flat belly.

Her tentative resistance slowly gave way to wonder as she explored this man to whom she was united by the law, by God, and by the strange mixture of hate and passion. His deep groan told her of the pleasure a woman could give a man, and the knowledge was an overwhelming assault on her senses. Her limbs intertwined with his, and her fingers locked in his long curls.

"Love me, Simon!" she begged as the pain became unbearable pleasure and pleasure unbearable pain.

Somewhere out in camp a rooster heralded the dawn with its onomatopoeic crow, even though the morning's first light had yet to filter through the slits of the curtained doorway. Kathleen stirred drowsily and nestled closer to the strong arms that enfolded her. Playful lips brushed the lids of her eyes, and the tip of a tongue tickled her ear, sending a flood of rapturous shivers coursing through her. Her arms came up to encircle him, and she whispered, *"Mi indio,* take me again!"

Simon laughed softly. "You're greedy, Catalina. And so am I. I can't get enough of you. Each time I make love to you, I dissolve inside. I drown in the warm wine of your eyes—in the warm juices of your lovely body."

"Then show me," she whispered, and her body arched upwards to meet his, giving as he gave.

The morning was growing old when Kathleen finally awakened. She turned slightly and put out a hand, but the place next to her was empty. For a long moment she lay there, reliving the previous night. It was incredible! Unbelievable! That she could behave in such an abandoned fashion. What ever had caused her to make such wanton love, to let Simon have his way with her? Why hadn't she realized the power of passion? She cringed with embarrassment. To think she had actually enjoyed herself—in the arms of the man she most detested.

She remembered the first time he had taken her, at La Palacia, and she had thought with disgust that that was what sex was all about. But to have Simon teach her! Irony of ironies. To be enslaved by passion to one's own husband! To be enslaved by a man whose dark, Indian skin and flashing, mocking eyes she found loathsome.

Ohh! She flushed with shame with each memory that assailed her. That she could have found that hitherto undiscovered pleasure in the arms of the scoundrel. Perhaps she indeed carried the taint of her mother's blood. How often had she heard the hurled accusations from her father that her mother had whoring blood. But, dear God, was her father any better, with his perverted lusts? And where did that leave herself but with the inherent passion of the senses?

Damn her senses. And damn Simon! She could imagine how out of proportion his male arrogance would be this morning. Well, she would show him! Let him just once swagger about her, and she would treat him as if he were dust beneath her feet!

But Simon did not return to the wickiup that morning, and when noon came Kathleen dressed and, taking a towel with her, went outside, ostensibly to bathe. She saw the grisly Angel, whom she noted had been careful to keep out of her way since he found that *el jefe* had claimed her as his wife. She repressed a scornful smile, recalling how quickly the bandido's bravado had disappeared.

Concha passed by, with the tiny Chela toddling behind her, and stopped Kathleen with an outstretched hand. *"Niña,* the worst has happened! Margarita's man, Najo, didn't return from the last raid."

"Oh, no!" cried Kathleen. "Should I go to her? Say something?"

"No, not now. She will be preparing for mourning. She's marking her face now with charcoal."

As Kathleen continued on toward the glade, sorrow for Margarita, heavy with Najo's unborn child, clouded her thoughts. Why, oh why, couldn't it have been Simon who didn't return? And with the thought of him, the memories of the night before returned. Fool! To have been so easy for Simon. Another conquest for his conceited male ego.

Nowhere did she see him. He probably already had ridden out of camp, spurring his horse toward the waiting arms of Francesca or Gemma. She cursed his name as she made her way through the maze of pines. Once she tripped over the gnarled root of a juniper, sprawling headlong in the carpet of pine needles and scratching her cheek on a prickly cone. Nothing was going right.

When she reached the banks of the stream, she removed her clothing and plunged into the water. But the relaxation she sought did not come; the chilly dip did not cool her boiling anger, did not soothe her feverish senses. She washed her hair and bathed, scrubbing abrasively at her skin as if to cleanse away a contagion. After she finished, she waded from the water, her wet hair swinging against the hollow of her back, and petulantly began to dress before heading back to camp.

Blinded partially by the late-afternoon sun, partially by her seething fury, Kathleen did not see the massive figure looming just ahead of her until it was too late. Heavy arms came around her, and a mouth smelling of garlic locked over hers, cutting off her scream of surprise.

Kathleen tried to push Angel from her, but his strength was too much for her. He slammed her down in the willowy grass and began ripping at her clothing. "I've been watching you, lovely lady," he grunted, and brutally rammed his knee between her thighs.

She moaned with the unexpected pain and drew up in a ball. "So, your beautiful body isn't good enough for the likes of me, eh? Well, I'll show you what a real man can do!"

He reared above her, but the ugly face contorted with lust underwent a rapid change to one of petrified shock.

"Get off her," a steely voice ordered.

Slowly Angel raised from his kneeling position to face the thunderous face of *el jefe*—and the leader's long knife that glinted in the sun.

"Your knife," Simon said, nodding at the man's leggings.

"I was only—"

"You knew my orders about the woman. Get out your knife."

"She was mine first!" Angel said, even as he whipped the knife from his legging. But he was not quick enough for the lean, lithesome leader, whose leg twisted about the larger man's so that he toppled like a tree at Simon's feet. Simon's shining knife arced upwards, and Angel begged, "No, *jefe!* I didn't mean to—"

Simon showed no leniency. The knife flashed downward to savagely bury to the hilt in the fleshy chest. Kathleen raised on her elbows to stare wide-eyed at the man who quivered in the throes of death, blood staining his dirty shirt and gurgling in his throat.

Simon grabbed her arm and jerked her roughly to her feet. "You little fool! I warned you about leaving camp alone. If Temcal hadn't seen Angel follow you, you'd be—"

"Be what, Simon?" Kathleen yanked herself from his grasp. "A piece of used flesh? Isn't that what I am already?"

Simon eyed her coldly. "Only you can tell me that, my wife." He bent and drew his blade from the lifeless body. "Your selfish stubbornness has caused me to kill a good soldier," he told her; once more sheathing the knife in his legging. "Now cover yourself and get back to camp."

Shaken, Kathleen half ran, half stumbled along the path that led out of the glade. At the camp everything seemed as usual, and it was hard to believe she had witnessed only a moment earlier Simon's compunctionless murder of one of his own men.

She retreated to the wickiup, nervously walking the floor. She had missed both breakfast and lunch, and her stomach growled with hunger. When the sun lowered and the smell of roasting meat on the evening campfires reached her, she could wait no longer and ventured outside the wickiup. But once again, Simon wasn't anywhere in sight.

Where was he? What would he do? Would he come to her that night? And would it be with his usual brusqueness, as if he took pleasure in her

fear? Or would he take her with the surprising ten-
derness of the night before? Regardless, she would
lay impassively in his arms, treating him with the
contempt that oozed from every pore in her skin.

She crossed to the nearest fire, where a huge
black kettle of beans bubbled and a jackrabbit
roasted on the spit. Concha, who dished out the
beans and corn cakes, handed Kathleen a tin plate
with a rabbit haunch, saying, "So you and *el jefe*
are at odds again, eh, *niña?*"

"He's a monster! A callous cutthroat! He killed
Angel without giving the man a chance!"

"And should he have?" Concha asked softly.
"His word is law, and must be obeyed to the letter.
How else would he control all these men? Without
firm leadership they'd soon split up into aimless
bands of marauders."

"Isn't that what they *are?*" she asked Concha and
turned away, leaving the woman to shake her head
after Kathleen.

Night's darkness covered the hidden valley and a
pumpkin moon hung low over the ridge of one
mountain. From one of the campfires came the vibrating beat of a drum accompanied by turtle-shell
rattles. In the firelight a young Indian, his body
painted in brilliant colors, leaped up and began
prancing in the center of gathered spectators as if
performing some tribal ceremonial rite.

Drawn by the music, Kathleen moved toward a
nearby flatbed wagon that was in the shadows and

seated herself at the base of one large wheel to eat her dinner.

As she chewed on the tough rabbit haunch, she watched while the youth sat down, giving way to a Mexican girl who took his place. A guitar and trumpet replaced the drum and rattles, and the girl moved sinuously among the onlookers, her hands intertwined high above her head, her back arched seductively. Her hips thrust forward suggestively with the music's beat. The girl's movements accelerated, keeping time with the rhythm as the music erupted in the sensuous fandango.

The staccato strains stirred something in Kathleen, and she felt her blood quicken in response. She longed to dance, herself, to exult in that momentary release of inhibitions, to cast off all restraint.

But as she half-rose to join the revelers, the sight of Simon moving among the men, clapping one on the shoulder, laughing at some jest by another, solemnly discussing something with still another, crushed her urge to dance. And when, with a cursory embrace, Simon caught up the girl, who was dancing with obviously flirtatious movements meant only for him, Kathleen swung around and headed for the wickiup.

Once inside, she picked up Simon's saddlebags and dumped their contents on the dirt floor. One by one she began hurling his razor, his brush, and other personal articles against the wall.

She was suddenly yanked around to face him. "You little witch! What's gotten into you now?"

"Don't touch me! You murderer! You and your high ideals. Tell me, *el jefe,* what will you do when you've disposed of all who stand in your way? Set yourself up as California's first emperor?"

Simon's green-flecked eyes studied Kathleen for a long moment. "I could take the time to explain the political situation to you, Kathleen. But I don't think that's what's eating at you."

She tried to jerk away, but he held her firmly. "I'm right, aren't I? It's eating your insides that you want me as much as I want you. But you're incapable of admitting it."

Kathleen's mouth parched suddenly. "No," she whispered.

"Oh? Then prove it." And he swept her up against him. His mouth slanted across hers recklessly, forcing her lips to yield.

Kathleen tried to push him from her, but his hands slid down to cup her buttocks, pressing her against him so that she could feel his urgency. One hand came up to tangle in her waist-length hair, jerking her head backwards.

"Say you want me, Catalina."

"Never!" she replied.

But her hands caught at the curls that fcathered at Simon's worn collar and pulled his head down to meet hers.

24

"Tell me you'll miss me," he teased, leaning down from Salvaje to catch her hand. Kathleen had forgotten how elegant Simon could look when dressed as the ranchero—the tight black breeches and bolero jacket over the frilled white shirt that lay open at the neck and the flat-brim hat set low over the mocking eyes.

She jerked her hand away. "Like the pox I'll miss you, Simon Reyes!"

He laughed aloud. "I'll put that to the test when I return, *mi vida.*" He spurred the horse forward and, with a company of his men, rode out in a flurry of dust.

Kathleen could have hurled her half-eaten orange after him. Of all the insufferable conceit! To ignore the hatred that could not help but inflect every word she spoke to him. Was he so insensible a man that he didn't feel the contempt in which she held him?

Each day grew worse, her humiliation greater, her degradation lower. And the fact that Simon could arouse passions in her which she could in no way repress was the worst of it all. The desire to escape gnawed at her brain, relentlessly plagued her every waking moment—and seeped into her dream-filled sleep to mingle with visions of laughing green eyes.

But there was one small hope. While Simon was gone, she might be able to persuade Renaldo to help her—to call off Simon's watchdogs. She had no idea when Simon would return, and therefore there was not a moment to waste.

She tossed the last of the orange away and headed to the far side of the camp where in an open field Renaldo drilled six or seven men in target practice. Two, Indians, used yew bows that were almost as large as they, while the Mexicans fired muskets. Kathleen waited until the next fusillade reverberated among the large boulders of the encircling mountain and the men were reloading, to approach Renaldo.

"Renaldo, can I talk with you—alone?"

The intelligent eyes studied Kathleen for a moment, then he said, *"Ciertamente, señora."* He turned and called out to Temcal to take his place, then rejoined Kathleen, who had moved a little aside. "Shall we walk a ways?"

Kathleen nodded her assent, and, as if by mutual agreement, the two began walking toward the river, but circumventing the camp and whatever curious eyes might be watching. After a while Renaldo said, "What is it you wish to talk about, señora?"

Kathleen heaved a sigh and stooped to pick a poppy from among the sheets of purple and gold flowers before continuing on. "Renaldo," she said finally, "if I'm to make anything of my life—if this is to be my life—well, you can see, surely, that I can't remain in this limbo."

She raised her gaze from golden petals of the poppy and fixed troubled eyes on Renaldo. "You must explain to me what this—" she indicated the camp with her free hand—"is all about. I realize you can't tell me everything. But enough for me to understand . . . to make some sense of all this."

Renaldo's velvet-brown eyes narrowed as if he expected some trickery, but the guileless expression in the lovely face convinced him that *el jefe*'s wife was sincere.

As he hesitantly began, trying accurately to explain the principles of his people's cause, Kathleen could only hate herself for the deception she played on the gentle man—but, dear God, if she didn't escape she would go mad, as mad as her father claimed her mother was.

But her pretense at interest changed to genuine attention as Renaldo continued his discourse. "And as you can see, señora, we have no choice. What can we do when the soldiers that Mexico sends— and they are ex-convicts for the most part, *rateros* that Mexico wants to get rid of—steal from us, or even murder, at the slightest provocation? Why, our wives and sweethearts can't even appear on the streets, so many rapes have occurred. Then there is Mexico's own unstable government. They change presidents every six months. If they can't adequately rule their own country, how can we, Californios, expect them to rule us justly? I ask you, señora, can you blame us for wanting home rule?"

By this time they had reached the river's edge. Kathleen tossed the heat-wilted flower into the gurgling water. "You speak as only a man of high principles would speak, Renaldo. And that is all very well. But I can only answer you as a woman would."

Renaldo's eyes flickered with surprise.

"Yes," she continued, "what of the women? You speak of a sweetheart. Would you have her postpone her marriage year after year until the day you finally gain your desires? And what of her desires? What of the tiny *niños* she desires to cradle in her arms? What of the husband she wants to prepare a home for? If one day a bullet should find you, what then? Oh, your ideals are very noble. But there must be a place in your life for practicality also. Because when you get down to it, Renaldo, life isn't noble. It's a harsh, practical existence. So how great would your love be? Would it be a second-rate love—second to your grand cause? Can you answer me truthfully?"

Simon's second-in-command walked a little apart from Kathleen before turning back to her. "Señora, what are you saying? Why do you bring all this up?"

Kathleen dropped her pretense. "Because I also am being practical. I can't live this existence—of a kept woman. And that's what I am in spite of papers declaring the contrary. What happens when your leader tires of me? What then? Tell me, Renaldo, is this your idea of nobility? What kind of life could I possibly make for myself?"

A pained look crossed Renaldo's face, and she hurried on: "I'm telling you this because I can help you—help your cause, if you'll let me."

She went to Renaldo and touched his arm imploringly. "Within the year, upon my father's death, I'll be heiress to a vast sum of money. A fortune, Renaldo! Think of it! What it could do for your cause. What it could do for the sweetheart you'll one day take as your wife. No more groveling. No more risking your life—and that of your family. I swear every penny will be yours—if you'll only help me. God knows, I don't care about the money. It's only brought me unhappiness."

"And do you think the money'll bring me any better chance at happiness than it has you, señora?" Renaldo asked softly. "Do you think I have so little honor? I could never hold my head up if I did such a thing. I could not betray the trust of a man like *el jefe*."

At that moment Kathleen could not remember a time in her life when she had ever felt so small, so humbled. But even those feelings were overcome by her own helplessness, her own sense of injustice— the utter futility that faced her.

"Well, *I* would," she said, pronouncing every word between clenched teeth. "I would betray your precious leader at the drop of a coin—and I swear by God I'll do just that if I ever get out of this valley."

Her voice rose to a shrill pitch. "I'll see him face an execution squad if I have to crawl, and beg, and bribe right up to the President of the United States."

"Then God help your soul, señora."

"He can't," she cried. "Simon has possessed my soul!"

The day immediately following her discussion with Renaldo Kathleen was to leave the valley. But not in the way she expected . . . not in escape.

She had gone along with the women and children

to the river to wash the clothes, when a gradual hush settled over the area. The lack of noise from the forest animals caused some of the women to lift their heads as if, like deer, they scented trouble.

Kathleen herself halted in her bathing of little Chela and looked up with a frown on her face. Chela stopped splashing the water and raised her little round face to Kathleen. "Da?" she asked.

Then, within the darkness of the forest on the river's far side, Kathleen's eyes caught the glint of metal. And in that same moment came the yell of "Charge!" and a horde of Mexican soldiers, in their brilliant blue uniforms and waving their gleaming sabers on high, swept down out of the forests on their great mounts and thundered through the river's rushing waters.

For the length of a heartbeat the women and children remained paralyzed. Then the mothers grabbed up their babies and shoved their children before them. Shrill screams pierced the still air. Screams of fright—and then screams of death's blows as sabers plunged into tiny brown bodies or slashed at women's thighs, bringing them tumbling to the ground in flowing blood.

Kathleen caught up Chela to her breast and ran on ahead of Concha, and amidst the roar of the muskets and the pitiful cries of the victims dying, Kathleen heard a man shout: "The golden one! Don't kill her! She's for me!"

Her heart pounded and her breath came in short

gasps, as she dodged a heaped body or a charging horse. Immune now to the swords and guns, Kathleen might have escaped but for the burden of Chela, which grew heavier with each step.

And then Kathleen was surrounded by the mounted soldiers. Panting heavily, she clutched the girl against her, waiting.

"It seems the circumstances have changed since our last two meetings," Aguila said, dismounting from his horse.

"Not that much," Kathleen snapped. "You're still the slimy snake you always were!"

Aguila crossed to her and placed the tip of his blood-red saber at the base of her throat. Kathleen felt its prick. "And you're still the haughty little bitch, Señora Reyes. But I imagine imprisonment will take the high-and-mightiness out of you . . . after I've taught you a few things first."

He lowered his saber. "Take the child," he ordered, and one of the soldiers stepped forward and pried loose the crying child from Kathleen's arms.

"Shall we return to camp, Señora Reyes, and confront your beloved husband?" Aguila sneered.

An insolent smile curved Kathleen's full lips. "You're slightly tardy, Lieutenant. Simon's not in camp."

Aguila's reptilian eyes flared briefly. "Bring her along," he rapped out. He swung upon his palomino and, bringing his quirt down viciously across the animal's flanks, bounded away.

Kathleen was roughly pushed forward by the butt of a bayonet rifle and almost fell. "Get moving, *puta!*" the beady-eyed soldier ordered.

A desolation of horror mounted with every step Kathleen took. Blood was everywhere. In a ravine she sighted Imelda, who had outrun even herself. The girl lay spread-eagled, her blood-stained skirts bunched above her thighs. She moaned, and Kathleen stopped. But a soldier said, "Keep moving—or the same'll happen to you—no matter what the lieutenant ordered." A hideous leer creased the filthy, beard-stubbled face. Kathleen cringed inwardly and immediately joined the few survivors, none of which was Concha, in the forced march into camp.

Kathleen could have cried from sheer relief when she saw trudging ahead of her Margarita, carrying Chela piggyback. The pregnant girl's face crumpled with tears when Kathleen caught up with her. "Oh, señora, señora!" she intoned.

"It's going to be all right, Margarita," Kathleen said, and took Chela from her. "We're still alive, at least."

Another burden was lifted from Kathleen's shoulders when they reached camp and she saw that the men of Simon's who had remained behind had been spared. She found Renaldo among the prisoners and caught the flicker of relief pass over his own countenance when he saw that she was unharmed.

The women and children were herded into a circle with the men and forced to sit on the ground by guards who wielded their rifles like clubs.

From one of triumph, Aguila's mood switched to a sullen nastiness. He came over to Kathleen and said, "Where is your husband, señora?"

"I don't know."

Gladly she would have liked to tell the lieutenant. It was her chance to even the score with Simon. The coward! He had ridden off to leave his followers to this massacre. Oh, if she only knew where he was!

Aguila nodded at one of his soldiers, and the man lifted his musket and fired into the sitting crowd of prisoners. There was a scream as a vaquero Kathleen had seen often about the camp slumped forward.

"Each time I ask you, señora," Aguila said with a silky smile, "and don't receive my answer, one of them will die."

"For God's sake," Kathleen cried, "I don't know where he is! None of us know! Do you think Simon would be so stupid as to inform anyone of his plans?"

The unblinking eyes studied her and then slid over to the huddled mass. "Move them out," he called sharply. "Then fire the wickiups."

He turned back to her, and she whispered, "What will you do with us?"

"For them—slave labor. Our illustrious grandees

will pay a great deal for someone to do their work
for them. Yes, labor is much better than death,
wouldn't you say?"

His hand crawled up her waist to squeeze brutally one breast, and Kathleen cried out, swaying in
pain.

"For you I have other plans. And afterwards—
perhaps death would be better, señora. For I do not
take slights lightly."

The march out of the camp began that same afternoon. It was something Kathleen was never to
forget. Ringed by the mounted soldiers, she and the
other prisoners were driven like cattle up out of the
valley. She paused once to look backwards at the
flaming wickiups, committing the place to memory
before stumbling ahead again.

Often one of the prisoners would slip on the
rocky trail, and the bull whip used on oxen and
jackasses would descend across their backs. Kathleen kept Chela close to her side, and herself
twisted an ankle trying to lift the girl over a rock-
strewn ravine. But when she paused to rub the rapidly swelling leg, a one-eared soldier prodded her in
the ribs with the butt of his rifle. She would receive
no blows across her face, for word had already
been given out that the "golden one" was to be
given no visible markings.

That first evening, camp was made near Placerita
Canyon, where Margarita told her a large quantity
of gold had been discovered nearly three years ear-

lier. In the craggy walls could be seen the dark holes of mine shafts, gaping eerily in the twilight. So different from the tranquil evenings of the *ranchería*. And Kathleen surprised herself by longing for the *ranchería*'s peacefulness.

Simon may have been harsh and merciless at times, but he was not a sadist. And if she had trembled with fear then, she shook now as if she were in the throes of an ague. Renaldo, thinking the cool mountain air chilled her, offered his jacket.

"Gracias, Renaldo, but it isn't the cold that makes me tremble."

His face was badly puffed where he had been beaten, but the swollen eyes still looked out at her with kind concern. "Don't worry, señora. *El jefe* will find us. He'll save us."

"Where was he when the others were shot down like mad dogs?" she asked bitterly. "Did he save them? No! He hightailed it out of camp ahead of time to save his own hide!"

"I won't believe that, señora."

"Your loyalty is admirable, but will it keep these pigs at bay? No, you know it won't. You make a good but foolish friend, Renaldo."

Kathleen looked down at Chela's tousled head cradled in her lap. The child slept so peacefully, unaware of what suffering might lay ahead of her, and Kathleen thought that it was better so. Chela was too young to miss the mother, who now lay dead somewhere along the river bank. And too young to be afraid yet. "As I am," Kathleen said to herself. "I'm the cowardly one. I, who always scorned timid people."

"Mujer!" a gravelly voice called. *"El teniente* wants you."

Kathleen looked up at the beefy soldier who stood over her and wished at that moment she was back there at the river bank . . . dead along with Concha and the others.

25

Kathleen handed the sleeping Chela over to Margarita and wearily pushed herself up. She followed the corpulent soldier across to a tent that had been hastily erected in the lee of a jutting glacial boulder. Taking a deep breath, she pulled aside the tent flap. A candle flickered on the table with the breeze that ushered in, casting the giant shadow of Aguila in every corner of the tent.

He crossed to her and stood before her so that she could smell the sour reek of wine about him. He thrust the half-empty bottle at her. "Drink it."

She turned her head away with a grimace.

"I said drink it!"

Kathleen knew Aguila was looking for the slightest reason to exert his brutality, to find an outlet for his anger at letting Simon slip through his fingers. She took the wicker-covered bulbous flask. But when she gingerly held the bottle to her lips, Aguila grabbed it and tilted it upright so that the purple liquid overflowed her mouth and ran down her neck into the cleavage of her breasts, staining the white, low-cut blouse.

Aguila's fair hand slid down the sticky trail of wine to cup one breast. "Now, *mi amor*," he whispered thickly, "I wish to sample the charms you've given so freely to your *cholo*."

Kathleen took a step backward and encountered the canvas wall of the tent.

"Strip," Aguila snapped, "or I'll have my men do it for you."

His eyes narrowed above the thin smile. "In fact, I might like that even better."

"No—no, I'll take off my clothes."

"I thought you would."

When the clothes lay in a mound about her ankles, an opaque film seemed to slide over the hooded eyes. "Now get on your knees."

Slowly, unbelievingly, Kathleen went down as the officer fumbled at his belt. What followed Kathleen succeeded in blanking from her mind, as if she stood apart from the depth of debauchery the girl was forced to sink. But after that night the scenes would return to haunt her, to drive her to what she thought must be the limits of madness, as she would hear herself silently laughing—laughing at the preposterous but wholly true idea that had she been a virgin when she entered Aguila's tent, she would have left a virgin; for the officer was impotent.

But with the return of these memories, the name she would curse would not be that of the lieutenant. It was the name of Simon Reyes. For it was he who had tricked her into marriage, who had held her as a captive. And it was he who had deserted her, leaving her to face Aguila's licentious cruelty.

When she left the tent at dawn, Aguila's heavy snores following her, a heavily armed guard outside escorted her back to the circle of sleeping forms. Renaldo sat up immediately, but she could not meet the questioning look in his eyes. For a long time now she had suspected he was half in love with her. She would not inflict pain on the idealist now.

She dropped to the ground and buried her head in her arms. "I'm all right," she mumbled, before drifting off to a numbing sleep.

Within two hours she was roused once more, with only bits of jerky to serve as breakfast, and the march resumed. Moving westward, the company of soldiers and the depleted remainder of Simon's camp set off along the Santa Susana foothills. When noon came, the prisoners were allowed a brief rest beneath lofty firs and were given one canteen of water, which they passed around—but no nourishment.

Then, jabbed by the soldiers' rifles, they were on the move again; walking, scrambling up stony inclines, walking, and walking. Kathleen, carrying Chela on her back, concentrated on putting one foot before the other. Blisters bubbled on the soles of her feet which the huaraches did nothing to alleviate, and perspiration soaked her clothing. Though the evening mercifully drew near, she felt her skin crawl with goosebumps that alternated with hot and cold flashes.

But it was Margarita who suffered the most, for her strength was rapidly reaching its end. Renaldo and Temcal had taken turns supporting Margarita, but were forced to let her walk on her own when Temcal, pausing for Margarita to catch her breath, was whacked across the jaw with a rifle.

"Get moving," the soldier ordered.

Blood flowing from his mouth, the Indian youth spat out two teeth. Renaldo crouched to jump the soldier, but Kathleen grabbed his arm. "Getting yourself killed won't help Margarita," she hissed.

And so each hobbled forward on their own under the watchful eyes of the guards.

The soldiers, who were mounted, were less affected by the march, but they too were weary, and were relieved when Aguila at last gave the signal to halt at the bottom of a high, barren bluff. Kathleen helped make a grass-tufted bed for Margarita, who moaned softly and held her rounded stomach. She tried to give the woman a little of the water that had again been portioned out for the prisoners, and some bitter acorns she had surreptitiously gathered along the march that day. But the young girl turned her head away, and her cracked lips trembled. "I'll not live, señora, to have the child."

"Of course you will, Margarita. But you need to eat—at least for the sake of your *bebé*."

"*Por qué?* Najo is dead. And what hope is there for our child . . . if he survives the white man's diseases? To be looked down upon because he is an Indian. That is all there is for him. No, it is better that I should die. Leave me be, señora."

"No! You're talking foolishly. You're just tired. I won't leave you until you eat something."

But Kathleen was forced to leave Margarita only a few minutes later. A shadow came to halt over her kneeling form. Slowly, apprehensively, she looked up to find the same beefy soldier who had escorted her to Aguila's tent the previous night.

Kathleen's insides shriveled into palpitating knots. Unsteadily, she stood and wordlessly followed the man. She saw Renaldo half rise, and warningly she shook her head.

By the time she reached the tent, Kathleen was in a near state of self-induced hypnosis. Her purple eyes were as glassy as the hooded eyes of the man who waited for her within.

"*Ven aquí*," he said when she entered.

Kathleen crossed to the cot he sat on, and he said, "Ahh, *mi amor,* you're much more obedient than you were last night. Perhaps I am teaching you something."

She made no reply, and Aguila gave a loud, raucous laugh that terminated abruptly. "Take off your clothes."

Stiffly she complied, inwardly cringing with disgust as his gaze crept over her like a fat, repugnant caterpillar. When she dropped the chemise, he said, "I find I'm too tired to participate in our lovemaking tonight."

Kathleen almost swayed with relief, until she saw the sly expression slide over his face.

"But I'm sure I shall enjoy watching you and my corporal."

"Pablo," he said, and there was a rustle from the shadows in the far corner of the tent as the gorillalike man rose and shuffled toward them.

"No!" she screamed and threw herself on Aguila, knocking him backward on the cot.

His knee caught her on her pelvis with a sharp crack, and the corporal jerked her off Aguila, bending her arms behind her in such an awkward position she thought surely her bones would snap from their sockets.

Aguila's smile was almost kind, and Kathleen felt an insane urge to laugh at the parody.

"You can't know how pleased I am that you prefer me over my corporal. And, of course, you'll show me your appreciation, won't you, Señora Reyes?"

When Kathleen made no answer, he shoved the butt of his quirt in her stomach.

Kathleen gasped and doubled over, clutching her sides.

"Well?"

She nodded like the dumb animal she felt, and Aguila barked at his corporal. *"Váyate!"*

Then she and Aguila were alone.

26

When Kathleen returned to her companions at dawn, she found that Margarita had died quietly during the night. Kathleen's own strength was sapping rapidly with the little sleep she was getting and the harrowing nights she underwent.

Renaldo, seeing the dark shadows beneath her violet eyes and the hollows that contoured her cheeks, crossed to her and led her to a comfortable spot beneath a Spanish oak, where Chela slept curled up against the gnarled trunk. He ignored the glare from the guard. "Try to keep up your strength, señora," he whispered. "By tonight we shall reach the mission of Buenaventura."

Kathleen's eyes widened. "Simon is there? They plan to capture him?"

Renaldo shook his head, and put a finger to his lips. "No, I don't know where *el jefe* is. But there is a way station at the pueblo there, and the owner is sympathetic to our cause."

"Of course," Kathleen said, remembering the little monkey-faced man and the enigmatic exchange between him and Simon about the vulture, the *cóndor*. "Juan."

"*Sí*, Juan. His stables serve as one of the warehouses for the artillery we're importing."

Then Nathan, Kathleen realized, was also involved in the revolution. And the venture of his and Simon's in the importation of household goods was a front. But before she could question Renaldo, he said, "Juan is our only hope. Through him we maybe can get word to *el jefe* before it's too late— before we're shipped out."

"Where, Renaldo? Why?"

"Who knows where—Mexico, the Oregon Territory. Wherever there is a market for slaves."

A grim smile broke the frown of concentration on Kathleen's face. The way she looked now—her face bronzed by the sun and her hair darkened with grime and hanging in heavy braids over her shoulders—she could be easily sold off as an Indian slave. How ironic it would be to find herself on an auction block in Virginia or North Carolina.

"I don't understand, Renaldo," Kathleen whispered tensely, huddling closer to Chela against the early morning chill. "How can Micheltorena do anything with us when he hasn't any real proof all of you are the revolutionaries he's hunting?"

"He doesn't need any proof, señora. He's already established his own form of law. He'll probably wash his hands of the matter and hand us over to a local official to dispose of as the man wishes . . . except for you."

"Me?"

"If Aguila gets to Micheltorena—if he can persuade *el gobernador* you are the wife of El Cóndor—then you'll be held as a hostage. When *el jefe* comes for you—"

"He won't."

Renaldo's eyes were no longer soft. "I don't know what's between your husband and you, señora, but I know *el jefe*—the man he is. His pride alone would never allow Micheltorena to hold you."

"Then you don't know the man entirely," Kathleen said, hating the waspish sound of her voice. She turned away and lay on her side, hoping to get some rest before the camp would be awakened for the day's march. But she was soon on her feet again as the soldiers on horseback encircled the prisoners and herded them along the main trail that led through the Santa Susana Pass northward toward the Santa Clara River.

Whenever Kathleen slipped on the rocky path

that at places was hemmed in by sheer cliffs, Renaldo was always there to catch her elbow, supporting her until she could regain her balance.

"Renaldo, will you forgive my sharp words?" she asked when the march at last broke for the siesta on the banks of the Santa Clara.

Renaldo smiled. "Your words were whipped away by the winds before they ever reached my ears, señora."

The river was now only a thin trickle of a stream after the drought of the dry season, but the water was a luxury to Kathleen. It soothed her aching feet and washed away the blood that oozed from the broken blisters. She sat on the bank with four other women who had survived the raid and the subsequent march, but since she did not understand their Indian dialect that well, she felt totally isolated but for Renaldo and Chela, who played delightedly in the water.

Kathleen badly missed the companionship of Margarita. The friendly Indian girl, her babe still in her womb, lay in the grassy fields beneath a crudely constructed wooden cross. Kathleen could not help but wonder if the woman was not better off.

Sadly she rose, only to encounter Aguila astride his palomino with two of his soldiers in attendance. She refused to look at the officer but could feel the hooded gaze crawl over her skin as he and his men passed on to the front of the line.

The sun, which had been an ominous red

throughout the day, was in Kathleen's eyes when she and the prisoners crested the ridge and looked down upon the pueblo of San Buenaventura and beyond it the blue-gray horizon of the Pacific Ocean.

Kathleen halted there at the ridge. In the orange-red twilight she could dimly perceive the way station. Renaldo had told her he had overheard that the soldiers would bivouac there that night. That night. Kathleen shuddered at the abhorrence that awaited her there that night. Her stomach churned in a nauseous roll.

How foolish and naïve she had been six months ago! To think that she alone could outwit her father, elude the machinations of Edmund, and still manage to escape unblemished. She had only blundered into one predicament after another, each worse than the preceding one.

Kathleen straightened up, and her eyes narrowed into purple slits of resolution. No, she was no longer the innocent young virgin who had left Boston so blithely. But she was a woman now, stronger—more endurable. Capable of surviving anything. She would survive to see the man whose very existence had plagued her from that first night at La Palacia. Who had betrayed her time and again. She would survive to see Simon Reyes's downfall.

The moon rode high in the cloudless sky by the time the prisoners and their captors reached the manure-spotted yard of the way station. Like wild horses, the prisoners were corralled in the wooden pen while the soldiers forcibly entered the adobe ranch house and ordered its patrons outside. The patrons, most of them bedraggled peons or scruffy-looking vaqueros, eyed the prisoners curiously before scurrying off in the darkness to their homes.

Some hours passed before Juan came out, lugging two kettles in his hands. Behind him his son carried pails of sloshing water. The guards permitted the two to pass inside the corral. Kathleen half rose, intending to talk to Juan, see if she could get him to help them, and all the while knowing it would be useless.

But Renaldo's restraining hand at her wrist prevented her. She turned to him, but he merely shook his head. "You will endanger all of us, señora."

Kathleen slumped back against the wooden slats. When Juan and the boy returned to the house, drunken laughter poured outside. Then there was the sudden scramble of the prisoners for the kettles as the guards gave them permission to eat. It was the first hot meal they had eaten in more than two days, and Kathleen found herself among the others, greedily dumping the kettles' contents into the wooden bowls, spilling the steaming soup all over them in their haste. As she carefully carried her bowl back to her corner of the pen, she thought with shame how low she had sunk, fighting over food like a yard dog.

She fished out the bits of meat and vegetables

first, dropping the tenderest in Chela's open mouth
just as if she were feeding a bird. With only the
juice left, Kathleen put the bowl to Chela's lips,
then her own. But before she could swallow the first
mouthful, she saw the corporal Pablo enter the corral. His beady eyes searched among the prisoners,
coming to rest on her. Slowly she lowered the bowl
to the ground.

"Go to Renaldo and stay with him," she told
Chela thickly.

The large black eyes gazed in unblinking puzzle-
ment on Kathleen, but at last the child said, *"Sí,
'Lina,"* and scrambled away.

Then the guard was there, standing before her.
"La puta is to follow me," he said with a leer that
reminded her of Aguila.

Kathleen got awkwardly to her feet. Her legs were
like wooden stilts under her as she moved forward.
The others in the corral made way for her, a
pitying look in their eyes.

Once inside the rancho, the laughter stopped,
and the soldiers set down their glasses and jugs of
fiery *aguardiente* at the sight of Kathleen. *"El teniente* is waiting for you—there," Pablo said, and
pointed toward the bedroom where she had once
changed her clothing.

Aguila watched the woman enter. In the flickering light of the wall candle she looked like a golden
apparition. He had already had his revenge on her.
Why did he continue to demand her when another

woman prisoner would have done just as well? But that wasn't true. Only this one. Perhaps it was her pride that fascinated him, for no matter how he debased her, she seemed to remain apart, her spirit untouched and unfettered, like some golden eagle.

Or maybe it was the contempt with which she regarded him, out of those deep purple eyes that were like chilled wine, so that he felt compelled to humiliate her, to prove that he, the Castilian, was better than the Californio's wife.

The Californio. Simon Reyes was a cross he had shouldered far too long. But by the time he reported to Monterey, that cross would have been thrown aside. If all went as planned, the lovely Kathleen Reyes would serve as bait for the fish. As flame to singe the drawn moth.

Aguila nodded curtly to Pablo. "Leave us."

The corporal frowned at not being included in the night's activities as *el teniente* had alluded to the previous evening, but he did as he was told, fearing the stinging whip of his superior.

Aguila removed his scabbard and tossed it along with his quirt on the leather-bound chair while Kathleen stood waiting with a quiet dignity that irritated him. "Come here and entertain me."

"And if I refuse?" Kathleen nodded at the sheathed saber. "Will you draw your sword, Lieutenant Aguila, and slay me?"

"No, Señora Reyes. That would be too easy a death for the likes of you. A slut deserves to be treated as a slut. No, if you fail to please me, you shall wish that you had begged me to slay you. Now, get rid of those stinking clothes and come here."

As Kathleen began to remove her clothes, he moved to the chair and once more picked up his whip. He fingered the flays thoughtfully.

"Maybe a woman like you needs to taste the bite of the lash to know her true place." He laughed as he saw the sharp intake of Kathleen's breath but noticed that she admirably held her tongue.

He let the whip drop to the bed. "But I hope that will not be necessary, for any kind of marks would lessen your value on the market."

Kathleen's eyes dilated to mere points.

"We have a convenient way to rid ourselves of Indians who fail to fit in with the mission's concepts, you know. We sell them."

"But I'm not an Indian," she pointed out.

"The sun, Señora Reyes, has tanned your skin as dark as one. A little dye on your hair, and only your eyes would lead your purchaser to believe you may have mixed blood in you. Now unless you wish me to try my hand with the whip, come here and show me what you've learned these past few nights . . . and unbraid your hair. I can't stand squaws."

Kathleen lay staring up at the adobe ceiling. The candle had long since gutted, leaving the room in total darkness so that she did not have to endure the sight of the man who lay half sprawled on her. Only the odor of his ejection on the sheets.

The sword he laid so carelessly on the chair was only a few feet away. She would run Aguila through like a stuck pig if it were only possible to reach the sword without disturbing him. She closed her eyes, wondering how much longer to dawn, hoping Aguila was finished for the night.

Scenes of that night flashed behind the closed lids, and her eyes flew open with revulsion—to meet light-green ones that glittered just above Aguila's head.

Kathleen lay frozen as she felt something hard slide between her breast and Aguila's head. In the darkness she could barely see the shape of Aguila's quirt. Then there was the abrupt sound of staccato gurgling as the whip was tightened about the soldier's neck. She felt Aguila jerk spasmodically atop her, and one hand groped blindly along her shoulder, digging into her skin as the gurgling came to a halt. And finally the shuddering ceased, and Aguila was rolled from her.

Kathleen found herself swept up into Simon's arms. "It seems, *mi esposa,* that I'm continually finding you in strange beds."

27

Kathleen found herself enfolded in the turquoise
woolen blanket Simon tore from the bed, and carried out into the dark stillness that surrounded the
way station. Somewhere near, a horse snorted,
echoed by the wine-reeking snore of a soldier who
lay stretched out at the door.

As Simon, dressed once more in the leather
chaps and brush jacket of the vaquero, moved
silently across the wheel-rutted yard, the night's
fresh air wafted over Kathleen's face, reviving her,
and she wondered why she didn't call out, alert the
guards. She told herself it was because she would
only be endangering herself. Had not Simon once

before forced her to choose between himself and his men? Then for the moment she would choose him again over the soldiers who would surely tear her apart without Aguila to lord over them. Yes, she would bide her time.

Once inside the stone rubble of the mission's walls, Simon spoke softly to someone, and Kathleen recognized Armand's French accent. Did Armand already know of Concha's death . . . or that his daughter Chela slept safely within the confines of the corral? And how had Simon slipped through Aguila's posted guards and the sleeping soldiers inside the way station?

Suddenly she found herself thrown astride Salvaje. "Where are you taking me?" she demanded in an angry whisper.

Simon looked up at her and grinned, displaying in the dark the even, white teeth. "Do you know, Catalina, you look like Lady Godiva right now?"

Imagining how she must look, mounted on the powerful horse with only her gilt tresses and the draping blanket to partially cover her nudity, Kathleen smiled in spite of herself, but said with a stern voice, "If I do, Simon Reyes, it's all your fault."

Then she leaned down, her face only inches from his, so that Simon found it hard to raise his gaze from the rounded breasts that gleamed so enticingly.

"It's all your fault, Simon!" she said harshly. "Everything! Your people there,"—she nodded toward the way station—"what about them? Will you desert them . . . as you deserted us before?"

In the gray light she saw the rugged features draw together in a frown. "So that's what it is," he said, as if talking to himself.

He swung up into the saddle behind Kathleen and quietly urged the horse forward. When the way station was several miles behind them, he said, "In answer to your question, I'm taking you back to del Bravo."

"And how do you explain my two-month absence?" she asked tartly.

"*Our* absence. Aren't a bride and groom allowed a *luna de miel*—a honeymoon? The last two months have been spent blissfully alone, in a mountain cabin, getting to know one another."

Kathleen could imagine Simon's insolent smile and refused to say anything.

"And in answer to your second question, my men are waiting on the beach. Armand'll see that Renaldo and the others are freed. Now," he said, his warm, tobacco-scented breath stirring the wisps of curls at her ear. "I want to ask you a question. Why are you so concerned about the people back there?—the people you would've looked down your nose at back in Boston."

"I—I . . ."

Kathleen bit her lip and fell silent. She was puzzled by the man who was her husband; and keenly aware of his maleness—the wide expanse of shoulders at her back, the clean scent of leather that clung to his clothing, the soft mat of hair that peaked through the open flannel shirt and tickled the nape of her neck . . . and the way his arm encircled her waist, just lightly enough to remind her she was one of his possessions.

Just before dawn, when the slate sky was burnished with faint streaks of purple, Simon reined in Salvaje at a small stream lined with twisted willows and dismounted. Kathleen slid into his upraised arms. For a fleeting second she thought the green eyes searched her face there in the darkness, but he turned away and released her.

Kneeling at the creek's bank, he splashed water on his face and dried it with the back of his sleeve. Then he crossed to Salvaje and, taking a packet from the saddle bag, produced what looked like to Kathleen thin strips of dried, lean meat.

"Goose liver," he said. "Eat some. It'll be almost eight o'clock 'fore we reach the cabin."

Warily Kathleen took the stringy-looking meat and bit into it. It was about as tasty as an old boot. But she was hungry, and she seated herself on a grassy knoll to eat the rest. Simon hunkered off to one side, and when he had finished his portion of the pemmican, he rolled a cigarette and lit it, all the while watching her.

Uneasy under his scrutiny, she said, "Without a watch—or the sun—how can you tell what time it is?"

"El reloj de los Indios," he said, a smile briefly touching the solemn lips.

"The clock of the Indians?"

Simon gestured to the fading light of the stars that were still scattered throughout the sky. "The two stars—there on the front side of the Big Dipper—they point to the pole star. By watching the swing of the Big Dipper around the North Star, you can hit within fifteen or twenty minutes of the correct time."

"And if it's a cloudy night?"

"Then you go by the time it takes to roll and smoke a cigarette."

"You're joking with me."

"Nope. The shepherds and vaqueros spend enough time on the range to have their inner timing down pat." He flicked his cigarette away and stood up. "Time we get going."

Kathleen wiped her hands on the blanket that covered her and followed Simon over to where Salvaje stood quietly grazing. After he hefted her up into the saddle, he mounted behind her. But instead of heeling Salvaje forward, he spoke, his voice low.

"Were you hurt, Kathleen?"

She turned her head and raised her violet eyes to meet his steady gaze. Understanding the underlying meaning in his question, her own gaze dropped. Her voice when she spoke was barely audible.

"I was not raped—if that's what you mean. Aguila's impotent."

There had been physical pain, she thought bleakly, but not anything that wouldn't heal. It was the mental torture, the unbearable memories that she could never mention to anyone. How could the arrogant Simon ever understand such degradation? Understand the meaning of humiliation, defilement, debasement.

The grimness that etched her face at that moment matched the midwinter gleam in Simon's eyes.

Several times, as the dawn lengthened into the crisp light of day, Kathleen was aware that she fell asleep, her head on Simon's shoulder, only to be jerked awake as Salvaje plunged down a *barranca* or scrambled up a rocky hill like some mountain goat, always surefooted.

Then they were there, on the mountain's pine-forested crest with the small log cabin standing in the clearing like a refuge for hunted animals, accentuated by the golden shafts of the morning sun.

Once again Kathleen found herself cradled in the cedar-bough bed, smelled the sweet, fresh scent of the ferns growing through the pine boards, and heard the musical flow of the stream that cut through the cabin floor.

As Simon moved about the room, she lay on the bed, not wanting to disturb her deep, drowsy contentment. But she suddenly jerked upright when Simon took hold of her right foot.

"Romero weed," he said, spreading the pungent

paste over her lacerated sole. "It speeds the healing and eases the pain."

"Another Indian remedy?"

"Um-huh," he said, ignoring her barbed tone as he picked up her other foot and rubbed the soothing unguent into the reddened flesh.

"Simon."

He looked up at her.

"Let me go—now. I can make my way to Santa Barbara and leave the country. I swear I'll never utter your name to a living soul."

Simon sat back on his haunches. "Even under torture? I'm afraid I can't take that chance. Too many other lives hang in balance besides my own."

The purple eyes frosted over. "So that's why you came for me tonight. You couldn't afford to have me give you away."

"Nope. I don't intend to share my wife with anyone. For that Aguila died."

Kathleen shuddered at the cool indifference in Simon's voice. She saw again the white bulging of Aguila's eyes and heard the wheezing rasp from deflating lungs. Simon, in his way, she thought, was as merciless as Aguila had been. And it was Simon's bed she would have to share for God knew how long. Simon's bloodstained hands she would have to endure.

"Your derringer's in my saddlebag," he said, breaking in on her thoughts. "From now on I want you to keep it with you—at all times."

"You're not afraid I'll use it on you?" she taunted.

He rose and hooked his thumbs in his belt.
"There's still Edmund," he reminded her. Then:
"We'll bed down until evening."

Kathleen's mouth parched suddenly. The agony
of Simon's intentions seared her soul like a hot iron.
Could she again make her mind a blank when Simon came to lie by her?

And what would happen when he found her
body rigid and unyielding?

28

Kathleen reclined on the mound of goose-down pillows. Over the powder-blue satin cases her bountiful mane spread in studied disarray like tangled skeins of apricot-colored silk. Her thoughts drifted over the day that stretched ahead of her, sorting the details that would have to be taken care of before the reception that evening.

There was a soft knock at the door, and Amelia entered, bearing Kathleen's usual morning breakfast—a cup of rich hot chocolate and sugar-powdered sopapillas. *"Gracias,"* she told the girl as Amelia sat the tray on the night stand.

"De nada, señora," Amelia said cheerfully, and

bent to collect the clothing that Kathleen had heedlessly dropped on the chair the night before.

When the girl had left, Kathleen picked up the cup with trembling hands. Did Amelia and the other house servants whisper of the fact that Simon did not share his wife's bed? As she herself wondered. Had he already grown tired of her? Or, dear God, did he despise her that she now had been used, that her body had been soiled by the leavings of another man?

The moment she had been dreading—that afternoon alone with Simon in his cabin, after he had stealthily whisked her from Aguila's stronghold—had all been for naught. Before, he would have taken her without thought, his lovemaking cursory yet consummate. But that afternoon they slept apart, their bodies only inches distant on the cedar-bough bed—yet never touching. And since then Simon had treated her with a cool politeness. Not once had he even entered her bedroom.

Was it out of disgust or pity that he ignored her? There were times when she would swear he didn't even know she was there—except for the occasional moments when she would catch the long green eyes resting on her in a speculative manner . . . as if she were an irksome insect that bore watching.

But this evening would be the worst she had so far had to endure since her return to del Bravo—to smile graciously at the guests Simon had supposedly invited in honor of his bride—and which she knew was merely a pretext for another of his political meetings.

Simon, the loving husband! Kathleen set her cup on the tray, sloshing the chocolate into the saucer. To pass her off as his wife in order to silence her knowledge of his identity; to masquerade as the respectable ranchero while he plotted against the Mexican government . . . that was her loving husband! Why, she was nothing to him but a pawn to be sacrificed at the right moment—and when would that be?

"I've the news you've been waiting for, Simon," Gemma said, inclining her head close to Simon's cupped brown hands as he lit her thin cigar.

Kathleen caught the meaningful look that passed between the two. And when Gemma slowly exhaled and flicked a questioning glance in her direction, Kathleen's lips curled in a contemptuous smile, and she said sweetly, "I'll take the cue and mingle with the guests—while you two conspire."

Actually, she wanted nothing better than to remain at Simon's side and watch the frustration crack Gemma's cool and lovely mask. But she would forgo that satisfaction in exchange for the precious opportunity to speak with Larkin, who at that moment was alone at the buffet table. The merchant, Simon had told her, had just been appointed by Polk as American Consul to California.

Here perhaps was someone who might be able to help her—one of her own countrymen.

Ignoring Simon's frown, she bypassed the matrons clucking like hens in the *sala*—a rude but necessary gesture, she knew, if she were to catch Larkin alone. But just short of her destination Dimitri Karamazan moved into her path. His olive skin was flushed and the black eyes glittered angrily. "So life is not so blissful for the bride?"

"I'm not sure I understand you," Kathleen said, trying to edge past Dimitri.

The Russian officer took another gulp from the champagne glass in his hand. "Oh, you don't have to pretend with me, Señora Reyes. Your secret is safe—I'm leaving tomorrow. Returning to Sitka."

"Leaving California? But why? I had thought—"

"That I'd marry Francesca? I assumed the same, señora. But her father turned my offer down today. Didn't you know that I'm a penniless opportunist?"

"But surely if Francesca loves you, something can be arranged, Dimitri."

"Ha! Francesca—like all the other women about—is charmed beyond reason by that snake you've married!"

Kathleen drew up her skirts to move around the young man. "I won't hear of such talk in del Bravo, Dimitri! Now if you'll excuse me."

Leaving the Russian with his mouth open in surprise, she reached Larkin just as he came to the end of the buffet table, his hands ladened with food and drink.

"Let me help you, sir," she said, taking the plate from one hand and setting it on the mahogany drop-leaf table that stood in one corner.

"Ah, Mrs. Reyes," Larkin said, looking over his veined and bulbous nose at her. "You can't imagine what good it does me to see an American woman gracing a Mexican household. Have a seat with me, madam. As I was saying, it just goes to prove that your race is a hardy breed."

He stuffed his napkin over the knot of his mulberry-colored cravat while Kathleen seated herself opposite him. "Yes," he said, taking up a fork and knife, "the American woman can make a life under the worst of conditions. Why, look at my wife, coming here, not knowing a soul—not knowing a word of Spanish. And do you realize, madam, she'll soon give California the first child of American parents? Marvelous opportunity here in—"

"That's what I wanted to talk with you about, Mr. Larkin," Kathleen said. She cleared her throat and hurried on before the consul could launch into another tirade about the grandeur of California.

"I—I don't think I'm the pioneer type. I've found it hard to adjust to the life here." She lowered her voice. "You see, Mr. Larkin, I'd like to return to the United States. But my husband—being so much like the Mexicans—is extremely jealous."

What lies, she thought, even as she lowered her

black forest of lashes in coy distress. "He wouldn't think of letting me return—even for a brief visit. So you see, I was hoping perhaps you can give me asylum—the protection of the American Consul?"

Kathleen raised pleading eyes, and Larkin jabbed agitatedly with his fork in the mound of tender spiced cabbage. "A man should never refuse a lady's request, but surely, madam, it's just a passing pang of homesickness, isn't it? Why, I know my wife cried often those first—"

"But you will refuse me," Kathleen said, not trying to keep the dejection from her voice.

"You must see, madam, with your husband being a Mexican citizen—"

"But he's not! At least I don't think he is. He may even be an American—a Texas scout, I think Father Marcos said."

"What he was is neither here nor there, madam. To own land in California, he would have been required to have either embraced Catholicism, Mexican nationality, or one of the local ladies—which he did not. And you must understand, in this dispute between the Californios and Mexico, the United States can not afford to get involved. Not openly at least. Not until the Californios have asserted and maintained their independence."

"And then?"

"Why, then," he blustered, "we shall render them all the kind offices in our power, as a sister republic."

"Of course," she said icily and rose from the table. But as she turned, Simon said at her side, "I hope my wife has been entertaining you, Thomas."

How much had Simon overheard? she wondered wildly as his arm encircled her waist, pulling her against him as if to flaunt his possession of her.

"Oh, yes, yes. She most certainly has, Simon," Larkin said, rising hastily and dropping his napkin in his plate. "A most charming hostess."

"You've got to be careful with Kathleen, or she'll turn your head."

Both Kathleen and Larkin looked guiltily up into the hard emerald eyes.

Kathleen eased into the sun-warmed spot on the bench. "Diego?" she asked softly.

Beneath the thatch of bone-white hair one eye cocked open. "*Sí, hija?*"

"You once advised me not to judge Simon too harshly. But this marriage of ours—this farce between Simon and myself—I can't stand it any longer. I thought I was a calm, steady person. But my hands tremble now, tears fill my eyes at the slightest irritation. And Simon—I think he's nerveless. Diego, it's asking too much of any woman. I'm his wife—and he humiliates me before the servants by avoiding my bed." And, Kathleen thought, by sleeping with another woman under the same roof, for she had seen from her bedroom window Gemma leaving early that morning in her black buggy. With Amelia watching, it had been all Kathleen could do to keep from slamming the shutters.

"And would you share your bed with him, *hija?*" the old man asked, with a candor that matched Kathleen's.

"Why—no. Of course, not! I can't stand him! It's just that—"

"You can't stand him—because you won't understand him."

"What's there to understand in him? He's a common cowboy that somehow wrangled his way into possession of del Bravo. A selfish, inconsiderate outlaw with illusions of ruling California. Escandón called Dimitri an opportunist last night. But Simon makes Dimitri look like a philanthropist."

"Then Simon is not the child I knew."

Kathleen sat forward. Her hands, which had been clenched in a tight ball, now cupped over the edge of the smoothly worn bench in expectation. "And who *is* the Simon you knew?"

"He couldn't have been more than ten when I first saw him. But it was his mother I remember more clearly."

Diego paused and reached for the half-carved stick of wood and razor-edged knife that lay at his side. "The Indians were herded daily out into the mission grounds," he said, resuming his whittling. "I was a soldier then—a good Spanish soldier, *hija*. And I stood guard that day they brought the Mariposa Indian woman in. A beautiful woman, tall and slim and stately, with black hair that fell below her waist—like a cascade of India ink. She didn't struggle between the soldiers who held her; nor did her son. It was probably their scornful attitudes that made our captain order the harsher punishment for her—flogging."

"Why? What had she done?"

"She was the mistress of a ranchero."

"And for that they flogged her?"

"I'm sure her dignity—which the padre mistook for haughtiness—irritated them. But you have to understand the times then, *hija*. The Indians had no rights. They were slaves. No sooner had the ranchero died than his wife sent word to the *soldados* at the presidio that there were Indians in the valley who needed converting. And she pointed a finger at Tocha, Simon's mother, accusing the Indian woman of adultery."

Diego broke off and spat a stream of tobacco juice onto the sun-baked earth. "So Simon was forced to watch while the soldados cut away Tocha's long black hair and shaved her head. To this day I can remember the awful way her head glistened as she stood under the broiling sun—proud and disdainful.

"Then the padre who stood at the top of the mission steps begged Simon's mother to realize and confess her sins. His voice droned on so long that we—and the mission Indians, who couldn't completely follow the Spanish words anyway—shifted from one foot to the other. We were anxious for the ordeal to be over.

"But Simon remained as impassive as his mother—except for the narrowed eyes. I would've sworn, *hija,* they were as dark and fiery as the flames of Hell.

"When Tocha refused to speak, our captain ordered the flogging to begin." Diego's rheumy eyes clouded over with memory, and he said, "It was the hardest thing I think I ever had to do . . . to lay the lash on the proudly held back . . . to strip away the threads of flesh.

"When she collapsed on the stone steps, the captain realized Simon had disappeared. A platoon found Simon in the mountains a day later. That's when they pierced his ear with a copper earring—to mark him as a runaway—a *huido.*"

"Dear God!"

"It didn't stop Simon, though. He began to disappear regularly after that. And each time he ran away, he'd be brought back and flogged. The last time he ran away, it was I who found him. He carried a knife, and I think the boy would've killed me if he could have. But I wrestled with the cub and got the knife away. He looked real surprised when I returned it along with a dozen or so *reals.* 'Hightail it out of California,' I told him."

"And he went to Texas," Kathleen said softly. "What happened to his mother—Tocha?"

"She wasn't the same after the flogging. One

night, when I was off duty, I helped her escape. Took her to that cabin of hers in the mountains. She died that same year."

"You were in love with her, weren't you?"

"I've talked too much. Must be getting soft in my old age."

Kathleen rose and laid a hand on the old soldier's still-straight back. "What you've told me, Diego . . . it helps me to understand Simon a little better. But there's too much between Simon and myself to change our feelings about one another."

"Time has a funny way of changing things, *hija*."

"There are some things, Diego, that time will never change."

29

The afternoon sun slanted across Kathleen's closed lids as she dozed in the rickety rocker outside her veranda door. Visions of Simon as he must have been as a boy drifted lazily through her half-thoughts, visions that Diego had conjured up earlier that morning.

Being half Indian, Simon would have been able to track a deer as well as any of the other Indian youths, she decided. And would have known the secret mountain recesses where the angry gods lived. But he was also half white. Who had his father been, who had given Simon the cactus-colored eyes and the white man's education? And what must it have been like to be an outcast of both the Indian and the Anglo societies?

Caught up in her speculation on Simon's past, Kathleen erringly assumed that the lone rider who thundered up the road, bringing her out of her reverie, was Simon himself. But when the dust settled and the rider dismounted, she recognized Dimitri. With the back of his hand he brushed the dust from his short, black beard before starting up the steps. Kathleen rose from the rocker and met him midway across the veranda.

"I'm surprised to see you here, Dimitri. I'd have thought you'd be well on your way."

"I would have been, Señora Reyes—Kathleen," he amended, catching her hand. "But I felt I owed you an apology for my ill remarks last night. I couldn't go without asking your pardon."

Confused, Kathleen drew back her hand, smoothing out her crumpled skirts, and said, "I've already forgotten the incident."

"I never should have said what I did, but my thoughts are still the same, Kathleen. I see the bitterness in your eyes. I know you're not happy here." He stepped closer so that his knee-high Wellington boots were lost in the folds of her crinoline skirt. "Come away with me."

Startled, she looked up into the handsome face, but saw instead another. One with a nose that had been broken, a brow that had been slashed, eyes that looked as bitter as hers must. *Why not?* she thought. This was the opportunity she had been searching for.

She looked now more intently at Dimitri. He didn't deceive her. She had met many of his kind in Boston. Francesca's father had labeled the Russian rightly. An opportunist.

The thought suddenly came to her that Dimitri was here just for that reason. Perhaps he had learned of the wealth that would be hers—if Edmund didn't arrange to get his hands on it first.

But here was a way to shake Edmund from her trail and escape Simon at the same time. Who would ever think to look for her at a Russian settlement in far-off Alaska? Surely she could somehow manage to rid herself of Dimitri once there, and make her way back through Canada to New England. How uproarious it would be to be sitting comfortably in Boston while Edmund continued to traipse through the California wilderness looking for her!

"You're right, Dimitri. I'm not happy here. I'll go with you—but only on the condition that you understand there's nothing between us—and there will be nothing. If you deliver me safely to Sitka, I'll see to it you receive a draft for six hundred American dollars within six months."

By then, she reasoned, she would be past twenty-one and entitled to the small savings her mother had set aside for her. And her father, if still alive . . . Well, she would worry about that then.

Dimitri hesitated, then said, "Readily agreed to, Kathleen. Shall I wait for you while you get your things together, or is Simon likely to return soon?"

"Better you wait for me down the road—where the mustard fields overgrow one side. I'll be there within the hour."

An hour. So short a time to change into her riding habit, to pack a few things—and her pistol that Simon had insisted she keep with her. So short a time to say good-bye to the people she had come to care for—Diego, Maria Jesus, and Amelia. It was better that she couldn't anyway. Still, they would wonder at her leaving with her things in hand.

She found Maria Jesus in the kitchen, stringing bunches of white onions on a line with *ristras* of scarlet chiles. *"Hola,* Señora Catalina," she called as Kathleen crossed the flagstoned tiles to the table covered with baskets of brown beans.

"Maria Jesus, Señor Karamazan has brought me word that Francesca would like me to spend a few days with her while her parents are away."

"Then I'll need to go with you, *patrona*. It would be unseemly to go alone."

"No, no, I'll be all right." Kathleen fidgeted, toying with the beans. She hated herself for deceiving the old cook. "I'd rather you stay and take care of Señor Simon while I'm away."

At last Maria Jesus accepted Kathleen's lie, and Kathleen hurried to the stables. Estrellita was back, brought there undoubtedly by one of Simon's men, Kathleen thought. Who? Renaldo? Armand?

And, thinking of Armand, she remembered Chela. Would she ever see the child again? And Temcal? And the others? Kathleen shook her head, as if to shake the memories from her.

"This will be our last ride together," she whispered against the horse's mane. For she could not take what had not been hers to begin with. Somehow she would make sure Estrellita was returned to Simon.

And with the realization that Simon might any moment ride in, she hastily buckled the saddle straps and mounted the mare. When she reined in some minutes later beneath the shadows of overhanging mustard vines, Dimitri stepped out of the tangled undergrowth, leading his roan.

"You took so long," he said, "that I was worried Simon had returned. I don't trust your husband. I've the feeling that, whether you two love each other or not, he'd kill me anyway for taking you away."

Kathleen had the same feeling. And even though she and Dimitri covered more than twenty-five miles, riding hard, by the time the sun deserted the sky, she still felt anxious. She had not forgotten the last time she had tried to escape Simon and how easily he had tracked her. Several times that evening she had a strong urge to look back over her shoulder but repressed it and spurred Estrellita faster through the narrow valleys and along the rocky paths of the Topotopo Mountains.

When Dimitri called a halt at the wooded crest of a red-streaked gorge of porphyry, the pale moon was already attended by its entourage of twinkling stars. "A fire'll be a welcome comfort tonight," he said, dismounting and tying the Appaloosa's reins to a scrubby thicket.

"No," Kathleen said. She ignored his offer of assistance and slid from Estrellita's back on her own. "A fire might draw someone's attention."

"You still fear your husband? He probably hasn't even had time to check out that tale you told your cook—about visiting with Francesca. You're a quick and resourceful person, Kathleen."

"I've learned to be. As you obviously are." It was a pity, she thought, that Dimitri was so corruptible when it came to money, because she basically liked the fickle young man.

Briskly she moved about, tying her horse next to Dimitri's and unstrapping her saddle, forestalling the nagging worries that would come with inactivity. But she began to be aware of Dimitri's Eurasian eyes hungrily watching her.

"Tell me," she said, hoping to set his mind on other things, "how do you plan to get us to Sitka?"

"By the day after tomorrow—if we push it—we should reach Monterey. From there it's only a matter of finding a brig bound for the North. There's enough whaling ships in the bay that we shouldn't have too much trouble."

Kathleen was busy spreading her saddle blanket in a spot where the grass grew more profusely between the rocky crevices when she felt Dimitri's arms encircle her from behind. She twisted from him, but he lunged and they both fell headlong on the blanket.

"I told you no, Dimitri!"

His mouth found her cheek instead, when she turned her head away. She pressed uselessly against the greater weight of his chest. Panting with the exertion, she said, "I swear—if you don't release me—you'll not get a cent from me, Dimitri!"

Above her the handsome face pouted. "I can't help it, Kathleen. It's your fault you're so desirable. The way your purple eyes shine so invitingly, the way you move, and your mouth—my God, Kathleen, a man's only human!"

He slipped into his native Slavic language, mumbling words of passion that Kathleen could only guess at. Handling the young man was going to be more difficult than she thought. Frantic, she tried rolling from him as his hands groped at her skirts, yanking them up about her thighs. Then suddenly his heavy weight was shifted from her.

Simon held the flintlock pistol on Dimitri. "Your scheme didn't work, Karamazan. Why would I pay to get my wife back when I can just as easily take her?"

Dimitri eyed the tall, spare man warily. "You weren't to get the message until tomorrow."

Kathleen scrambled to her feet. "What are you two talking about?"

Simon's eyes fell on Kathleen with exasperation. "Did you seriously think your friend here wouldn't try to make the best of the opportunity you gave him? While you were packing, he left a note with Diego. You were to be ransomed—and he'd get in touch with me—at the proper time."

Simon's angry gaze switched back to Dimitri. "But you didn't know Diego could smell a fox a mile away. It didn't take long for him to figure something was up and send for me. And it shouldn't take long for you to get on your way, Karamazan. Unless you want to test my patience—and my accuracy."

"You wouldn't take that chance, Reyes. Because it would destroy—"

"Dimitri," Kathleen cried, "Simon doesn't bluff! Do what he says!"

The Russian officer glanced at Kathleen, weighing her words. "I know when to bow out," he said with a grin. "Kathleen, Reyes, *adiós.*"

Under Simon's watchful eyes, the young man quickly saddled his horse. Kathleen gnawed at her lower lip, dreading the moment he left her alone with Simon. Dimitri she could've somehow handled. Simon, no.

When Dimitri rode down the hill into the gorge

and was out of sight, Simon turned on her. "Damn it, Kathleen, you're not worth the powder it'd take to blow you to hell!"

He grabbed her by the shoulders. "Do you realize if I'd had to kill him that it'd take just one word in the ears of the Russian government and it'd give 'em reason to come pouring back into California again! It'd wipe out all our plans—our months of work."

"Then why did you come for me?" Kathleen shot back.

Simon's lips stretched in a thin line, and he shoved her from him. "Damned if I know."

30

In the western heavens the burnt-orange moon lay cradled in luminous silver clouds. There was a harvest chill in the night air, and Kathleen slumped deeper in the saddle, trying to absorb the steamy warmth rising off Estrellita's sweat-soaked flanks.

Instead of retracking southward toward del Bravo, Simon's quarter horse climbed the westward slopes leading out of the valley, scrambling the stony protuberances at a pace that jarred Kathleen's teeth with each step. "Where are we going now?" she called out. She was cold and hungry and miserable.

Simon dropped back to ride alongside Kathleen. "To Frémont's camp. The revolution's begun."

"Was that the news Gemma said you'd been waiting for?" As much as Kathleen disliked bringing up the woman's name, her curiosity was stronger.

"That—and the word that Micheltorena and Sutter—he's been made the captain of the civil military now—are on the march with their armies toward Santa Barbara."

Kathleen's wingswept brows raised in surprise. "The United States is getting involved in this?"

"Technically, no. Frémont's men—and the sixty-odd that came with his scout, Kit Carson—are to be mainly a show of force. To give Micheltorena something to think about."

He shoved his hat to the back of his head and continued. "As Larkin told you, the United States can't afford to give Mexico any reason to complain—at least not till Polk gets the Texas annexation problem out of the way."

So Simon had overheard her conversation with Larkin the night of the reception, when she pleaded with the consul for help. No wonder Simon overtook her and Dimitri so rapidly—forewarned, he had only to set his watchdog, Diego, on her.

Chagrined, she said, "Little good your stupid revolution'll do you! Mexico'll only quarter more and more troops here. Then the Californios'll know what it is to suffer under a real yoke of tyranny."

"Mexico won't be able to garrison more troops here—not if she's in a war with the United States. Which she soon will be. And after the United States wins—and it will—the Californios'll petition for statehood."

"That'll be marvelous!" Kathleen said acidly. "Especially for the people who survive your revolution—if many do!"

Her heels dug into Estrellita's flanks, and she pushed ahead to take the lead on the narrow trail. Simon's low chuckle reached her as she passed him, and her back stiffened while she silently fumed at being the object of his amusement.

An hour later the light of the scorching moon gave Kathleen her first glimpse of Frémont's camp. Ghostly gray tents dotted a small plateau rimmed on three sides by steep canyon walls. In the camp's center, instead of the stars and stripes, waved a red and white flag with a red star and a grizzly bear.

"Some of the mountain men must've already got the jump on declaring California a republic," Simon muttered, his face displaying obvious displeasure.

As they headed upward toward the encamped mesa, a guard called out from among the boulders that encroached the path, and Simon signaled back with a burst of three successive shots from his pistol.

Kathleen and Simon were allowed to continue along the path unchecked. However, once inside the camp, they were approached by a man in buck-skin with hair slicked down by bear grease. He held a lantern high in his hands. "Captain Frémont's been expecting you," he said, and led them toward a tent standing toward the rear of the encampment.

Inside, Frémont sat at a makeshift desk of crates. A different Frémont than the one Kathleen had met at Simon's cabin. He wore the blue uni-form of the United States Army, and his sandy-brown hair had been clipped just below his ears.

"Simon—Mrs. Reyes," he said, rising. He took Simon's outstretched hand with a grin. "As usual, you're late."

"And tired," Simon said. "Do you have a vacant tent for us, John?"

"Yes—and a tub of water that's chilled by now. But my men'll quickly heat some more water for you, Mrs. Reyes."

"Nothing could sound better," she said shyly as she brushed back the dusty wisps of hair that had escaped from her chignon. Apparently her marriage to Simon had caught Frémont by surprise. She could only be grateful for his natural courtesy and tact.

"Go on," Simon told her. "I'll come to the tent later, after John and I have finished talking."

The same mountain man guided Kathleen to a darkened tent but left the lantern with her. "I'll be back with buckets of hot water, ma'am," he told her.

Kathleen would have liked to soak for the rest of the night in the steaming water, but, knowing that Simon might return at any moment, she quickly bathed. Her long hair she was forced to wash without soap, since there was not enough water to adequately rinse it.

When Simon pushed aside the flap, she was already dressed—in a long-sleeved, high-necked white muslin gown—and sitting on the one cot in the tent. If Simon was startled by the sight of her in a nightgown, her hair falling in tangled curls among the gown's folds, he gave no indication.

Kathleen continued to painfully comb the snarls from her hair while Simon wordlessly shucked his dirty clothing before her. As if the two of them had always shared bedrooms, he stepped into the battered tin tub, totally unconscious of his nakedness.

Like a wall of gold, Kathleen's thick hair fell over her shoulder as she brushed it, concealing the flush of embarrassment that tinted her face. She was confused by the forced intimacy that had steadily grown between them.

"You'd better get some sleep," he said. "We leave tomorrow for Santa Barbara."

Kathleen peeked through the cascade of hair. "I'm to go also?"

Simon picked up the cake of soap and began lathering the bronzed skin of his chest and arms. "There's going to be fighting there. You'll stay at La Palacia where it's safe."

"Safe for me—or for you?" Furious, she slammed her brush on the cot and advanced on Simon. "What you mean—isn't it?—is that I'll be a prisoner again so that I can't give away your plans."

Simon took a deep breath. "Kathleen, you're beginning to sound like a shrew."

And before she realized what happened, one of Simon's arms snaked out and wrapped itself about her legs. She fell forward across the tub and was only saved from a nasty bruise against its edge by Simon's other arm.

"Let go of me! You're getting me wet!"

"What you need is a whipping," he said. He threw up her gown to reveal the firm mounds of her buttocks.

Kathleen thrashed about, twisting and flailing her arms. "Don't you dare!" she shouted. But his hand came down heavily across her bare rump, and she gasped with each sharp, repeated whack. Then, although Simon's blows were just as hard, Kathleen ceased her struggling, as if welcoming the deliverance of each strike like a lashing caress.

Simon's hand came down once again, and remained on her buttocks for a breathtaking moment. Kathleen waited, suspended in an interlude of time, for what she did not know. From above her, Simon's voice came like the gravelly rasp of flint against the blade. "Get up, Kathleen."

The tone of his voice, his distant manner, were

almost as humiliating to her as the nights she had endured with Aguila. Abruptly she shoved herself from him, trying in what was anything but dignified to pull her wet gown down about her ankles.

But for once Simon did not seem to find her predicament amusing, did not mock her as she half expected. He rose from the tub and, in the strained silence that permeated the tent, pulled on the same dusty pants and flannel shirt he had discarded.

"I'll come for you early," he said over his shoulder as he turned to leave.

For a long moment Kathleen sat there, stunned, not quite sure what to make of Simon's actions. Then she flung herself across the cot, her anger at Simon spilling out in all the oaths she had ever heard—the guttural curses of the sailors, the vivid swear words of the vaqueros. But nothing drove away the haunting ache that gnawed inside her.

It seemed to Kathleen that morning came just as she finally fell asleep. In the pre-dawn darkness, Simon squatting at her side was only a shadow against the dimness of the tent. "It's time to go," he said as her lids swept open. Then he was gone.

When Kathleen had pulled the brightly patterned skirt and low-cut blouse over her shift, she joined Simon outside where he stood gently quieting the saddled Salvaje and Estrellita.

"The others?" she asked. "Frémont's men aren't coming?"

"They'll join mine in Buenaventura at the right

time," he said, and took her by the waist, throwing her up over the mare's wide back.

The westward journey over the Santa Ynez Mountains passed in a heavy silence that puzzled Kathleen. Simon's face was set in an expression as stony as the sheer cliffs that rocked in both sides of the passes they negotiated.

Warily Kathleen watched him as suspicion grew within her. What if La Palacia was not her destination? What if Simon intended to rid himself of her along the way to Santa Barbara rather than leave her alive to warn the soldiers at the presidio?

Noon came, and Simon halted on the rocky banks of a swift-flowing mountain stream. From beneath the cool shade of an evergreen—as darkly green as Simon's eyes now were—Kathleen watched with growing fear as Simon deftly whittled a spear from the limb of a fallen pine. Was this the moment she would be sacrificed on Simon's altar to revolution? Had she not come to realize that Simon could be ruthless when it came to the Californio cause?

However, the moment of danger passed when Simon knelt at the stream's bank and, after some moments of concentration, jabbed the spear into the water.

"Trout," he said, rising with the still-wriggling fish impaled on his spear. At that moment, Kathleen thought he looked years younger than the thirty-odd she had at first judged him to be.

She sat contentedly watching him clean the fish and prepare the fire, all the while marveling at his skill in wilderness survival. The fish had a wonderful smoked flavor, and Kathleen stuffed herself, so that when she finished she stretched out, wanting nothing more than to sleep the long, lazy afternoon through.

Simon, setting on his haunches, watched her from across the fire. When Kathleen heard him rise and cross to her, her heart began to thud expectantly. Slowly she raised her lids. He stood there above her, his thumbs hooked in his belt.

"You tempt me," he said. And then, as if she might misunderstand, "I'd like nothing better than to stretch out for a nap. But we have to be on our way. Rain clouds are climbing in the west."

He bent over and took one of her outstretched hands, pulling her to her feet. "We'll stop early tonight." He turned away abruptly, as if her nearness repulsed him.

Throughout the rest of the afternoon they rode through one pass after another. And as the sun dropped from sight, the horses trotted along a winding corridor of stone which opened into a path leading out onto the saddleback of the mountains. The moisture-laden wind blew from the sea, whipping the hair from its knot at Kathleen's neck.

Turning around in the saddle, she saw the valley behind her nearly sheathed in darkness. Farther down the mountain they had just ascended, a band of antelope grazed.

On the western side of the mountain there was still enough sunlight to follow the mossy path that plunged a short distance into the green cover of the firs. Minutes later, Simon reined in before one of the larger brush-covered hills of chaparral that ridged the mountain. Dismounting, he untied the saddlebag before coming over to Kathleen and helping her down.

"What is it?" she asked when he released her.

"A cave." He began to thread his way through the shoulder-high bushes. Every so often he would stoop to gather broken twigs and limbs. "This is where we'll spend the night."

Reluctantly Kathleen followed and found herself swallowed up by a cool darkness. "Simon," she called out. She was half-afraid some kind of bat would sweep down upon her, like in the stories she had heard as a girl.

"It's all right," his voice said at her shoulder.

She heard the strike of a match, and the cave was filled with soft light.

"It's little more than a gouged-out portion of the mountain . . . but it'll be a dry place to sleep for the night," he said as he set fire to the dead brush he had gathered. "Dig some food out of the bags while I tend the horses."

Kathleen found the remains of the smoked trout and some hard biscuits to munch on, by the time

Simon returned. She was reaching for the canteen when he sent it skidding across the cave's damp floor with a kick of his boot.

"Scorpion."

He crossed to her and, stooping to take her hand, which already prickled, he held it to the firelight. Then he surprised Kathleen by placing his mouth against her palm. The sucking tickled her skin, and she tried to draw away. He held her firm.

After a moment he spit. "I doubt the venom's had time to travel. You'll probably be feverish tonight, but that'll likely be all the effects you'll suffer."

Kathleen watched as his dark head bent over her hand again, and an unexplicable tremor passed over her. She felt slightly lightheaded but suspected it was due more to the realization of her weakness at Simon's mere touch rather than any affects of the sting.

Covertly her gaze followed him as he put away the remains of the meal and spread out the saddle blankets. Using one of the saddles as a pillow, he stretched out his long frame. He glanced at her and said, "We've got another day's ride to Santa Barbara. You'd best try to get some sleep."

Cautiously Kathleen lay down on the other blanket, only inches from Simon. Half afraid of him, of herself. But whatever moment she feared never came. Only, after an interval, the steady rhythm of his breathing. At once reassuring and frustrating to her.

For a while she lay there watching the puffs of smoke from the dying fire stream upward to some concealed outlet in the cave's ceiling, and listening to a cicada chirp somewhere just outside the cave's entrance.

Then at last sleep came, but with it dreams. Dreams of Simon, dressed as the vaquero, in Gemma's office—and Simon the ranchero giving his full attention to Francesca's words. Then a curious oppression seeped into the dreams, which soon turned to nightmares as the faces of Angel, Edmund, and Aguila drifted before her.

"Kathleen! It's all right—it's all right."

She opened her eyes to find Simon leaning across her.

"You were moaning," he said softly, "and thrashing about like a sick calf."

He put a hand to her head. "You might be, at that."

Kathleen felt nearly half-frozen, as if the cold glaciers of a million years earlier were rising through the floor of the cave. Her teeth chattered. "I'm cold, Simon."

But she was only partially aware of the warmth that enveloped her as Simon gathered her body up against his.

31

Unconsciously Simon ground out the half-smoked cigarette with his boot, leaving an ash-stained circle on the hardwood floor of Gemma's office. He was in an ill humor, and he knew it had nothing to do with the foray he was to lead in four days at Buenaventura.

If the bit of intelligence Nathan had gleaned from the governor's palace was correct, Micheltorena and Sutter had marched out of Monterey with a combined force of almost three hundred men. And by the time they reached Santa Barbara, the presidio's roster had added another fifty-seven. Yet with Castro's forces soon to arrive, and backed by Frémont's show of force, there was a good chance of defeating the governor.

Nor was his ill humor due to the report that Edmund Woodsworth had been seen at the presidio talking with Micheltorena. What was the man up to now? So far, his own spies had served him well, supplying him with information not only about Woodsworth's movements in California but the man's life in Boston. Sweet Jesus, no wonder Kathleen was disgusted by a man's touch when she had practically been sold to someone like Woodsworth!

But then, he himself hadn't made the situation any better. Why had it taken him so long to admit to himself the truth of that first night? Maybe if he hadn't been so drunk, if he hadn't willingly let himself be deceived into thinking Kathleen was Aguila's paramour—maybe his bestial behavior that night he raped her would never have occurred . . . and she would not hate him as she did.

Simon rose from the leather chair and began pacing the office, lighting another cigarette to dangle from the corner of his mouth. It was Kathleen, he knew, who was responsible for his ill humor. A vision of her came to him, and he chuckled aloud, remembering the silly way she had squinted behind those damned spectacles. Her ridiculous disguise hadn't fooled him for a moment, hadn't hid the spirited beauty that had so disarmed him.

Dios mío, how he wanted her! It wasn't just the innate sensuality that pervaded her every move-

ment, from the guileless way she would glance at
him from beneath lowered lashes to the sinuous
swaying of her hips. Nor was it the strong courage
of her convictions, or the way she fought him at every turn in spite of her obvious fear of him.

Maybe Kathleen was right. Maybe he was an animal. God knows he had been forced to grow up
like one. If he cared at all for this one woman, he
would be unselfish for once, think of someone else
for a change.

The door opened, and Gemma entered the room.
"It's all taken care of. I've put her in the best room
we have."

"And the guard?"

Gemma settled back in the chair behind her
desk. "You can be sure she's safe, Simon. I've sta-
tioned one at each end of the hall."

Simon crushed out the cigarette. "Gemma, you're
a rare woman. Never asking anything of me. I'll
find a way to repay you one day."

Gemma's smoky brown eyes rested on Simon's
dark face. "You know what I want from you, Simon. But——" She shrugged. "I'll settle for your
friendship, if nothing else."

Simon put on the sombrero, pulling it low over
his eyes. He paused at the door. "You understand,
Gemma, if the attack should fail, it's up to you to
see to it that Kathleen is safely aboard the *Tempest.*"

"You're sure Nathan's ship will put in?"

"At the week's end—if all goes well."

"He's to take her back to Boston?"

"He's to take her wherever she wants." Simon's face was expressionless, but Gemma did not miss the wintry look that hardened the green depths of his eyes.

She waited until she was sure Simon was well out of the building, then she made her way back to Kathleen's room.

At the sharp rap on the door, Kathleen reached for the towel and rose from the porcelain tub with a regretful sigh. It had been so long since she had had a long, soaking bath. Since the day before she had fled Valle del Bravo.

"Who is it?"

"Gemma. May I come in?"

Kathleen grimaced. She didn't like at all waiting at La Palacia for Simon to return. She would rather have waited at his camp, braved the dangers of the battle, than to stay with the woman who eyed her with such hate.

"Yes, certainly," Kathleen answered. Quickly she slipped back into the dirt-stained skirt and blouse.

Gemma swept in, her dark hair piled high and her rose satin skirts rustling with her graceful walk. At once Kathleen felt ill at ease, the barefoot peasant before the regal lady. She watched Gemma move to the marble-topped bureau and pick up a tortoise-shell comb, idly playing with the curls before her ears. After a moment the woman looked in the gilt-edged mirror at Kathleen.

"You know Simon and I have been in love with each other for years."

"Why are you telling *me* this—his wife?"

Gemma turned to face Kathleen, her well-manicured hands locked on the bureau's edge. "You are an intelligent woman, Miss Whatley, so there'll be no need to mince words. I didn't get where I am now without some bit of shrewdness. I always place my bet with the winning side. Simon's side will win—eventually. And when it does, *I* intend to be the woman at his side—not you."

Kathleen planted her fists on her hips. "And if I'm not willing to give up Simon?"

"Then that's most unfortunate. Because, however unpleasant I find it, I feel it is to my own benefit that I follow Simon's instructions."

An instinctive feeling of danger seized Kathleen. "Which are?" she asked, backing slowly toward the door.

Gemma smiled softly. "That you be silenced—permanently. You understand, of course, you know too much about the revolution. Simon naturally has to take this precaution."

"I don't believe you," Kathleen whispered.

"You should. I mean to see to it that you are kept quiet . . . but my way. A woman on the slave block as fair as you should sell for a goodly price, you know."

"No!" Kathleen shouted. She grabbed for the doorknob and jerked it open. A battered-faced man with a rifle gripped in his hands filled the doorway. Kathleen opened her mouth to scream. The man raised the butt of his gun and slashed it downward across her jaw.

Kathleen slumped to the floor in a pain-filled mist of unconsciousness, and Gemma carefully picked up her skirts as she stepped over the inert figure. "Make certain she's securely bound and gagged before loading her into the wagon, Guido."

When the wagon had quietly set off from the rear entrance of La Palacia, Gemma returned to her desk. Within the hour Edmund Woodsworth was ushered in. "You have her?" he asked, drawing off his gloves.

Gemma drew on the thin cigar, then said, "I want your assurance that you'll immediately remove her from California—where she and El Cóndor—Simon—will never chance upon each other."

"Where is she?"

"The money first. I'm not such a fool to keep her where you'd find her, Woodsworth. How you get her is your problem."

Edmund took out his purse. "You ask a high price."

"You can afford it—with the fortune you'll soon have control of, if I understand the rumors correctly."

For the first time a frown crossed the lineless face. "Not quite. James Whatley died last month."

At that same moment Kathleen's eyes flickered open to encounter a blurry, gray haze. The throbbing ache that accompanied her distorted vision was so great she immediately closed her eyes, willing herself to a semi-unconscious state again.

But the flies that swarmed about her and the stench that seemed to invade every pore in her skin were too great to be ignored. Once more she tried opening her eyes. Her head still ached acutely, but her vision presently focused, and she knew with a sickening horror that she must be in the women's barracks of the presidio compound.

The adobe brick room she found herself in could scarcely be more than fourteen feet square, and even that space was reduced by the plank bunks that lined the walls. The one single high window admitted little fresh air to drive out the fetid odor that came from the center of the room, where human excrement overflowed the improvised latrine.

But what frightened Kathleen more than anything was the apathetic looks given her by the eight other women in the room. Most of them appeared to be of Indian origin, although she thought two or three could have been Mexican. But all of them gave her only disinterested glances when they saw that she had awakened, before they turned away to stare lethargically at the walls.

Kathleen wondered wildly whether there was so little hope that the women had resigned themselves to their animallike existence. And with that thought came another—the realization that she could rot there in the cell and no one would ever know it. Rabid panic seized her, and she leaped from the bunk and flung herself against the foot-thick wooden door. Her screams rent the stifling air, but the other women seemed oblivious of her outburst.

When the seizure of fear had consumed her strength, Kathleen slumped to the dirt-packed floor. Spittle beaded her lips. And when she wiped it away, the name of her husband rose to take its place. "Damn your black soul to hell, Simon Reyes!" she shouted repeatedly, until her voice was hoarse and her curse dwindled to a faint croak.

If Simon had wanted to insure that she did not give him away, why had he not killed her instead of condemning her to this miserable existence?—she asked herself over and over in the long days that followed. Or did Simon detest her so much? From the very first he had believed her to be a deceitful, treacherous woman of the streets. And she had said nothing to change that opinion. But, dear God, did she deserve this? Death was infinitely preferable!

She lay her head on her knees, and the tears fell from her eyes as quietly as the curses from her lips.

"The presidio," Woodsworth instructed the driver, and he settled back to muse over the situation as the carriage made its way out of the throng of other carriages parked before La Palacia.

Why had he not thought of it before—at Gemma's office when she inadvertently mentioned Simon and El Cóndor in the same breath? Woodsworth permitted himself the slightest smile of satisfaction—a smile that lingered on the lipless mouth even as he alit from the carriage and was presented to the ramrod-stiff governor. The same satisfied smile transferred itself to the usually stern lips of Governor Micheltorena as Woodsworth explained his dilemma.

"So you can see, Your Excellency, we are obviously in accord concerning this man—El Cóndor. With his capture, an annulment, I'm quite sure, can be effected. I will once again be Miss Whatley's appointed guardian—and you will once again have a completely stable provincial government."

Micheltorena drummed his square-tipped fingers on the oak desk. "You may be right," he said after a minute. "The Whatley woman may serve as bait to ensnare her husband—the man you claim is El Cóndor."

32

His lean body flattened against the adobe brick, Simon silently slid over the wall of the compound and dropped down into the darkness of one corner. His gray poncho, like the skin of a chameleon, blended with the gray presidio walls.

It was sheer stupidity. Every moment he delayed the attack at Buenaventura, he not only endangered Renaldo and the men who lay hidden in the chaparral thickets just outside the town but also jeopardized the entire hope for independence. All this folly for the white woman who hated him with every separate nerve in her body.

That lovely golden body. It had nearly driven him insane to think that Aguila had laid his foul hands on it. But to learn that Kathleen was held prisoner in the presidio compound to be branded and sold as a slave . . . the thought was more than he could endure. Would the horror of the compound never stop? First his mother—and now Kathleen.

It had been all he could do to act rationally, to think logically, when Renaldo had ridden his lathering horse into camp that morning and tossed the edition of the *Novedades* at him. The headline seemed to expand before his eyes: WIFE OF REVOLUTIONARY IMPRISONED FOR PART IN CONSPIRACY.

The memories of his childhood terror of the compound had risen to suffocate him, and he had crumpled the newspaper in his hands as if he would crumple the memories.

He turned to Renaldo then, his voice coming in a dry rasp. "Take the men to the thickets outside the town. If I don't return by morning, mount the attack without me. Understand?"

Renaldo's eyes were brown stones in the thin face. "Let me come with you."

"No! We can't risk it. One of us needs to lead the attack. And this is something I have to do, Renaldo."

Now Simon could only wonder, as he edged along the wall, if he had been foolish, placing his own selfish desires above the welfare of the Californios. And yet, he knew he could have done no differently.

"We've been waiting a long time for you, Cóndor."

Simon whirled, cursing his carelessness, even as his hand whipped to the knife tucked in his legging. Damn her treacherous heart! How clever his dear wife was with men. First Aguila, then Dimitri, and now Edmund. But the little bitch *had* warned him . . . had sworn countless times she'd have her revenge on him.

The captain whistled to summon the soldiers waiting just beyond the courtyard. "Not yet, Mejia," Woodsworth told the captain. "My turn first. Then you can have your revolutionary."

As quickly as Simon had drawn his knife, Edmund drew out his sword and leaped backward. The two circled each other, each sizing up his opponent. Simon had ridden hard throughout the night and knew his strength was no match for that of Woodsworth. And he was at a disadvantage with the shorter weapon. He would have to take the offensive rather than let Woodsworth wait him out. His long knife flashed in the night, and Woodsworth leaped backward.

The Englishman's lipless mouth twitched in what could have passed for a smile each time the point of his sword scored a red path along his opponent's body. When Simon tried moving in closer, Woodsworth cut the sword through the air, keeping Simon at arm's distance but continuing to nick him, drawing blood.

"Shall I slash your other brow for you?" he taunted. And at once a scarlet line cleft Simon's right brow. Blood spilled over, blinding him.

Simon struck then, while the man was careless with success. Throwing up his left forearm, he used his poncho as a shield to entangle Edmund's sword. The sword clattered to the ground and, caught off balance, Edmund stumbled forward.

From behind him Simon heard a whooshing sound as one of the soldiers lunged at his back. Simon dodged and whirled just as the soldier's saber drove into Edmund's stomach. The man pitched onto his knees. His hands clutched his torso as the intestines poured forth like slippery, writhing snakes.

There was shouting then, and the soldiers converged on El Cóndor.

Kathleen looked out between the wooden spindles that barred the window of Captain Mejia's office. She tried to make her mind lucid, to gather her senses while she waited on him. Why had he summoned her? What did he plan to do with her? What other horrors would she now face?

The door opened, and she turned her back to the window. The balding captain entered. With him was a man she did not recognize, a man with a stringent mouth, curving nose, and thick grizzled brows that sloped downwards, concealing the expression in the eyes.

He seated himself behind the desk, and the captain went to stand at the door. "Have a seat," Mejia said, indicating one of the cane-backed chairs.

Kathleen knew she must look a sight with her grimy hair straggling over her shoulders and her bedraggled clothing and dirt-encrusted nails. But she moved toward the chair with her head held high. There was open admiration in the captain's face, but the other man's was shrewdly bland.

When she had seated herself, the captain said, "This is our governor and commander in chief of the military forces, Manuel Micheltorena, señora. He wants to help you."

Both men mistook Kathleen's silence for obstinacy. They did not know how frightened Kathleen was of cells, that she was so desperate she could not speak, for fear that the captain's mention of help was a trick.

The two looked at one another, and after a moment the governor cleared his throat and said: "Señora—Miss Whatley. Yes," he said, noting her startled look, "Mr. Woodsworth informed us you're the daughter of the United States ex-minister to Spain, the late James Whatley."

"My father—he's dead?"

"I thought you knew. I'm sorry. As I was saying, Miss Whatley, Mr. Woodsworth appeared before me to clear up the charge against you."

"What charge?" Kathleen demanded, gripping the reed arms of the chair.

"The charge of theft that Señorita Gemma Chavez brought against you. Unfortunately Mr. Woodsworth—who was to serve as a character witness in your behalf—met with an accident in the early hours of this morning."

Kathleen sat there, incredulous. "Edmund— dead," she half whispered to herself.

Micheltorena bowed his head. "I know the death must be hard to take, coming on the heels of your father's death." He looked up again at the young woman across from him. "However, I am prepared to offer you some consolation—immunity. Here," he said, rising, "come to the window."

He pointed a large-knuckled finger to the parade ground outside as Kathleen came to his side. Several Indians now stood waiting under the baking sun, bound to one another by heavy chains at their wrists and ankles.

"Do you recognize one of them?" The shrewd eyes watched her carefully.

Kathleen looked again. Dressed only in the breechcloth, they all looked alike. Yet . . . one—as thin as the others, but with a more powerful build. Her breath came in a gasp as the sun glinted off the mahogany-colored hair.

"It's your husband—the one they call El Cóndor, is it not, Miss Whatley?"

Kathleen looked back to Micheltorena. "What is it you want from me, Governor?"

"We merely need your confirmation that the man

outside is the revolutionary—El Cóndor. You, of all people, would know. In exchange for your testimony against him, I am prepared to offer you immunity from the theft charge."

"What will happen to him?"

Micheltorena studied her. "I am a just man, Miss Whatley, as far as my office allows me. The man will be executed for treason."

Kathleen turned away and returned to her chair. She leaned her elbows on the chair's arms, resting her head in her hands. Confusion. Her thoughts were jumbled, with visions of Simon. Simon removing her wet clothing that first night in the cabin; Simon tackling her in the mountain stream, laughing; Simon rubbing salve on her blistered feet.

"If you'll just sign this statement," Micheltorena said, breaking in on her thoughts, "we can have it witnessed. We wouldn't need to detain you any longer. You'd be free to go."

Free! Kathleen couldn't believe it. She was free from her father, from Edmund. And all she had to do was sign the paper and she could walk out of that hellhole. She could at last return to Boston. The joy that suddenly coursed through her was as sweet as the wine of the country.

She took the paper Micheltorena thrust at her and picked up the pen on the table. How many times, she asked herself, had she sworn vengeance on Simon? Her opportunity was here. At last.

The fine print swam before her eyes. The chance for revenge didn't taste as sweet as she thought it would. No, it was like sour wine in her mouth. The pen dropped from her hand.

"This piece of paper would be a fraud, Your Excellency, if I put my signature on it. I don't even know that man outside, much less lay claim to him as my husband. For a moment I was desperate enough to get out—I would sign anything. But not an innocent man's death warrant. I'm sorry."

Micheltorena frowned. Had Woodsworth tricked him in order to lay his hands on this woman? *Carramba!* He'd just have to wait until he returned from Buenaventura to find out what was behind it all.

"That's too bad, Miss Whatley," he said, not trying to conceal his anger. "I have no other choice but to let you serve out your sentence as a slave."

He snapped his fingers at Mejia, and the captain crossed to the door and called the guards.

Once inside the cell, Kathleen slumped to her knees, rocking back and forth. Four days in the mission compound had driven her beyond rational thought. Even now she trembled with the knowledge that her mind would surely snap if she endured one day more in the lice-infested cell.

Oh, God, if there was only some way she could kill herself. If the captain's office had been on the second floor, she would have thrown herself from the balcony onto the shards of glass that lined the presidio walls.

Kathleen saw again the blank eyes of her mother. She realized her mother had been spared the horrors of the asylum by the insanity that had indeed finally claimed her. If only she herself could seek the forgetfulness of insanity!

Fool! Fool! The tears coursed bitterly down her cheeks. She had sacrificed all for a man who had betrayed her time and again. And why? That was the bitterest part of all. To have to admit that she loved him, Simon Reyes, a man who had scorned her from the very first, used her and tossed her aside.

She could only hate her weakness more. As long as she might live, she could not wipe out the memory of his lips on hers, the taste of his salty skin, the feel of his muscles rippling below her fingers, the whispered words of passion that fell from the hungry lips.

What woman was sharing them now? Gemma? Francesca? Some dusky Indian maiden?

Fool! Fool!

33

It was not yet dawn when Kathleen heard the first sound of distant cannonading, scarcely twenty-four hours after she had been returned to the compound.

Like the other women, she scrambled to the wall containing the single high window. One Indian woman scrambled atop another's back, grasping tightly at the wide sill of the window.

"*Que pasa?*" a squat, stringy-haired woman asked.

"*Mira!*" the one at the window answered. "The sky is bursting with lights—there in the south, toward Buenaventura."

Kathleen hugged the opposite wall, its adobe

warm to her icy hands, and saw flashes of light that
periodically filled the tiny window. The revolution
was under way. And where was Simon? Had he
been released? Was he now leading his men into a
battle that would end in death for some?

What if Simon were killed? Kathleen shuddered,
hanging her head in despair. Wasn't that what she
had wanted?

Restlessly she moved about the room, wringing
her hands, wishing there was something she could
do—anything to take her mind from the shelling
still going on. If only daylight would come. The old
Mexican woman would bring the bowls of *atole*—
perhaps she would know something.

But the morning sunlight filled the window, and
the old Mexican woman did not come with the
breakfast. The soldiers seemed to have deserted the
fortress. With the onset of night an ominous silence
claimed Santa Barbara.

Kathleen lay on her bunk, listening to the other
women conjecture. "It's French pirates," one declared. "They've attacked from the sea."

"Bah! You've been in here so long you've lost
your mind," another said. "It's some kind of holi-
day. The soldiers are setting off fireworks."

And on it went through the long night.

Then, with the advent of morning and the mission bells pealing out the matins, there came the
clanking of keys outside the wooden door. Slowly it
swung open. A sailor stood there, a muzzle-loader

clutched in one hand and a brass ring of keys in the other. He looked as stunned as Kathleen.

"Nathan!" Kathleen cried out, and pushed among the women until she was at his side.

Nathan dropped the ring of keys and caught the young woman up to him. "You all right, lassie?" he asked gruffly.

Kathleen shook her head affirmatively and moved away to see his face. It was as ruddy as ever, but there was a pallor beneath the skin and fatigue in the crinkly sea-bright eyes.

She looked around her at the sailors in their striped red shirts, holding pistols on the few remaining soldiers lined up against the wall. "The revolt?" she asked. "It succeeded?"

A broad smile broke out on Nathan's face. "Aye, lassie."

As he led her toward the captain's now-vacated quarters, he related to her the events of the past two days. ". . . And after Simon slipped free yesterday, he made his way to the *Tempest*. He charged me with holding Santa Barbara, while he joined Renaldo and Castro at Buenaventura. They finally defeated Micheltorena and Sutter at Cahuenga, a place a few miles north of the pueblo of Los Angeles. Simon's with Micheltorena now, drawing up the list of demands by the Californios."

Kathleen took a sip of wine from the glass Nathan handed her to still her trembling lips. No doubt Gemma was at Simon's side . . . as she promised she would be. Wearily, she leaned back in Mejia's high-backed chair. "So Simon's won—and I'm no longer a threat to him. What does he plan to do with me now?"

Nathan's brows knitted. "Simon doesn't know you're here—or else . . . Well, he thinks you betrayed him to Micheltorena. I've never seen anger get such a hold on him. The mention of your name makes those eyes look like green flames. I didn't even know you were here until I opened that—"

Kathleen shot up in the seat, spilling her wine. "He thinks *I* betrayed him?" she sputtered. "He— and that whore of his—betrayed *me!* That's why you found me here!"

Nathan frowned and sucked on his briar pipe. "Kathleen, I don't know what's all between you and Simon. He's my friend. But you're—well . . . The *Tempest* is taking Micheltorena and his men back to Mexico next week . . . and I'd like to take you with me—to be my bride—if it's over between you and Simon."

Kathleen twirled the stem of her glass between her fingers. *Why not?* she thought. *At last, here's someone who cares about me, a New Englander like myself. Someone I can understand, who understands me.*

She put out her free hand. "I'm so tired, Nathan. I could sleep a week. Will you take me to the mission?"

"Ah, so you've finally awakened, my daughter."

Kathleen raised her eyes from her reflection in the well water to watch Father Marcos cross the sun-dappled courtyard. "I didn't know I was so exhausted, Father. I was tempted to sleep another twenty-four hours."

The gaunt padre perched on the stone rim opposite the young woman and tucked his hands in the wide sleeves of his habit. "A lot has happened the last twenty-four hours to risk sleeping another day through."

The wine-colored eyes widened with forced interest. "Such as what, Father?"

"The talk of Baja California—Francesca Escandón has run off to join that Russian officer that was courting her."

"Dimitri Karamazan?" A genuine smile lightened Kathleen's face. "The man doesn't give up! But you, Father—I'm surprised at your gossiping. Still, tell me more."

Father Marcos watched the lovely face across from him. "Gemma Chavez has wisely chosen to return to Mexico with Micheltorena and his troops. You know that she, and not Simon, was responsible for your imprisonment at the presidio?"

Kathleen's hand gripped one of the wooden posts that bridged the well. "I don't want to hear about Simon!"

"Then you're being willfully blind, my daughter.

Selfish and narrow-minded. You're refusing to see Simon's side, but only your own, dwelling on your own hurts. If I sound harsh, it's because I care too much about you two to watch you foolishly throw away something precious. And, while I'm at it, I might remind you that you two are married in the eyes of God—and what God has joined together, no man may divorce."

"Then you know about Nathan's request?"

"Yes."

"Let me put your worried soul at rest, Father. I dispatched a note to Nathan an hour ago. I told him I couldn't be his wife. I'm returning to Boston tomorrow on another brig, the *Yankee Gull*."

"And Simon?"

"How can you defend him! No, don't tell me I'm being unfair. We won't talk about what's happened between myself and Simon. But that still leaves the kind of man he is. A man the Church would certainly frown upon. Or is killing now condoned? And what about deceit? Or isn't taking over the land belonging to Andrew King's widow—Doña Delores, or whatever—a fraudulent scheme? And what—"

"My daughter, why must you be so perverse in seeing the truth? What is the surname King, translated into Spanish?"

"*Rey*," Kathleen answered slowly.

"Or, plural—*Reyes*. Simon is Andrew's son by an Indian woman. I know—I baptized Simon at

Andrew's request. Thereby making Valle del Bravo rightfully his."

"Oh, no," Kathleen whispered. "Then—"

"Kathleen, child, Simon is but a man. He sometimes makes mistakes. Don't you? Will you make one now by leaving him, by returning to Boston?"

Kathleen looked down at her left hand. It lay in her lap in a tightly balled fist. "I don't know, Father. So much has happened between us. We've both changed. I'm not the same person I was six months ago. I don't know if I can erase the bitterness. . . . And then there's Simon's side, which you insist I see. Since the moment we first met, Simon's willfully chosen to think the worst of me. And I guess he has reason to. I just don't think anything can be done to change what has happened."

"Love can do anything. But this is a decision I can't make for you. I'll leave you to think on it, Kathleen."

The mist had cleared from the Santa Barbara Channel, so that the "queen of the missions" once more shone splendidly in the morning sun.

Kathleen watched from the deck as an oarboat rowed toward the *Yankee Gull* the last of the boarding passengers . . . and her oppression grew with each wave that receded behind the small oarboat.

She had what she wanted, she told herself fiercely. She was free—free from her father, from

Edmund—from all male domination. She could now go her own way, independent at last. And Simon? Her attorneys in Boston could arrange some sort of annulment.

They could change the law, but they couldn't change her heart, her feelings, her love for the one man who didn't want her . . . the one man that was everything to her.

Unshed tears finally spilled over while there was no one to see them; to splash on her hands that clutched the railing with such an aching longing. A yearning that was as sharp as a knife thrust.

There was only the ridiculous copper earring, shining on her third finger, to remind her that she was still legally bound to Simon.

Kathleen began to work the ring off. It would stay in that land at the end of the world, where she should never have come in the first place. She raised her hand to hurl the ring into the wave-tossed Pacific.

A brown hand gripped her fist.

Kathleen turned to find Simon, once more dressed as the elegant ranchero, the flat-crowned hat set low over cactus-green eyes that gleamed wickedly.

"Do you think, Catalina, that by ridding yourself of the ring, you rid yourself of me?"

Then, before the curious eyes of the sailors and passengers, Simon swept the startled young woman up into his arms.

"Where are you taking me this time, Simon Reyes?" Kathleen demanded, with an equally wicked gleam in her eyes, as he moved among the people to the boarding ladder.

"To bed, *mi vida*. To bed."

In spite of the laughter that rippled among the people there on deck and the ribald remarks among the hands, Kathleen pulled Simon's dark head down to hers and kissed the long lips with a passion that would last through the years.

FREE
Fawcett Books Listing

There is Romance, Mystery, Suspense, and Adventure waiting for you inside the Fawcett Books Order Form. And it's yours to browse through and use to get all the books you've been wanting... but possibly couldn't find in your bookstore.

This easy-to-use order form is divided into categories and contains over 1500 titles by your favorite authors.

So don't delay—take advantage of this special opportunity to increase your reading pleasure.

Just send us your name and address and 25¢ (to help defray postage and handling costs).

ALL TIME BESTSELLERS
FROM POPULAR LIBRARY

☐ ALWAYS IS NOT FOREVER—Van Slyke   04271-0   2.25
☐ DIANA ROSS—SUPREME LADY—Berman   04283-4   1.75
☐ YOUR SINS AND MINE—Caldwell   00331-6   1.75
☐ THE HESS CROSS—Thayer   04286-9   2.25
☐ THE UNORIGINAL SINNER AND THE
   ICE-CREAM GOD—Powers   04287-7   1.95
☐ HOW TO MEET MEN NOW THAT
   YOU'RE LIBERATED—Gellis   04288-5   1.95
☐ AFTERNOON MEN—Powell   04268-0   1.95
☐ MARINA TOWER—Beardsley   04198-6   1.95
☐ SKIN DEEP—Hufford   04258-3   1.95
☐ MY HEART TURNS BACK—Patton   04241-9   2.25
☐ EARTHLY POSSESSIONS—Tyler   04214-1   1.95
☐ THE BERLIN CONNECTION—Simmel   08607-6   1.95
☐ THE BEST PEOPLE—Van Slyke   08456-1   1.95
☐ A BRIDGE TOO FAR—Ryan   08373-5   2.50
☐ THE CAESAR CODE—Simmel   08413-8   1.95
☐ DO BLACK PATENT LEATHER SHOES
   REALLY REFLECT UP?—Powers   08490-1   1.75
☐ THE FURY—Farris   08620-3   2.25
☐ THE HEART LISTENS—Van Slyke   08520-7   1.95

Buy them at your local bookstore or use this handy coupon for ordering:

POPULAR LIBRARY
P.O. Box C730, 524 Myrtle Ave., Pratt Station, Brooklyn, N.Y. 11205

Please send me the books I have checked above. Orders for less than 5 books must include 75¢ for the first book and 25¢ for each additional book to cover mailing and handling. I enclose $_____ in check or money order.

Name_____
Address_____
City_____ State/Zip_____
Please allow 4 to 5 weeks for delivery.